Olympus High: The Lost Gods

HOLLY KELLY

This is the dedication: For those who pursue their dreams, even when no one else believes in them.

Let it be known to all Gods and Goddesses on Olympus, that Zeus, formerly known as King of the Gods, has been found guilty of heinous crimes has been duly punished.

His crimes were as follows:

Ð He seized the throne of Olympus from Petros, the true King of the Gods (eldest brother to Zeus, Poseidon, and Hades) and he did so through treachery.
Ð He erased the memory of our great king from all on Olympus and throughout the world.
Ð He stole newborn gods and goddesses from their parents.
Ð He erased all memories of these children from the minds of their families.
Ð He stole the powers of the young gods and goddesses to keep for himself.
Ð To cover his crimes, he hid the children in the human world.

As punishment for his offenses,
The Betrayer has been thrust into the deepest pit of Tartarus.
Any allegiance sworn to the Betrayer is now null and void.
All who do not renounce their loyalty to him will suffer his same fate.

It is now imperative that we find the lost gods and goddesses.
They are having their powers restored and as a result, are a danger to themselves and all those around them.
If you see evidence of a lost god, please inform the ruler of your realm.
All will be done to return the lost gods or goddesses to their families of origin.

Remember, the gods may be lost in plain sight.

Sing no more this bitter tale
that wears my heart away.
—— *The Odyssey*, Homer

THE MOST LOATHSOME and powerful beings in the mythical world come in threes—the Moirai, the Sirens, the Gorgons, the Oneiroi... each of them unique in their power, a threat.

Zeus looked down at Peisinoê as she lay in a plush four-poster bed, her body draped in a white coverlet, her shape outlined clearly—a shape he knew intimately. Her forehead still held a sheen of sweat from childbirth—it did nothing to diminish her beauty. Zeus glanced at the two infants in her arms, and then looked down at the third he held loosely. His hackles rose. This woman had just borne him three daughters. Triplets. The mother, herself, was a triplet. Three born of three, this was an unprecedented risk.

"Are they not beautiful?" Peisinoê said.

"Yes, they are," he said, forcing a smile. If only he'd known there would be three, he could have ended this months ago. He could have prevented their birth. By the time he found out, it was too late to end the pregnancy, but not too late for other plans.

"They're not identical like my sisters and me," she said.

"No, they're not," he agreed. "They each have distinctive features."

"And power. Can you not feel them? Each so different, but perfectly balanced."

"Yes."

"They're so beautiful." She glanced at the child on her right. "This one looks like you."

He had to agree. She had eyes as blue as a clear sky and a halo of blonde curls.

Then she looked at the one on her left. "And I dare say, this one looks like me."

Indeed, she had her mother's black hair and porcelain skin. Zeus nodded. "I think you're right." He then turned his gaze down to the infant in his own arms. She looked back at him. A jolt went through him at her watchful gaze. Power and intelligence shone from her amber eyes, eyes that seemed to defy him, even now. "But this one..." he said, narrowing his gaze, "has a unique look all her own."

"Does she?" Peisinoê tried to sit up to get a closer look.

Zeus brought the child over to her.

A smile lit Peisinoê's face. "She looks like your grandmother."

Zeus frowned. "Why, yes. I think you're right. I can see Gaea's features. That's a bit disturbing. It's almost like a part of my grandmother has escaped the pit of Tartarus."

"Oh, hush. She's perfect. All our babies are perfect."

"Yes, they are." He agreed to placate her.

"You must promise me..."

When she hesitated, he said, "Promise you what?"

"Swear on the River Styx..."

He tensed, wondering what would be required of him.

"...that our three daughters will grow up on Olympus."

He hid his reaction to her request. It was appalling. It was intolerable. There was no chance he would give in. But how could he make her *think* he has? A realization almost made him smile. A loophole. He would be saved by semantics.

"I promise on the River Styx that our daughters will grow up on Olympus soil." As he vowed, he pictured a mountain range—one far from his own familiar peak.

He knew he'd succeeded in his deception when she said, "Thank you." His lover smiled and then yawned. Her eyes drooped; she looked exhausted. He brushed the thought away like an annoying gnat. He had more important things to think about—his daughters. He must do something about them. But because of his oath, he could no longer kill them. It would be a shame to destroy them regardless. All that power would go to waste. And they were powerful; at mere minutes old, he could already feel their power. Of all the beings who had a chance of usurping his rule, these three babes were the most likely to do it. They simply had to be dealt with. But before he could, he would have to deal with their mother, and that he must do carefully. Crossing Peisinoê would be like dancing on the edge of a razor.

Zeus looked to the open door and said, "Handmaidens, can you please take the infants and care for them so their mother can rest?"

"No, I—" Peisinoê protested.

"It's okay, my sweet," he sat beside her and caressed her cheek. "They will be well cared for." He arched his eyebrows and said, "And you need to rest."

Once the infants were safely away, Zeus said, "I have to go, but just for a moment. Not to worry, though. I have someone special to care for you. Under her watchful eye, I have no doubt you'll rest as you've never rested before." He leaned over and kissed her one last time. He savored the taste of her soft lips as a tinge of regret pulled at his heart. Leaning back, he opened his eyes. Peisinoê's eyes remained closed; contentment warmed her face as a hint of a smile splayed across her lips.

"Stheno," he said, "you may come and take care of her." Whispers caressed the air as Stheno stepped into the room. Zeus turned his gaze to the marble floor, noticing for the first time, the veins of gold running through the white, though that was only a passing thought. He couldn't ignore the two powerful women before him. The risk of what he'd orchestrated for this moment was immense. Yet, he dared not look up while it played out.

"Who is—" his lover questioned, her voice cutting off when a chorus of loud hisses erupted above him and then faded.

Moments later, Stheno said, "It is done, my king. I expect Medusa to be returned to us in one piece within the day."

Zeus's temper sparked, it sounded as though she'd given him an order, though this was not the time to respond in anger. If retribution were warranted, that would come later. Instead, he kept his eyes down and said, "I swear it shall be done."

Stheno's footsteps faded as she retreated.

Zeus turned back to his lover's stony gaze, frozen in a look of confusion. He was struck by the color of the stone. He'd seen many of the Gorgon's statues, they were dark, splotchy and none too appealing. The statue of Peisinoê was white, iridescent, and of the purest alabaster. It was stunning, nearly as stunning as her face. If he could get away with it, he'd add this statue to his art collection. One day, perhaps he might. "You truly are beautiful, my dear, but the risk is not worth saving your life." He once again laid his hand on her cheek, the marble still felt warm against his palm. He jerked his hand away when he felt her life force vibrate from within, the anger unmistakable.

No, it wasn't just angry. It was enraged. Stone held no emotion. Yet this stone did.

This woman was powerful.

Too powerful.

He could never display her; he would have to hide her away. Somewhere no one would dare venture. A smile spread as he thought of the perfect prison for his lover, a prison he used for another powerful being. Decision made; he looked through the door as he rose. First things first, he must make sure his daughters would give him no trouble.

Chapter One – Jemma

We men are wretched things.
——*The Iliad*, Homer

JEMMA'S HEART did backflips against her chest wall as she chanted in her mind. *I can do this. He's just a boy, nothing more. I can totally do this.*

Actually, he was her lab partner. The fact that he was the hottest guy at Olympus High and she'd had a crush on him for as long as she could remember meant nothing to her. Absolutely nothing!

Adjusting the heavy box in her arms, she looked through the throngs of students making their way out of the school. When she spotted Joal at his locker, her heart took a stuttering beat. He was blond, stood several inches over six feet tall, and was built like the swimmer he was—lean, muscular, altogether too good looking. And his green eyes with sweeping lashes had broken more than his share of hearts, including her own.

She was about to lift her foot to take a step in his direction when Brooklyn slinked up behind him and wrapped her arms around his waist. A crack in Jemma's damaged heart widened a bit.

Since when were they an item?

Joal smirked, glanced back at Brooklyn, and said, "Hey, babe." Then he shut the locker door. Turning to face her, he pulled her into his arms and said, "I only have a few minutes before practice."

"I only *need* a few minutes," she said, her tone teasing. "I'll make it worth your while."

Despite the insane urge for Jemma to turn and escape the situation, she took a deep breath and forced one foot in front of the other until she was standing beside him. "Joal?"

"Yeah?" he said looking down at her and narrowing his eyes.

"I wanted to make sure you remembered. We're supposed to meet in the library. You told me you had a few minutes to spare."

He raised an eyebrow, not speaking for a long moment. "And you are...?"

Her heart sank. *Why am I not surprised?* "I'm your lab partner. We've been working on our project together?"

"Jemma?" Brooklyn said, "Do you really have to do it now?"

"You two know each other?" Joal asked.

"Of course, silly," Brooklyn said. "Jemma's on my cheer squad. She's a flyer."

"It's due tomorrow," Jemma said, keeping her eyes on Joal, "...a week before the last day of school. This is beyond cutting it close."

"We wouldn't want you to lose your perfect four-point grade average now, would we?" Brooklyn said, flipping her hair over her shoulder.

"I thought we were already done," Joal turned and pressed a kiss at the base of Brooklyn's throat.

Brooklyn moaned. "Mm. Come on Jemma, couldn't you just finish it yourself?"

"We're nearly done," Jemma said, averting her eyes, "It'll only take a minute. I want to make sure we didn't miss anything."

"It's fine the way it is... uh..." Joal paused, his brows scrunching.

"Jemma," she said in a clipped tone.

"Right," Joal said as he turned to nibble on Brooklyn's ear.

Jemma wanted to pour an ice bucket over both their heads, instead, she looked away and said, "Forget it. I'll finish it myself."

"Thanks... uh..." he said, scrunching his brow.

"The name's Jemma!" She turned and stomped away. Joal never ceased to amaze her. Jemma knew he wasn't stupid. So why couldn't he remember her? Was she truly that forgettable?

"What a total and complete jerk-face," she mumbled as she strode toward the physics room. After trying the door, she felt like screaming.

It was locked.

Great! Now, what am I going to do? The box was too big to put in her locker. Admitting defeat, she started the two-mile trek home with the heavy package in her arms. Her back was killing her after the first block, and she had many more to go.

If Joal had come with her to work on the project—like he said he would— he'd be able to put the stupid box into his oversized, overpriced SUV. Now she'd not only have to carry the darn project home, but she'd also have to carry it back to school in the morning.

The wind whipped Jemma's hair as thunder rumbled. She looked up and her heart skipped a beat. Black thunder clouds churned in the distance. Picking up her pace, Jemma prayed that she would get home before the sky opened up and poured down on her.

Λ

Joal picked up his backpack off the locker room floor and ran his fingers through his wet hair. Practice went well today. Of course, it always went well for him. Swimming was more natural than walking. He slammed his locker shut and said, "You guys ready to go?"

Kahula and Tao both nodded and fell into step beside him as they exited the locker room. The comfort of having friends at his side was a stark contrast to most of Joal's life. Loneliness had been his constant battle until three years ago, when Kahula showed up at Olympus High. Kahula had ignored the invisible barriers between Joal and the other students as he swept him up in his friendship. Now, Joal was fully submerged in a tight-knit group of friends who would literally die for one another.

Tao, well, he was a different story. He spun around and strolled backward, facing Joal and Kahula as they marched out the door, entering B hall. "Did you check out my swim time for the fifty-meter freestyle?"

Joal smiled at Tao's cocky attitude. It was a real confidence booster to realize you're a demigod, and not just a freak others said you were. Joal had never had that problem. He'd always known who and what he was.

"It wasn't bad," Kahula said. "Someday you might be able to keep up with Joal."

"Not even in his dreams," Joal said shaking his head.

"He has an unfair advantage," Tao said.

"We all have an unfair advantage," Kahula said.

"He has more of one than we do. I'll have more of a

chance when Joal goes on his..." Tao's brows scrunched, and he turned to Joal. "What do you call it?"

"A prison sentence," Joal said.

"I wouldn't call training with the Nordic god of war a prison sentence," Kahula said.

"Be glad you don't know enough to understand what it's really like," Joal said. "I just want the summer to be over so I can come back."

"You never told me," Kahula said, "how did you get mixed up with a god of war?"

"Well, you know my mom is a Nordic sea-goddess."

"Yeah."

"She met Tyr at the Stream of the Dead, centuries ago."

"What is that?" Tao asked. "Sounds like a rock concert?"

Joal chuckled. "No. It's a river in Denmark. Anyway, Tyr's the only non-sea god my mom will talk to. I don't think she fully accepts him, but he's... useful. And he, of course, is smitten with my mom, so he'll do anything she asks."

"Fertility goddesses have that effect on people," Kahula said.

"And she's asked the war god to teach you to fight?" Tao asked. "How awesome is that?"

Joal scoffed. "Yeah, no."

"So, where does your training take place?" Tao asked.

"On a remote island in the Pacific," Joal said.

"A tropical island?" Tao said. "That doesn't sound so bad."

"An uninhabited island," Joal said. "I'd rather be in school."

"There *are* some pretty hot girls at this school," Tao said. "Speaking of..., who were you talking to in the hall?"

"You mean Brooklyn?" Joal asked.

"Naw, the other one."

"What other one?"

"The girl carrying a box that looked like it weighed as much as she did."

"I have no idea who you're talking about," Joal said as he pushed the door open, and stepped outside. The wind gusted and for a moment all Joal could see was his hair as it covered his eyes. He brushed it away and looked up. Black clouds billowed and churned in the sky. A wave of unease washed over him.

"Dudes," Joal said and cut a glance over to his friends; they both had their eyes glued on the sky.

"Gods, what's going on?" Kahula asked.

Joal shook his head. "I don't know. But that's not natural. I think we should get a closer look."

"Shouldn't you ask your father?" Tao asked.

Kahula scoffed.

"What?" Tao blinked.

"My father and I are not on speaking terms," Joal said, opening the driver's side door and climbing in. Kahula followed, getting in the passenger side. "And before you ask," Joal said, "I'm not running to 'mommy' for help either."

"I wasn't going to...," Tao's words dropped away as he climbed in the back seat. "Oh, forget it. I just hope we don't get our butts handed to us by Zeus or Ares."

Joal started the car and pulled out of the parking spot. "If I see any sign of them in the area, we'll get out of there quick. But it's not likely they'll be there personally. It's probably a skirmish between the sea-gods and sky-gods. They're forever fighting."

"It's not just Olympus High that has the rivalry?" Tao asked.

"That's an understatement," Kahula said. "Sky-gods and sea-gods loathe each other."

"I guess your mom never invited a sky-god to dinner?" Tao asked.

Joal chuckled darkly. "No."

"Why are we going at all?" Tao asked.

Joal shrugged. "In case it's something else."

"What I don't understand," Tao said, "is why you and your mom live on the surface. I mean, Kahula and I have to. But you—"

"Amphitrite," Kahula said.

"Who?" Tao asked.

"My dad's wife," Joal said. "She wouldn't be too happy to know that I exist. Though I don't know why I'd be to blame for my dad not being able to keep his junk in his pants."

"Oh," Tao said, frowning.

Joal didn't bother to counter the assumption that his mother lived here. He hadn't seen her in about six months. She was always too busy to come. Or maybe she forgot she even had a son on this side of the world. Yeah, both of his parents pretty much sucked. Joal pressed his foot down on the gas pedal, anxious to get his mind off his thoughts.

The bay came into view in the distance. Waves rose and crashed below a billowing, purple-gray sky. Joal scanned the ocean for the source of the trouble. There was nothing obvious that he could see. The highway snaked along the shoreline like a serpent. The head of the serpent opened its mouth towards the waters. His heart pounded when he finally got close enough to see the problem.

A dark mass moved beneath the surface coming toward the shore. The water above bubbled and churned. Several cars had stopped, and onlookers stood at the shore pointing to the waves, their eyes glued on the scene. Joal pressed harder on the gas.

"Is that a sea monster?" Kahula asked.

"Don't be stupid," Tao said. "There's no such thing." He looked at Joal. "Right?"

Joal arched an eyebrow. "You still have a lot to learn." He paused a moment before saying, "It's not a sea monster."

"Then what is it?" Kahula asked.

Joal avoided the question. "I need you to listen to me. When we stop, I'll get out and Kahula, you take the wheel and get Tao out of here, fast."

"No!" Kahula said. "There's no way we're leaving you."

"You'll do what I say."

"And why would we do that?" Kahula asked.

"Because *you* can die."

"You think whatever that is, it can kill us?" Tao asked.

"They *will* kill you."

"What are they?" Kahula asked.

"Dagonians. And they don't tolerate the existence of 'half-breeds'.'" He made a quotation mark with his fingers.

Kahula's eyes widened. "You have to be joking. They never come on land."

"I wish I were."

"And why can't they kill *you*?" Tao asked Joal.

"They can try." Joal slammed on the brakes and the vehicle screeched and came to rest at the edge of the road by the sandy beach. He leaped out as he yelled, "Go!"

Joal's feet hit the ground and he raced to the humans gathered on the shoreline watching the churning sea. They were close enough to the water that Joal felt the spray of the sea as he skidded to a stop. "You need to leave, now."

A twenty-something, lean man with snake tattoos circling his neck looked him up and down and said, "And you are?"

"Someone who knows that bad things are about to happen."

"You know sh—" his voice cut off when the first Dagonian surfaced thirty feet away, his black eyes burned, and his face contorted in rage as he lifted a dripping sword above his head. Half a second later, a dozen other Dagonians rose from the waves, their tails cutting wedges through the water and then through the sand as their bodies hovered over the ground. Each of them had gold bands on their biceps. Joal remembered what his mother called them. *Maj bands.* They were infused with the power to offset gravity.

The humans screamed and fled—finally. Being a teenager sometimes sucked. No one ever took you seriously.

The Dagonian's eyes locked on him, and one sneered. *"Human."* He spoke Atlantean. Joal's mother raised him to speak the language in hopes that he would one day find a home in the sea—as if that would happen.

Joal answered him back in Atlantean, *"You wish."* Pulling a small, celestial bronze cylinder from his pocket, he lifted it and said, *"Eleftbérosi."* A metallic snap later and he grasped a gleaming trident in his hand, the three sharp blades glinting menacingly.

The Dagonian's eyes widened and then narrowed as he hissed, *"Traitor."* Other Dagonians quickly gathered at his side.

"I'm giving you one warning to hightail it back into the water before I wipe the arrogant expressions off all your faces," Joal said. *"If you go now, I'll forget you ever set foot, tail or whatever on land. Stay and harm even one human, and I'll personally introduce you to Hades."*

"Big words for an infant," the Dagonian said, his eyes glistening in amusement. The Dagonian raised his sword and swung. Joal deflected the strike that was meant to sever his head and came back around with his trident. The Dagonian turned in time to miss decapitation himself, but his shoulder didn't fare so well. Joal cut him so deep that he could feel the blade's tip nick the bone as it passed through. Blood poured from the wound as the Dagonian dropped his weapon, roared, and slapped his hand tight against the gash. In a heartbeat, the blades of countless other swords rained down on Joal as he

deflected each one, his movements so fast that human eyes wouldn't be able to track him. Tyr had taught him well.

Joal's trident clashed with sword after sword as sparks rained down on the rocky terrain. He moved, instinct taking over as he fought. He felt air shift as a sword sliced toward his back. He twirled his trident overhead and behind him, deflecting the strike and then pivoting to intercept another strike that came from his right, the blade clanged between the prongs. It took a simple twist of Joal's weapon to snap the blade in half. Another block and snap of a blade on his left, and then one directly in front. All of this happening in the space of several heartbeats.

Joal continued to move forward, blocking, sweeping, slicing, and snapping blades as he neared the surf. Occasionally, he drew blood, but not one Dagonian could land a strike against him. In less than a minute, most of the Dagonians were left with broken weapons and damaged egos. Joal continued to drive them toward the sea. He would not be satisfied until they'd gone back to where they'd come from. The misty spray of a wave coated his face, and then as quickly as it started, the battle was over. The Dagonians backed away from him, horror written on their faces.

"*Son of Poseidon,*" their echoing voices breathed. And then they were bowing their heads. *"Forgive us. We did not know who you were."*

Son of Poseidon? How did they know?

Joal caught his reflection on his blade. The image of a trident glowed aqua-blue across his cheek—his father's mark. Wow. Looks like the jerk remembered he existed. Joal wondered if the mark would be permanent, or if his father made an exception this one time because he didn't want his son sliced to ribbons. Truth be told, the Dagonians were not much of a threat, especially not for one who was used to fighting a god of war. But humans against these battle-trained creatures... that would be another story.

"Go back to the sea," Joal said, *"all of you. Before I summon my father."*

He didn't need to ask them twice.

In less than two seconds, the last of the Dagonians disappeared beneath the waves, leaving him alone on the beach. He stooped down and picked up each piece of the broken blades and threw them far out to sea. He didn't want a hapless human to slice their foot on the razor-sharp shards. Once the beach was clear of debris, he pulled out his cell phone and called Kahula.

"It's over," Joal said in lieu of a greeting. "I could use a ride." He didn't wait for an answer as he ended the call and strolled back toward the road.

Chapter Two – Jemma

For a friend with an understanding heart
is worth no less than a brother
—— *The Odyssey*, Homer

TWO MONTHS LATER...

Jemma found her best friend, Cassie, waiting for her on the swing hanging over the wide front porch of her modest brick home. A drizzle misted across Jemma's face as the wind picked up, cooling her skin and raising goose pimples—typical Washington state weather, especially on this side of Mount Olympus. Jemma hurried up the steps and out of the rain.

"I'm really glad I'm graduating this year," Cassie said, scooting over to make room for her. "I'm so done with school."

"Um, Cass," Jemma said, sitting down. "It hasn't even started yet."

"Yeah, don't remind me. Soon enough, my life will once again suck. I'm just glad it's my last year of school."

"You still have college, and I hear their classes are not an easy stroll through the park."

"Yeah, but then I'll have college guys to take my mind off my troubles. One make-out session with a twenty-something hottie will make all the studying totally worth it."

"I'll take your word for it. I, for one, am more concerned with getting a degree than swapping saliva with some hormonal, sweaty guy."

"You wouldn't be saying that if we were talking about Joal." Cassie gave Jemma a sideways glance.

"Oh, no. Don't even say his name. Joal is history. He's not worth my time."

"Oh, really?"

"Yes! Absolutely."

"Okay, princess. But you've been obsessing about him since the second grade."

"Yeah, well, the obsession is over," Jemma said. "I'm through pawning over someone who doesn't even know I exist. I thought for sure when I made the cheer squad, he'd finally see me. But no, he still can't even remember my name."

"Yeah," Cassie said. "He seemed to date every cheerleader *but* you. You know, it's interesting that he never settled on one."

"Yeah," Jemma said. "You should have seen how mad Brooklyn was when he left on some summer trip and didn't even say goodbye."

"I just had a thought," Cassie turned to face Jemma. "Maybe he's dated so much just to maintain an image. Maybe he isn't what he says he is."

"You mean like he's a spy? You think the government sent a spy into Olympus High." Jemma arched an eyebrow. Here she goes again—Cassie and her crazy theories.

"No. Not exactly a spy, I just wonder if he has a secret. Like a big secret." Her eyes widened. "Maybe he's the son of someone really important."

"Like a billionaire?"

"No. Someone more powerful, like royalty… only more."

"You think Joal is some kind of prince?"

"Yeah, and he's not allowed to marry any of us lowly humans."

"Humans?"

"People, whatever."

"I think you have a vivid imagination."

"Dismiss me if you want, but I know that Joal is hiding something."

"Enough about Joal. We need to make plans. School starts in only one month."

Cassie perked up. "Okay, what do you want to do?"

"How about a movie?"

"Naw, I looked at the listings and everything at the theater is likely to put you in a coma. I was thinking something more daring."

"Like what?"

"Adventure in the cemetery," Cassie's eyes sparkled with mischief.

"What kind of adventure?" Jemma frowned.

"Ghost hunting."

Jemma laughed. "How are we supposed to hunt ghosts? I don't think bullets work with the corporeally challenged. Besides, don't you hate guns?"

"We're not going to use guns. I've got a ghost hunting app on my phone. It has a thermal camera, an EMF detector, and a voice recorder that detects and translates electronic voice phenomenons or EVP's—that's voices you can't hear with your ears but shows up in a recording."

"Are you serious? You can't possibly believe in ghosts."

"Of course, I do! One of these days we need to do a *Ghost Quest* marathon. You'll be a believer too. Though, we'll have to do it at your house. My mom won't let me watch it on the TV. She thinks it's *evil*. I have to sneak it on my phone when she's not looking."

"This is what you want to do?"

"Yes. Come on, it'll be fun."

"Alright." Jemma shrugged. "Ghost hunting it is."

Hours later, she and Cassie stepped under a wrought-iron sign that read, "Heavenly Gates Cemetery." They found a stone bench nearby and sat; cold seeped through Jemma's jeans, sending a shiver through her.

The moon hung over a perimeter of pine trees, adding a silver glow to the gray slashes of vine-covered tombstones, and rusted, iron fencing. A low fog crept over the ground and around the tombstones, bringing with it the scent of moss and wet grass. Crickets chirped, and an owl hooted from somewhere in the distance. They had all the makings of a horror movie.

Goosebumps sprouted on Jemma's arms. "This is seriously the number one creepiest place I've ever been to. I don't get why we couldn't have gone to Garden Grove Cemetery."

"Are you kidding," Cassie said. "That creepy feeling is *them*."

"Them?"

"The ghosts."

"Right," Jemma said, drawing out the word.

"I found this place last year while helping my mom do some genealogy on her family," Cassie said. "Great uncle Herbert is buried somewhere over there." She pointed to the right. "As soon as I saw this place, I knew it would be the perfect place to go ghost hunting."

"And you think because it's spooky here, that there are ghosts?"

"Absolutely. Okay, it's time." Cassie pulled out her phone and opened the app. A garbled whirring sound emanated. Jemma had to stop herself from laughing. She didn't want to hurt Cassie's feelings, but good gods, the thing sounded like a device built fifty years ago, not the latest iPhone.

"See here." Cassie pointed to a green bull's eye overlapping a negative black-and-white image of the cemetery in front of them. A robotic voice said, "Ghost detected." Cassie panned around, stopping when her phone caught the image of what looked like an alien at the center of the bull's eye.

"Here we go," Cassie whispered.

The device said, "Communication detected."

"Oh, cool," Cassie said. "It's translating."

"Help us," said a ghostly voice.

Jemma had to admit, it did sound eerie, like it didn't just come from the phone, but from the fog around them.

"Wow," Cassie said. "It sounds way cooler out here than it did at home."

Jemma rolled her eyes and mumbled, "'Help us?' That's original."

"Shh. Of course, it's something ghosts say a lot. They're dead."

"Right."

"I'm going to try to talk to it," she whispered and then said loudly, "Hi. My name is Cassie. What's yours?"

They waited a long time as the alien figure continued to hover on the screen. *"Angel."*

"Cool," Cassie said loudly. "Your name is Angel?"

"Maybe it's Angel from *Buffy the Vampire Slayer*," Jemma said as she nudged Cassie. "He's really hot."

"We could only be so lucky," Cassie said. "I wonder if there's any reality where we could make out with a ghost?"

Jemma laughed. "I don't think so."

"Angel."

"This is awesome," Cassie whispered to Jemma and then raised her voice. "So, Angel, how did you die?"

A third time they heard, *"Angel."*

"Yes, I know your name is Angel," Cassie said, "but how did you die?"

The screen darkened. A few seconds later they once again heard, *"Angel."*

"This thing isn't working right," Cassie said, shaking her phone. "I swear it worked great at home. It said some crazy stuff—answering questions only a ghost in the room could answer."

"It's probably a glitch," Jemma said.

"Save us, angel."

"Now *we're* the angels?" Jemma asked.

"Maybe I can work with that," Cassie said as the wind picked up. Leaves fluttered around them. "Come spirits, come to me. Speak to me. Let nothing hold you back. Let no barrier keep you in." Cassie's dark hair whipped around her face. She was really getting into this.

"Save us, angel." The volume rose.

"I wonder what they need to be saved from?" Jemma asked as the fog thickened around them.

"Save us, angel."

"Save us, angel." They chanted.

"Go," Cassie shouted, "Go..." She turned to Jemma and whispered, "This is a Catholic cemetery, right?"

"I think so."

"Go to the gates of Saint Peter," Cassie bellowed.

"Save us, angel."

"Save us, angel."

"I *am* saving you," Cassie said. "I told you where to go."

"Save us, angel."

"Save us, angel."

"Listen, if they won't let you in at the pearly gates," Cassie said, "there isn't anything *I* can do about it."

"Save us, angel."

"I think the app's broken," Cassie said. "I'm going to restart it."

"Save us, a—"

A feeling of dread seeped into Jemma's skin, emanating from the cool air around her. For a moment, she couldn't breathe as a charge, like an electric jolt, shook her body. She dropped to her knees, gasping at the strange sensations overcoming her. A face materialized from the fog. A white, ghostly figure floated in the air in front of her. She was beautiful—ethereal, with large almond-shaped eyes and long, black hair floating in a halo around her exquisite face. Her hand pressed against the base of her throat, and her mouth gaped open as her eyes darted from Jemma to the back of Cassie's head to the cemetery surrounding her. From the fog behind her, white, skeletal hands reached out. The ghost's confusion turned to terror as the hands grabbed her and pulled her back into the mist. Jemma's eyes were wide as she stared at the swirling fog. The ghost had disappeared.

"Okay," Cassie said, turning back to face her, "I restarted the app. Let's try this again." She looked down at Jemma and wrinkled her nose. "What are you doing on the ground?"

Jemma cleared her throat and rasped, "I tripped."

There was silence for a moment, and then the same voice said, *"Save us, angel."*

"Save us, angel."

Cassie swore. "I think it's stuck in some kind of loop."

"Save us, angel."

"Hey, Cass?" Jemma tried to swallow the lump in her throat.

"Yeah?"

"We need to go." Jemma rose up from the ground and

stood on trembling legs as she fought back an insane urge to run. There was something seriously wrong with this place. Her stomach lurched.

"Save us, angel."

"Yeah," Cassie said dismissively as she continued to mess with her phone. "This app is garbage."

Jemma grabbed Cassie's hand and pulled her toward the car. "Come on. We need to go. Now!"

"Okay, okay," Cassie answered. "You don't need to manhandle me."

Once they reached the car, Jemma opened the passenger side door as she looked up toward the cemetery. Darkness overshadowed it and then that darkness appeared to swirl. It looked like a black hole in the forest. And it felt so... wrong. Unnatural.

"Woah," Cassie said, pausing as she held the driver's side door open. "Do you feel that?"

"Just get in," Jemma said.

Cassie paused for just a moment and then she ducked into the car. A heartbeat later, they were on the road, headed back toward town.

Cassie chatted away as she drove. Jemma only half-listened, concentrating on her breathing as she fought back nausea. What did she see? Was it some kind of vortex? And then did she truly see a ghost? Being in a cemetery at night trying to communicate with spirits was a recipe for feeding an overactive imagination, right? That had to be it. She *had* to have imagined all of it, including the ghosts, which must have been the fog. With all Cassie's crazy talk, Jemma's mind conjured up the images. That was most definitely it. It had to be.

Jemma felt foolish. She'd never known she was that susceptible to the power of suggestion. Finally, Jemma said. "I'm sorry the ghost hunting thing didn't work out."

Cassie shook her head. "It's not your fault. What can I expect from a five-dollar app? I need real equipment."

"You want to try this again?" Jemma asked.

"Absolutely," Cassie said firmly. "I think the location was great, but I need to do some research before we go again. And I need the proper equipment."

"No, next time let's do a different location," Jemma said, her heart once again pounding, "there was something creepy about that place."

"Not a chance. The reason it *was* creepy is that there were ghosts there. We're totally going back."

Jemma suppressed a shudder. *Best friend or not, Cassie's on her own.* Even as she thought it, Jemma knew she couldn't abandon Cassie to whatever was at that cemetery. She would just have to convince her to stay away. And if she had to, she'd puncture Cassie's tires to keep her from going.

Chapter Three – Kronos

Say not a word in death's favor;
I would rather be a paid servant
in a poor man's house and be above ground
than king of kings among the dead.
—— *The Odyssey*, Homer

DEEP IN THE PIT, beneath the world of man, beneath the world of Hades, the king of the Titans stirred. *An ancient power has awoken.* Stretching his long limbs, he put his sandaled feet on the icy floor and stood. *Who is this primordial deity whose power summons me?*

With purposeful steps, he strode toward the entrance to the seer's cave.

"Kronos," Phoebe said in greeting, but she did not look at him. Her eyes were on her basin—the pool of prophecy.

The Titan king stepped into the light cast by the pool; his glowing red eyes turned the pool's blue glow a deep violet. "Who is it?"

"I'm not sure," Phoebe said, reaching into Pandora's box. Her arm disappeared past her elbow into the small container that appeared to be no more than a hand deep. Kronos frowned. This box's power was nothing to trifle with. He studied Phoebe's face, looking for any hint of doubt, but all he could ascertain was that the Titan goddess of foresight looked as if she'd not slept in eons. "Something has been hiding her from my sight," Phoebe said as she pulled out a mirror. "Ha! I see her clearly now."

"What? Only now? How did they hide her from you?"

"Oh, the fates were clever, but I've been playing this game much longer than they have. I have a few tricks up my sleeve."

"Does this trick involve my son?"

"Zeus?" She arched her brow and then chuckled. "You know me so well. Yes, he'll be playing an integral role."

"And the fates? They are hiding a goddess?"

"Not exactly. She's more powerful than a goddess, but she's also young and inexperienced."

"What is she to us?" Kronos sneered.

"She is our salvation. Soon, we'll be free. We just have to bide our time. Patience is key."

Kronos cracked a smile. Freedom. It was the sweetest word he'd tasted in many millennia. "I've been waiting for thousands of years. I can wait a bit longer, as long as my freedom is sure."

"We shall be free, if all goes as planned."

"When do we start?"

"Fate has already set events in motion," Phoebe said with a smirk. "I just need to change the trajectory a smidgen and do it without fate's knowledge."

"You speak as if fate were a person."

Phoebe smirked, "Oh, she is. And she's going to learn an extremely valuable lesson."

Chapter Four— Jemma

Perverse mankind!
Whose wills, created free,
Charge all their woes on absolute degree.
—— *The Odyssey*, Homer

THE STAIRS CREAKED as Jemma raced downstairs, making her way to the kitchen. Her stomach clenched in hunger. She stumbled across the cracked linoleum floor and grabbed the back of a chair as the room spun. She closed her eyes and focused on her breathing as the cracks in the plastic cushion of the metal chair dug into her fingers. Once she'd steadied herself, she opened her eyes and moved slowly toward the fridge.

Her stomach growled, demanding food. Wasn't vertigo supposed to make you nauseous? But all she could think about was the left-over pasta in the fridge. It called to her like a siren's song. The room finally righted itself, thank heavens. She couldn't afford to have dizzy spells today, of all days.

She opened the door of the old Frigidaire and pulled out the half-eaten container of Alfredo.

"Are you going to eat all that for breakfast?" her mother said, and Jemma froze. She looked up. Her mom's hair was wrapped in a threadbare towel and her face was washed clean of makeup—she looked younger without it, though Jemma knew better than to tell her that.

"What?" Jemma said. "I'm hungry." Jemma looked up and met her mother's cynical eyes as they narrowed.

"You're getting fat."

"No, I'm not." Actually, Jemma had no idea if she *had* put on weight. She rarely stepped on the bathroom scale. The last time she did, she came in well underweight.

"Yes, you are." Her mom grabbed her hand and pulled her toward the stairs. "Come on. Let's see how much you weigh."

Jemma frowned as her mom pushed her into the bathroom and nodded to the scale. "Go on. You'll see."

Jemma took a tentative step onto the device and the numbers spun. The scale practically gave her a heart attack when it stopped, but then it changed direction back to safer territory, and then back to a number still way too high, and finally settled on a number that left her speechless.

"See, I told you." Her mother said, looking over her shoulder.

"That can't be right. The scale is broken."

"It's not broken. And don't you have cheer tryouts this morning?"

"Yeah, but Brooklyn told me it's just a technicality."

"Was that on the phone or in person?" Her mom arched a brow.

Jemma didn't answer.

"Hm, I thought so. Your face is rounder. Your hips are huge, and so are your breasts—though *that's* not so bad. But still, you expect those cheer girls to catch you without breaking their backs? There's no way they'll let you be a flyer this year. I doubt they'll even keep you on the cheer squad."

"I'm not fat, mom. You'd be happy if I were anorexic."

"It'd be an improvement from what I see."

Jemma growled. "Check a BMI chart."

"Check what?"

"A Body Mass Index chart, it tells you if your weight is healthy." Jemma would do it herself if her mom had let her have a cell phone.

"My eyes don't lie," her mom said.

"Just do it, mom."

She pulled out her phone, her nails clicking against the screen as she typed a search. She scowled. "It's not so much the weight you are now," she said, letting Jemma know her weight was normal, "it's how fast you're gaining. At this rate, you'll be obese in no time."

Jemma threw up her hands. "You're insane."

"Yeah. And you're fat."

"I'm not fat! Seriously, I can't believe it... You know. Forget it. I have better things to do than stand here and argue with a grown woman who acts like a juvenile."

"Don't talk to me like that, young lady." Her mom put her hand on the door frame to block Jemma's exit. "You're grounded."

"Grounded? Seriously?"

"Yes."

"I can't go to cheer tryouts? What about school? It starts next week."

"You're grounded from that crazy best friend of yours."

"You're grounding me from Cassie?"

"Yes, until further notice. You are not to see her or talk to her. And you will not eat me out of house and home either, so starting right now, you're on a diet."

"You're the one who's crazy, putting me on a diet, and I'm

not even overweight."

"It's for your own good."

"Whatever." Jemma pushed past her mom, bounded down the stairs, grabbed her cheer bag, and stormed out the front door, slamming it behind her.

What kind of mother acted like hers? Not a good one. All of Jemma's life, her mom had been controlling everything in Jemma's world. Well, all except for the parts she couldn't control. When confronted with those, her mom would freak out, throwing out insults and criticisms at every turn. Jemma was desperate to see the day when she could move out from under her mother's thumb.

Minutes later, Jemma slammed her cheer bag on the bench in the locker room. Yanking at the zipper, she opened it and pulled out her uniform.

"Hey, J—" April's voice cut off as her eyes widened. "Um, you look different."

Oh, no. Not her too.

"Is that different in a good way, or bad," Jemma asked.

April shrugged, her eyes refusing to meet Jemma's. "I don't know, just different."

Jemma put her feet through her shorts and pulled them up. They squeezed her thighs, refusing to reach her hips. *What the...?*

She pulled out her spare jogging pants. They made the journey, but not without difficulty. Turning to the full-length mirror, she gaped at the figure before her. The elastic squeezed her waist, giving her an undeniable muffin top!

"Oh, no, no, no, no," she mumbled.

She glanced at April, who looked away just as their eyes met. Already dressed, April escaped out the door to the field.

"This cannot be happening to me," Jemma said. After

trying on the entire contents of her bag, she settled on the only clothes that she could squeeze into, never mind the fact it looked like she was about to burst out of them.

Wanting the ground to swallow her whole, she forced herself to step out onto the field. April must have warned the others. All eyes were glued to her.

Brooklyn strode forward, a deep scowl on her face as she approached Jemma. "You're late."

"I was having wardrobe trouble."

"Obviously." She looked her up and down. "What in the world did you do? Eat everything in Garden Grove? We can't let the new recruits see one of ours looking like this." Brooklyn shoved her back toward the door to the locker room. "We have a reputation to uphold. In fact," she glanced back toward the squad, "we've already chosen the bases and spotters. That only leaves the flyers. And as you well know, flyers must be small, light..., you know, easy to catch. It's a matter of safety."

Jemma's heart sank. "What are you saying?"

"Do I have to spell it out for you?" Brooklyn frowned at her, her hand on her hip. "Sorry, Jemma, but you didn't make the squad this year. I'd tell you to lose some weight and try again next year, but we're seniors, so, you know..." She shrugged.

Jemma blinked back tears.

"Don't expect any sympathy," Brooklyn said, jabbing her finger at her. "You brought this on yourself. I thought you were committed to the squad. Apparently, I was wrong. It looks like you were more committed to fast food." Brooklyn turned her back, flipping her hair, and said, "You know your way off the field."

Jemma stood in stunned silence as her throat tightened, and her eyes burned with unshed tears. Feeling utterly defeated, she turned away and went to change back into her street clothes—which ended up being another struggle. The clothes she arrived in seemed to fit tighter than they had when she got there. But how could that be?

What is happening to me?

Chapter Five – Joal

JOAL WOKE to the tantalizing smell of bacon. Denise! Gods, how he'd missed her and her cooking. If he didn't see another banana or coconut in his life, it would be too soon. Tyr might have been a god, but he was the lousiest cook in history. And truth be told, Joal wasn't much better.

Stretching his aching body, Joal attempted to climb out of bed. Everything hurt. You'd have thought that Tyr might have taken it easy on him these last few days, knowing Joal was to return home. Nope. The Nordic god of war didn't know the meaning of the word mercy. And you'd think, because Tyr was training him to fight, that as his pupil, Joal should have been confident that he was never actually in jeopardy.

Yeah. No.

Joal didn't have a speck of doubt that if he hadn't found a way to block every strike, Tyr would have sliced off his arm and then fed it to the sharks as punishment for being stupid. Tyr, having only one hand himself, let Joal know repeatedly that only one hand was needed to fight, the other was optional. Not to Joal. He was immensely attached to both of his hands.

Finally dragging himself out of bed, he pulled open his curtains and looked out his wide window, taking in an appreciative view of Garden Grove. His house sat on the side of Mount Olympus, perched on stilts above a small lake and waterfall. Through the mist, he could see the whole town. It spread out before him, the edges creeping up the foothills of Washington's Mount Olympus. An overcast sky drizzled rain across the gray roofs and checkered streets that blanketed a rolling landscape. Vehicles like ants darted along the roads, and people entered and exited buildings in an early morning frenzy. Joal closed his eyes and felt the buzz of power coming from the citizens below. There was a reason the mountain he lived on was called Olympus. The area surrounding it held the largest percentage of demigods in the US.

It was so good to be home.

He padded downstairs in his bare feet and there Denise was, standing in front of the stove, her hair speckled with gray and piled up in a messy bun. She turned to him and smiled, her blue eyes crinkling around the edges. His mom repeatedly commented about how old Denise looked. To Joal she was perfect—gray hairs, rounded body, and lined face in all.

"Hey, baby," Denise said as she wrapped him in a warm embrace. When she pulled away, she scowled. "You've lost weight."

"I didn't have your cooking," Joal said.

She frowned as she assessed him. "Well, I'll take care of that. Have a seat," she nodded toward the table, and he sat. She placed a plate in front of him, piled high with bacon, eggs, and hashbrowns. Then placed another plate with a large Mickey Mouse-shaped pancake, dripping with butter and syrup. Finally, she poured him some orange juice.

"Mickey?" Joal said. "Really? I think you forget I'm not five." He tried to frown but couldn't manage it.

"You'll always be five to me," she said, tousling his hair.

Joal chuckled as he jerked away and then ran his fingers through his strands to mitigate the damage she'd done. His phone vibrated. Even before he glanced at the screen, he knew who it was. "Hey, Kahula."

"Hello, oh great ruler."

"Let me guess. You want a ride."

"Yeah, for both Tao and I. But only if it fits into your busy schedule."

Joal chuckled. "Yeah, I've got an open slot right after you scrape the harpy sludge off my shoes."

"Man, you've got to stop hanging with the harpies," Kahula said.

"It's a step up from hanging with you," Joal said.

"Ooh, ouch! I guess I walked into that one."

"Yeah. You did." Joal laughed. "Alright. I'll see you at seven thirty."

"Um, actually we're already here. We wanted to save you the trouble of coming to get us."

"No. Guys. Denise is not cooking for you."

"Oh, hush," Denise said behind him, "we have plenty. Tell them to come on in."

"They don't deserve your cooking."

"And you do?" She arched a brow.

"After what I've been through this summer. Yes, I do."

Minutes later, they were laughing and eating. Joal felt as if he'd never left. And then forty-five minutes later, they were walking side by side as they strolled through the main entrance of Olympus High.

"Hey, Joal," said some kid with combed-back hair and a leather jacket.

"Hey, James Dean," Joal answered, cracking a smile as the kid beamed at him.

"Hi, Joal," a pretty girl who looked too young to be in high school, smiled brightly at him.

He nodded and cracked a smile. He could feel her heart take off in a sprint. There was no denying the effect he had on the opposite sex... and some of the same sex, for that matter.

Joal's eyes widened when he saw Brooklyn flirting with Evan, the captain of the lacrosse team and Evan was definitely flirting back. As if he felt Joal's eyes on him, Evan turned to glare at him. Joal raised a brow, not intimidated in the least. If Evan knew what was good for him, he'd stop posturing. He had no idea who he was dealing with. Still, it was a relief that Brooklyn found someone else to satisfy her needs. It had taken him about three seconds to grow tired of her mind games.

Joal had lost count of how many people greeted him before he made it to his locker. He'd just closed the door when he saw her, a girl he'd never seen before, at the far end of the hall. Something about her struck him. Hair the color of copper dipped in honey cascaded over her shoulders. Her body, lush, curved in just the right places. And her eyes... hazel, bright, round, and filled with a mixture of hesitation and confidence. Her lips were full, pink, and, if he were being honest with himself, looked entirely too kissable. She was stunning. If this girl wasn't a goddess, she should be. And today, he'd find out if she were.

Λ

Jemma strolled through B Hall and nearly ran into a girl climbing down a ladder. "Sorry," she muttered, and then she looked up. Banners announcing the approach of homecoming hung across the width of the hallway. Gods, it was the first day back and they were already prepping for homecoming.

She'd never missed that dance before, but then she'd never been ostracized from society before either. And given what happened at tryouts, she couldn't expect otherwise. She gave her chances of being asked to homecoming about a thousand to one. It would take someone either fearless or ignorant to ask her.

"Hey, Jemma," a familiar taunting voice made her cringe. Brooklyn.

"Have we put on even *more* weight?"

Jemma shot a look over her shoulder and shrugged. "Yeah, from the looks of it, you *have.*"

Brooklyn's eyes narrowed as she sneered. "You're an idiot. You're just angry that you got kicked off the cheer squad this year. You brought that on yourself, you know. Last year you were a flyer, this year, you're a big, fat nobody."

Jemma tried not to flinch. The last thing she needed was Brooklyn seeing how much her words hurt. But truly they did. She had loved being on the cheer squad. Flying above the crowd, twisting, and twirling in midair was as close to heaven as she'd ever come.

Jemma squared her shoulders as she decided to ignore Brooklyn's painful jabs.

"Hey, babe." Evan stepped to Brooklyn's side and put his arm around her. He turned and glared at Jemma.

What was his deal?

"I thought you weren't talking to her anymore." He shrugged toward Jemma.

"I'm not."

"Good, I wouldn't want her curse rubbing off on you."

Curse?

Evan pushed his meaty finger against the tip of his nose and snorted.

Jemma's face burned as she heard a rumble of chuckles around her. She turned her back on the crowd and strode purposefully toward her first-period class. *Stupid ignoramus! If I could get away with it, I'd punch him in the—*

"Hey, girlfriend!" Cassie intercepted Jemma and surrounded her in her signature best-friend hug.

"Hey," Jemma said.

Cassie leaned away, and her smile turned to a scowl. "What's wrong?"

Brooklyn laughed and hissed, "Freaks." She brushed by her with Evan at her side. They both got swallowed by the crowded hallway.

"Oh," Cassie said, frowning.

"You really shouldn't be seen with me," Jemma said, adjusting her backpack. "Don't you know I'm a pariah? Being around me is the equivalent of committing social suicide."

Cassie shook her head. "Don't be so dramatic. Oh, and you might want to know, I just saw Joal. Looks like he's back from his trip."

Jemma closed her eyes and groaned. "No. Why couldn't he just move away, preferably to another planet."

"Listen, I know you've had a major crush on him, since... well, forever."

"Yeah, and he's never given me the time of day. And now that I'm... good grief. He hasn't seen me since I—"

"Put on a few pounds?"

Jemma groaned.

"I don't see what the big deal is. If you hadn't been giving me updates on that stupid number on your scale, I probably wouldn't have even noticed."

"Yeah, right." Jemma shook her head. "It doesn't matter anyway. I'm so over him. I don't know why I ever liked him in the first place."

"He's nice to look at?" Cassie shrugged.

"Don't remind me. He's also egotistical, self-centered, condescending... need I go on?"

"Yeah, but he's not cruel, and he never bullies. He's just... confident and a bit oblivious."

"Too oblivious to see me."

Cassie scratched her head. "He doesn't see a lot of people.

But yeah, even when you were a cheerleader, he didn't notice you. I still think he's hiding something."

"He's not hiding anything. You're just being paranoid."

"Well, regardless, I predict that this year will be epic."

"Epically bad."

"Oh, don't be such a sourpuss," Cassie frowned.

The bell screeched. "I'd better get to class," Jemma said. "If I don't graduate, I won't be able to escape this hellhole."

"Hey, don't disrespect my hometown."

"It's my hometown too. I can disrespect it all I want."

Cassie scoffed, but her eyes were lit with amusement.

Minutes later, Jemma strolled into Ms. Kingsley's world history class and skidded to a stop. There he was, Joal Forseti, leaning against a desk on the other side of the room. He looked hotter than ever. His white shirt strained over his muscled chest, and his sun-bleached hair looked wind-blown —in a good way. Wherever he'd been must have been all kinds of sunny. He sported a warm tan that set off his emerald eyes. Those eyes immediately turned to Jemma and his eyebrows rose. Heat bloomed in her cheeks as she averted her gaze. Jemma kicked herself for her reaction. *Why is he looking at me? He never looks at me.*

Finding a seat as far away from Joal as humanly possible, she sank down and attempted to calm her racing heart. Keeping her head down, she ventured a peek. He was no longer looking at her, but still, her heart continued to thump hard in her chest. Jemma chewed on her bottom lip and forced her eyes to the front of the room.

"Okay class," Ms. Kingsley said, "I know this is our first day back, and I should cover all the class rules and other boring crap, but you know what? You're seniors. You don't need me to baby you. I had most of you in my classes before. You know what's expected by this time, and if you don't, check the syllabus or see me after class. After I take roll, I'd like to jump right in to learning, so get out your notebooks and be ready to take notes." Minutes later, she dove into her lecture. "This week, I'm introducing you to..." Ms. Kingsley pulled down a map over the whiteboard. "...the Greek Empire."

Jemma cracked a smile. She loved Greek history, especially mythology.

"It's an interesting fact." Ms. Kingsley continued, "that the ancient Greeks didn't call themselves Greek. Does anyone know what they did call themselves?"

When no one responded, Ms. Kingsley said, "Jemma?" As if Jemma had raised her hand.

She hadn't.

Regardless, Jemma said, "They were called Hellenes, named for Hellen, son of Deucalion and Pyrrha—the survivors of the great flood who repopulated the earth by throwing stones that turned into people."

"Thank you," Ms. Kingsley said.

"Ms. Kingsley?" a voice rose. Jemma turned around to see who it was and arched an eyebrow. It was Attie, at least Jemma thought that was her name. But whatever her name was, she rarely spoke up. This girl had an incredible ability to blend in and not be noticed.

"Yes?" the teacher said.

"Do you think there's any truth to the Greek myths?"

The class erupted into laughter. Jemma couldn't help looking at Joal. She wanted to know if he was laughing too.

He wasn't. But he did have a hint of a smile in his expression.

"Quiet class," Ms. Kingsley warned. "That's a good question." She scowled as her eyes quickly scanned the room. "One might ask if there's truth to Buddhism, Christianity, or any other religion. There are large bodies of people who believe the most fantastical stories—people who are not laughed at but honored for their beliefs. At one time, the Greek myths were put forth as truth by whole countries, whole civilizations, even. Just because *we* weren't raised to believe in them, doesn't mean they were any less feasible to their followers."

Attie nodded and looked down at her notebook as if it held the mysteries of the universe. A smile lit her face.

Forty-five minutes later, the bell rang. Jemma stood, and the room spun. She clutched the desk at her side to keep from falling. Squeezing her eyes shut, she willed her stomach not to heave. *What's wrong with me?* This entire month, she felt as if she were fighting off an illness.

A warm hand pressed gently on her shoulder. Jemma felt a jolt and jumped back. Turning to see who had touched her, she was surprised to meet Joal's eyes.

Smiling, he said, "Hi, my name's Joal. And you are..."

Jemma frowned. Of course, he forgot her name—yet again.

When she didn't answer, he said, "Are you okay?"

She shook her head. His clear eyes penetrated hers as if he was searching for something. She'd dreamed of this day, the day he finally noticed her. But instead of feeling warm and fuzzy, she felt completely unnerved. Glancing away, she said, "I'm fine." Her voice quivered. "I just got up too fast."

"Oh, okay. Good." He looked at her expectantly, a surprising warmth in his expression caught her off guard. "So, what *is* your name?"

Jemma sighed and finally said, "Jemma," just as someone shouted, "Joal."

A boy Jemma didn't recognize came up from behind him.

"You coming?" he asked Joal and then glanced at her and cracked a smile.

"Yeah," he answered. He looked back at Jemma and said, "It was nice to meet you." Then he turned around and left.

Nice to meet you?

Shoving her notebook in her backpack, tears stung her

eyes. *No! I am not allowed to cry.* It's not like this same situation hadn't replayed itself over and over again throughout the years. Though it seemed that this time he actually saw her. Really saw her. And that difference rocked her to her core.

Jemma flung her pack over her shoulder and rushed out of the room. Less than a minute later, she pushed open the door to a bathroom, stepped into a stall, leaned over, and pressed her forehead against the cool, steel wall. Tears leaked from her eyes as she focused on breathing steadily. Finally, after several minutes, she stopped shaking and the tears dried up.

This situation was *not* different. Her heart couldn't afford to think it was. He may have looked her in the eye and asked her name. But it would end the same, he would forget her, and she would survive it.

Am I truly that forgettable?

No. She wasn't going to think about it. If she did, she'd be crying all over again.

She stepped out of the stall and stood in front of the mirror. She examined her face. Her cheeks were flushed, and her eyes had a tinge of red, she had minor makeup smudges, but she was otherwise composed.

Jemma shook her head. This was exactly what she said she wasn't going to do. Why was she letting him affect her like this? Joal may be the king of jerks, but she shouldn't let herself care anymore.

She didn't care!

If she said it enough, that would make it true. Her betraying heart sank at the thought of swearing him off. She could do so much better. Why couldn't she just forget him like he forgot her?

Well, she'd just act like she didn't care. Her heart would catch up eventually, or she'd die a lonely old woman, forever pining after someone who didn't even know she existed.

Rubbing away the make-up smudges, she stepped into the

hall, it seemed emptier than she expected. How long was she in the bathroom? She looked at her watch and gasped. She'd missed the first two minutes of her class!

She stopped short when she heard a voice that sounded a lot like Joal's, coming from around the corner of B hall. It *was* Joal. The timber of his voice was unmistakable. He spoke low, his tone urgent. "Are you sure there's not another one at the school? A girl, a senior."

"Not that I'm aware of." A deep voice she didn't recognize spoke. "So, what is she?"

"I'm not sure," Joal said.

"How powerful?"

"Very."

Their voices grew fainter as the sound of their footsteps diminished.

"She must be..."

"...could you be..."

Jemma could only catch fragments of this conversation, and then the voices died off completely.

She peered around the corner. Joal and another student disappeared through double doors at the end of the hall, heading toward the gym.

That was weird. She wondered who he was talking about. The conversation sounded important.

For him.

One thing she knew, he definitely wasn't talking about her. She was the least powerful person in the school.

She shoved the thought aside and continued to her class. When she pushed open the door of room C23, all eyes turned on her—layers upon layers, row upon row. There was no sneaking into her choir class.

"Hello, Jemma," Mrs. Waters said, frowning. "I'm glad you could grace us with your presence."

Jemma lowered her blushing face and rushed to step up to

the soprano section. She was about to sit beside Lexi, but the glare of her steel-gray eyes stopped Jemma in her tracks. She moved to the next row up and stepped beside a girl she recognized but didn't know personally. This girl kept her eyes straight ahead but moved farther away from Jemma. She ignored the slight and took her place with the choir.

"Okay, advanced choir students, you know the drill. Let's continue our warmup. She turned to the piano player and said, "Give me a middle C." She turned back to the choir and sang out a standard major scale. Then she turned to the students and raised her hands. Jemma and all the other students opened their mouths to sing. The note rang out soft and hesitant from Jemma's mouth. She loved to sing, but today, something felt different. Her voice moved smoothly from the first note to the second. The sound seemed to gain a life of its own and filled her with—her voice choked off when she'd realized she'd left the others behind. They were all still singing the C note, dragging it out unnaturally long.

"Jemma!" the teacher shouted. Jemma could feel the concussion of her teacher's bellowing voice. It felt like it would knock her over. All the voices went silent.

"What in the name of the gods are you doing?" Mrs. Waters snapped angrily.

Jemma's eyes widened in shock at the reprimand in the teacher's voice.

"I... I'm just singing the scales," Jemma answered, her face heating.

"Do you think I was born yesterday, because now I know *you* weren't." Mrs. Waters shook her head. "Did you forget how to sing *with* the choir?"

"No, I..." Giggles bubbled from the other choir members.

"You may not take your actions seriously, but I do, and I have zero tolerance for it. Go down to the counseling office right now and transfer out of my class. And don't you dare sign up for another vocal class."

"What?" Jemma blurted, completely stunned. "But—"

"Go," Mrs. Waters growled as she glared sharply at Jemma, "Now," She picked up the classroom phone. "I'll call ahead and let them know you're coming."

Jemma wanted to argue, but things were bad enough for her this year, she didn't need to make enemies of the teachers too. So instead, she nodded her head, as she blinked back her tears. Choir was one of her favorite classes, and now that too was being taken from her. She felt like she'd stepped into an alternate reality this year—one that made no sense. Could things get any worse?

Chapter Six – Joal

Of the many things hidden
from the knowledge of man,
nothing is more unintelligible
than the human heart.
—— *The Odyssey*, Homer

JOAL PULLED out his phone and texted Kahula. *Missing practice today. I'll fill you in later.* He slipped the phone in his pocket and strode toward the office but stopped short when he saw *her* strolling out the door. Once again, he was struck by the warm perfection of her. He clenched his fists as his hands ached to touch her. Then he saw her expression. Sadness poured off her, and he found his heart breaking for her. *What happened?* An open door brought a gust of wind carrying her scent.

A moment later, Joal swore under his breath. How had he missed it? She smelled like a fresh breeze. *She was sky-born. Why in Hades did she have to be sky-born?* Now he really needed to find out what she was doing here at Olympus High.

When she disappeared around a corner, he forced himself to not follow, instead he waited a few minutes before he moved toward the office and pushed the door open. Taking a cleansing breath, he looked at Mrs. Otterson and grinned.

"Hello, Joal," she smiled sweetly. "What can I do for you?"

"This is somewhat embarrassing," he said. "I was supposed to give the new girl in my history class a message, but I'm afraid I forgot. I need to catch her before she leaves school today. Can you tell me where her last class is?"

"Sure thing, sweetie. What's her name?"

"It's Emma; I'm not sure about her last name."

Mrs. Otterson plucked away on her keyboard and narrowed her eyes. "Okay. Emma, Emma... Hmm. You say she's in your history class?"

Joal nodded.

"I don't see any Emma. There's a Jemma, Jemma Ryan."

"That's got to be her."

Mrs. Otterson shook her head. "She's not a new student; she used to be on the cheerleading squad."

"You sure?"

"Yes, either way, there's no Emma. And no one else in that class has a similar name."

"That's strange." Joal was baffled. If she'd been a cheerleader, he would've remembered her. He'd dated most of the cheerleaders at least once. Hades, he'd remember this girl regardless. Becoming aware that Mrs. Otterson was growing suspicious of his reaction, he returned his full attention to her and quickly said, "That must be it, then. Can you tell me what class she has last?"

"It looks like she's taking an optional seventh period, so she's here longer. It's Mr. Thurston's AP Calculus in B Hall room 18."

Wow, beautiful, and smart. Too bad, she's the enemy. "Thank you, so much."

"Anytime dearie. Is there anything more I can do for you?"

"No, thank you. You were very helpful."

"I'm glad," she said, her voice ringing with sincerity. "Can I give you a note to excuse your tardy?"

"I'd appreciate it."

She scribbled out a note and handed it to him.

"Thank you," he said, smiling widely at her.

A warm blush lit her cheeks. "Anytime, dearie."

Several hours later, Joal was peering around the corner, watching the door of Jemma's class. The shrill ringing of the bell signaled that the class had ended. A trickle of teens trailed out the door. They looked like Joal expected, scholarly, solemn —Joal raised his brow as the captain of the football team, a burly son of Ares, stepped out. He was followed a moment later by the girl that had to be Jemma Ryan. How could she not be new to the school? There's no way he'd forget a girl as beautiful as this.

Joal studied her as she stepped into view. He kept out of sight. She was stunning, flawless. It was obvious to him that she was no mere human. He needed to find out who she was and who exactly she belonged to. Was Jemma a full goddess, a demigod, or something else entirely? And most important, what was she doing here? She hadn't applied to the school as non-human through normal channels. According to Dante, she had no sponsor, no mentor, no paperwork... So why was she here? He would have to be discreet to unearth her secret.

Λ

Jemma made her way through the hall and pushed open the exit, eager to get out of the school building. This day was, by far, the worst first day of school she'd experienced in her entire life. *But Joal talked to me.* She mentally slapped herself. *No! I'm so not going to read anything more into that.*

When she nearly plowed over Evan, she realized that, unfortunately, her disaster-of-a-day was not over. Evan reached out and grabbed her arm. Something shot through her at his touch. It felt dark, slimy, like sludge creeping through her veins. Evan seemed to feel something too, as he hissed and drew his hands back.

He chuckled darkly. "Jemma Ryan has a secret."

"What are you talking about? Why is everyone acting so weird today?"

"Weird? Look who's talking. I know you're not one of *us*. But *what* are you?" He rubbed his chin.

"You're insane, now get out of my way. I have places to be."

"You're not going any—" he began angrily, and then his words cut off as his eyes drifted behind her. He tensed and stepped back.

Jemma glanced back to see what had spooked him, but all she saw was empty foliage.

"Fine. Run away. But I'll be watching you." Evan said and then turned and strutted back into the school.

His words echoed in her ears as she made her way home. *I know you're not one of us.* Well, duh. He thought she didn't know that? Brooklyn had made it perfectly clear.

Jemma felt eyes on her back. She turned and studied the walkway and empty yards behind her. There was nothing out of the ordinary. Quickening her pace, the feeling of being watched persisted. Her heart pounded with every step.

Was it Evan? He did say he was going to watch her. But sneaking around, spying on her as she walked home? That was over-the-line creepy.

Finally, Jemma stepped up the sidewalk leading to her old, leaning-tower-of-a-clapboard home. At least that's what she called it. Its entire two stories were tipped at a slight angle. The house looked like it should be condemned. But so far, it continued to stand.

"Mom," Jemma shouted, strolling in the front, and shutting the door firmly behind her. The feeling of unease left as a musty smell assaulted her. Their home was over a hundred years old. The fight against the old lady smell was a constant battle.

She dropped her backpack on the floor, turned on the wax warmer, and put two highly scented cubes in the tray. "I'm home." She made her way to the kitchen. Her stomach clenched in hunger. The dry, green salad she'd eaten three hours before was long gone.

Her mother was sitting at their laminate table drinking a glass of chocolate milk from her favorite "World's Best Underachiever" mug as she opened the mail. Her hair was pulled back into a ponytail, showing a rim of gray roots around her scalp. Looks like she was done working for the night. Her mom never wore her hair up if she was going out.

Jemma looked longingly at the chocolate beverage in her mom's hand.

"Don't even think about it," her mom said— as if she could read her mind. "There are carrots and celery sticks in the fridge."

Just kill me now. "I already had a salad for lunch. I need something more than just veggies, mom."

"Right," she said. "You say that all the time. But every time I see you, you look bigger."

Jemma pursed her lips, opened the fridge, and pulled out a Ziplock bag filled with dry vegetables. "Have you made me an appointment with the doctor?"

"You just need to stop stuffing your face."

"Mom," Jemma growled. "I haven't *been* stuffing my face. There's something wrong with me. I was adding up all the calories I've been eating, and it's not even five hundred a day."

"You're short, you don't need as many calories as most people."

"Mom, less than five hundred calories are not nearly enough, even for someone as short as me. And I'm not gaining weight anymore, but I'm not losing it either. You need to call the doctor."

"You know how I feel about doctors."

"Yeah, they're the devil. But mom, I don't know why *you* can go when you have a sore throat, but I can't go even when I'm on the brink of pneumonia?"

"Stop being so dramatic," her mom snapped. "You never get sick. Besides, I *know* you're sneaking food. There's no other explanation."

Jemma could feel her blood pressure rise. "I haven't been sneaking food."

Her mom shook her head as if she didn't believe her. Who was Jemma fooling? Of course, she didn't. She never did. "You are being so unreasonable, just like you were about my social security card," Jemma said. "I need it for my college applications."

"We can't afford college."

Jemma took a deep breath and attempted to calm her temper. After the day she'd had, she felt like she'd explode. But if she completely lost it, it would only make things worse. She needed her mother's cooperation if she ever wanted to escape this place. "Mom, I told you, I qualify for a Pell Grant and student loans."

Her mom shook her head. "You don't want to get into debt."

"Mom," she said attempting to sound as calm and reasonable as she could, "Pell grants don't have to be paid back, and I'll apply for a scholarship. I've gotten really good grades. If I'm lucky, I'll get a full ride."

"Nothing in life comes free."

Jemma huffed. "I know. Which is *why* I've worked my butt off in school. If I don't go to college, all my hard work will be for nothing. I'll be forced to work for minimum wage the rest of my life. Do you really want that for me?"

"Why do you want to abandon me?"

"Mom, this isn't about you."

"Of course, it is. Why can't you just be content to live at home and mooch off your mother? Most teenagers are happy with that. Why do you even need to keep going to school after you graduate? And why do you need a job at all? I'm working double shifts so that you can buy nice clothes and have spending money."

"I don't want spending money; I want a life. I don't understand you, mom. You want me to be a normal teenager? Well, why can't you be a normal mother? Most moms want their children to make something of themselves. You never have! You've always held me back."

"You don't understand," her mother said, tears building in her eyes.

"Then help me understand."

Her mom shook her head and stood. "I can't." She rushed toward the kitchen door. Jemma grabbed her arm and pulled her back.

"Mom. I've had as much as I can handle. I've already requested my birth certificate and as soon as it comes, I'm requesting my social security card. Whether or not you like it, I'm applying for college and getting a job. And then I'm moving out."

"I already took a risk for you when you got your driver's license. Do you *want* me to go to prison?"

"What are you talking about?" Jemma threw up her hands.

"Nothing," she shook her head. "Nothing at all. Do whatever you want, but I won't have any part of it." Her mom shook off her grip and fled the kitchen, leaving Jemma wrestling with a mixture of emotions. But through it all, her determination grew. Jemma would get what she needed herself. She couldn't count on her mom. She was crazy. But no matter what her mom did or said, Jemma was getting out of this house and away from Garden Grove.

Joal shook his head as he stood by, listening to Jemma and her mother's conversation. This girl's mom was seriously messed up. But the way Jemma stood up to her... well, it was brilliant. Still, the conversation had been strange. He looked at the old home she lived in. Yeah, this wasn't the house of a goddess. And her mom... there was something suspicious about that woman. Whatever the case, Jemma's mom was human. He could feel it. Did this mean Jemma was a demigod? No. That didn't feel right either. More likely, Jemma's mom was not really her mom. The level of power Joal felt at Jemma's touch was too much for her to be half human. Either way, there was something off about this whole situation.

Joal searched to see if there was anyone around. When he found the area clear, he emerged from behind Jemma's house and strode to the sidewalk. Pulling out his phone, he called Kahula. His friend answered on the first ring. *Practice must be over.*

"What's up?" Kahula said.

"Hey, brother," Joal said. "I need you to pick me up at the corner of Sycamore and Elm."

"I don't have a car," Kahula said.

"You can drive mine."

"I know the code, but where are the keys?"

"There's a spare in the glove box. You don't even need to use it, with the key close, you'll just need to push the ignition button."

"Aren't you afraid someone will steal your car?"

"The key's not always there; it appears when I need it."

"I'm not you."

"Doesn't matter, *I* need you to have it."

"Okay, but you owe me."

"I do not," Joal scoffed.

"Someday you might."

"Dude, it would take you a hundred years to do enough for me to owe you."

"Yeah, don't rub it in. Do you want to tell me why you of all people would miss the first day of practice?"

"Not on the phone."

"Okay. Do you want me to bring the newbie?"

"No. Drop him off first. I can wait."

"Now you've got my curiosity all peaked."

Joal smiled. "Don't hurt yourself."

Fifteen minutes later, Kahula pulled up to the curb, got out, and looked around. "What brought you out to the wrong side of the tracks?"

"I may have found another one." Joal got in behind the wheel.

"Another demigod?" Kahula got in the passenger seat and shut the door.

"No, I'm not sure what she is."

"She?"

"Yeah. "

"Is she hot?"

Joal shot him a glare. "Hands off her."

"Hey, dude." Kahula raised his hands. "I'm only human, well, half-human."

"Yeah, I know," Joal growled.

"Okay," Kahula swore under his breath. "I get it. You want her," he said, stating it as if it were a fact.

Joal shook his head. "She's sky-born."

Kahula swore. "Have you told Dante?"

"Yes, about her power. But no, about her being sky-born. I haven't had a chance."

"What did he say?"

"He told me to find out about her. He wants to know who and what she is. If she's a threat to the humans, he said he'd take care of her."

"That under-worlder scares me." Kahula shuddered.

"I wouldn't want to get on his bad side," Joal said.

"You and me both. How did you meet him?"

"My dad sent him to keep an eye on me."

"Why didn't he send a sea-god?"

Joal raised his eyebrows. "Are you really asking me that?"

Kahula frowned. "Your stepmom's a real piece of work."

"She is?" Joal's eyes widened as he turned toward Kahula. "Gods, why didn't you tell me before?"

"Shut up." Kahula punched Joal in the shoulder. "So, what's the plan?"

"We get to know her."

"That's it? That's the plan?"

He looked in his rearview mirror, back toward Jemma's house. The image of her face swam in his memory and his heart skipped a beat. "Until we know who she is and what she's doing here, that's all we do."

Chapter Seven – Jemma

There are two gates of dreams:
one pair is made of horn and one of ivory.
The dreams from ivory are full of trickery;
Their stories turn out false.
The ones that come through polished horn come true.
—— *The Odyssey*, Homer

"SHE REALLY SAID THAT?" Jemma eyed Cassie's fry as it dangled loosely in her fingertips. The rain pattered against the windows of the school cafeteria, the sound nearly drowned out by the commotion of the lunchroom.

"Yeah," Jemma said. "She really did. You know, I always knew my mom was a bit crazy, but prison? Like me going to college or getting a job would bring a SWAT team to our door."

Cassie's eyes widened. "I bet your mom's not really your mom."

Jemma huffed.

"Maybe she's a criminal. Maybe she kidnapped you and is hiding you away from your real family, because—"

"Cassie, please don't you start, too. I can only deal with one crazy person in my life."

There was a long pause and then Cassie said quietly, "I'm not crazy."

Jemma immediately regretted her words. "I'm sorry. I know you're not. It's just...it's been a horrible week."

"I know it has. I'm sorry I'm being so touchy. Are you going to do it anyway? Apply for college, I mean?"

"Of course, I am. I've already requested a copy of my birth certificate. As soon as that comes, I'm requesting a copy of my social security card. I'll just need to 'borrow' my mom's driver's license again. And then I'm gonna apply for college and hunt for a job."

"Borrow, huh."

"Yeah. It's for the greater good." Jemma shrugged and then caught sight of her old friends Hailey and Maddie entering the cafeteria. They looked her way and proceeded to sit at a table far from her. Jemma's heart sank.

"Do you really think you can do this without your mom's cooperation?" Cassie asked.

"I'm almost eighteen, soon I won't need my mom's cooperation." Jemma took another sip of her drink. Pain hit like a bolt of lightning slamming into her back. Jemma gasped, inhaling her pop. The burn of diet coke was nothing compared to the screaming agony of her body. She'd be wailing if she could get in some air. As fast as it came, the agony was gone, leaving her sputtering and coughing. She turned to see what had struck her.

"Whoa, be careful." Cassie patted her back as she continued to cough.

"What was that?" Jemma rasped, turning back and coughed several times more.

"You choked on your pop," Cassie said.

"No, it's my back. It felt like it was on fire. You didn't see anything? I didn't get struck by lightning, did I?"

"Uh, no." Cassie shook her head slowly. "I think that would have shattered the glass in the window. Not to mention, you'd probably be dead."

"That hurt," Jemma said, trying to look at her own back.

"Let me see it," Cassie said as she stepped behind Jemma and pulled her blouse away. "I don't see anything. Your back looks fine to me..." she paused, "...though."

"What?" Jemma said.

"No. It's nothing."

"What's nothing?"

"Your bones are sticking out a bit. Have you lost weight?"

"I wish." Jemma tried to look behind her, but she couldn't see what Cassie saw. "You sure it's not red? I could've sworn something burned me."

"Nope. Just your same old pale, fleshy self."

"Very funny, I'm not pale."

"Girl, you couldn't tan to save your life."

"Listen," Brooklyn snapped, appearing from behind Jemma, "if you freaks are going to go like all lesbian on each other, please wait until you're alone to tear each other's clothes off." Brooklyn said with a lunch tray in her hands. Jemma had the insane urge to push the tray into her face. Brooklyn turned and strutted away.

"We're not lesbians," Cassie shouted, clenching her fists. She seemed to realize what she said as her eyes darted around the cafeteria. "Not that there's anything wrong with it."

"Yeah," Brooklyn called over her shoulder and laughed. "Could have fooled me."

When she was finally out of earshot, Jemma said. "I'm really sorry."

"You're not the one being a total witch." Cassie dropped back down in her seat.

Jemma looked across the lunchroom at their old table. Every eye at that table was looking at her. Most were sneering, some were laughing. Jemma had wondered what effect she was having on Cassie's social life.

Who was she fooling? Her friendship with Cassie was ruining her best friend's social status. Cassie would be better off without her. *Things couldn't possibly get worse.* Jemma no sooner thought the words when she was proven wrong.

Joal came into view. He was flanked by two of his friends —other elite members of the swim team. At most schools, there were rivalries with other schools. At Olympus High, there were fierce rivalries between the school's own sports teams. And there were no crossover athletes. Three teams were the pinnacles: the football team, the lacrosse team, and the swim team. And at the top of the pinnacle of the swim team sat Joal Forsetti—unbeatable, untouchable.

Unbelievably, Joal's eyes fell on her, and he headed straight for Jemma and Cassie. Jemma's pulse beat against her throat. What in the world was he doing?

Joal raised an eyebrow as he stopped behind her. "You're sitting at our table."

Seriously? First, he forgets I exist, and now he's trying to intimidate me. Jemma's temper rose.

"Sorry," Cassie said as she lifted her tray.

"We are *not* sorry," Jemma snapped. "There are no assigned seats in this cafeteria. We got here first, so I guess you'll have to find somewhere else to sit." She waved him away.

"Ooh!" the boys howled in surprise. With wide smiles, they looked to see what Joal's reaction would be.

"Fair enough." Joal shrugged. He dropped his tray next to Jemma and sat beside her. "We can sit here together." His elbow brushed hers, and once again she felt a jolt. There was seriously a lot of static in this school.

"On second thought," Jemma said, standing. "I've got some studying to do before class. I'm going to head to the library."

"Oh, no you don't," Joal said, tugging her back down into her seat. "You wanted this table so much. You can have it. I don't mind sharing if you don't."

"O—kay," she said as she studied his tray. He had an insane amount of food.

Joal's friends stood smirking. He nodded toward them and said, "Sit."

Like trained dogs, they obediently sat, and the benches groaned with their added weight.

"Is that all you're eating?" Joal scowled at her plate of dry salad. He didn't wait for her answer, but said, "So, Jemma, why aren't you on the cheerleading squad this year?"

Wow. He remembered my name this time.

"She probably quit when she realized that they don't cheer at swim meets," said the tall, dark boy on the other side of Joal.

The other boy laughed and gave him a high-five.

"Be serious, Tao," Joal said.

"I *am* serious."

Joal looked at her curiously. The way his eyes penetrated hers made her insides feel like warm Jell-O.

"I couldn't be a flyer anymore," she said in a quiet voice. "I put on too much weight." *What am I doing? Why am I telling him my most embarrassing secret?* Though, it wasn't really a secret for anyone with eyes.

"That's ridiculous. It's just like girls to obsess over being skinny. I'm going to give you a tip about guys." He pointed a French fry at her. "We love curves on a woman. Besides, you're better off. Who wants to fly anyway? Swimming is much better." He popped the fry in his mouth.

"I like swimming *and* flying," Jemma said. "I like anything that makes me feel like I have no boundaries."

"I can understand that." Joal shrugged and then took a large bite of his hamburger.

Why is he being so nice to me?

Once he was done chewing, he asked, "How long have you lived here?"

"Longer than you." Technically this was true. Joal's birthday was three weeks after hers, and they've both lived here their entire lives.

"You're kidding, right?"

"Nope." Jemma's throat bobbed.

"How could it be that I've never seen you before? Have you been homeschooled all this time?"

Her chest quivered, and her eyes burned. *What game was he trying to play?* Jemma was appalled when she realized she was about to cry... in front of Joal. She'd literally rather die!

Jemma shot out of her seat. "I've got to go." Tears gathered as she offered a quick goodbye to Cassie and rushed away.

"Wait," Joal said, his words brushed her back as she dumped her tray and retreated into the hall. Jemma fought to hold her tears back. Crying in front of Joal might be the worst thing imaginable but crying in front of anyone else at the school was a close second. Instead of stopping at her government class, she took a detour around the gym and ran down to the end of an unused hallway. A rusty, steel door stood before her. She wrestled it open, slipped inside, and turned on the light. She'd found this room her first year of high school—after taking a wrong turn before cheer practice. It was a forgotten part of the building, an old biology lab, complete with cages, specimen jars, animal skeletons, aquariums, boxes, and dust. Lots of dust.

Jemma ignored the filth, lifted off a sheet that covered an old couch, and sank down. Her heart sat shattered in her chest as tears slid down her cheeks. Her world was crumbling around her. Her friends turned their back on her, the whole school turned their back on her, the one friend who didn't, should have, and her mother was wreaking havoc with her life plans. Even Joal was finally noticing her—as someone to intimidate and play mind-games with. To top it off, her body was blowing up like a balloon and giving her phantom pains. Everything in her world was falling apart.

Her stomach grumbled as tears continued to fall. She took in a ragged breath. She should just give up. Forget finishing high school. She should go home and eat everything in the fridge. Her mother wouldn't care—well, at least she wouldn't care if she quit school. She'd care a lot about the food. Being a high school dropout was nothing compared to putting on a few pounds in her mother's mind.

A creak sounded like claws against a chalkboard. Jemma jerked as her eyes darted up and met the last person on earth she expected to see.

"Am I disturbing you?" Joal stepped in and shut the door behind him.

Jemma jumped up and wiped the tears from her eyes. She was so dumbfounded she didn't answer, she just stood looking down at the floor. He moved with casual grace as he strode over and stood before her. She took a quick glance up. He seemed much larger, standing so close. Her head didn't even reach the top of his shoulders. Of course, at her height, most guys towered over her. Still, Joal was really tall. His warm, tropical scent wafted over and had her heart pounding.

He stepped to the couch and sank down. Reaching out his hand, he took hers and tugged her down to sit next to him. She didn't resist.

What would come next? Jemma could only imagine, but it couldn't be good. He'll probably laugh at her, tease her for crying. He likely thinks she's ridiculous, overreacting to nothing.

A feeling of panic hit her, and she stood. She couldn't take it. She really couldn't. It was bad enough when he ignored her. Having Joal, her life-long crush, mock her—it would destroy her. "I... I've got to go."

Joal's hand reached out and took hers. It was warm and calloused, and it felt so good. Fresh tears gathered. The familiar charge tingled lightly in her palm.

"Please stay," he begged. His voice seemed genuine, with no sign of mockery. Still, she was hesitant to trust him.

"Why?" she said. Her voice sounded so small; her eyes were glued to the floor.

"Because I... I need to apologize. I'm sorry for... well, I'm sorry for being a jerk." His voice rang with sincerity.

Jemma realized they were still holding hands, and she pulled her hand away from his. "Why are you being nice to me?" She ventured a glance at his face.

His eyes widened. He looked... hurt? No, she had to be wrong.

"I didn't know you thought so little of me," he said.

Those words flipped a switch in her head, and her temper rose. "Thought so little of *you*? You don't even remember who I am. We've been in the same school every year, been in the same classes since kindergarten."

His brows furrowed in confusion, but she continued as the years of hurt and disappointment fed her emotions.

"And in all that time, you couldn't even bother to remember my name. I must have told you ten thousand times, and every time you were unlucky enough to have to deal with me, you'd always forget who I was. We worked as partners on a biology project three and a half months ago, and every single day you'd inevitably get my name wrong. I don't know why you suddenly care about me now. And I have no clue why *I* care."

"That makes no sense," he said, echoing her own thoughts as he shook his head.

"Is this a dare?" She wiped away the tears from her cheeks. "Is that why you decided to talk to me? Did someone put you up to it? Did Brooklyn?"

He scoffed. "No. No one knows I'm here."

She shook her head and stepped away. "Of course, they don't."

"That's not what I meant," he said, rising from the couch. "I don't care who knows I'm here. Listen, I'm sorry. You have every right to be angry with me. I was stupid, selfish, and too self-absorbed to have noticed you." He surprised her with the intensity of his voice.

"Why?" she said. "Why are you wanting to talk to me now? Was I too small for you to see before, and now that I'm fat, you finally see me?"

He shook his head. "That's ridiculous. And what idiot called you fat?"

"Why do you want to know?" Jemma asked.

"So, I can punch them in the face."

Jemma shook her head at the impossibility of this conversation. "You'd have to punch everyone on the cheer squad." *And my mom.*

"They're jealous of you."

"Ha. Somehow, I doubt that. You never answered my question. Why now?"

He paused for a moment before he spoke. "You and I have a lot in common."

"Like what?" What did he know about her that he didn't know before? Probably everything, considering he knew nothing about her.

"You live with one parent, and you've never met the other, right?" he asked, catching her off guard.

"What? How did you know?"

He raised an eyebrow and cracked a smile. Her heart flipped over in her chest as his piercing green eyes focused on her.

"So." She shrugged. "We both have an absent parent. There are a lot of kids who live with only one parent."

"Yeah, but their absent fathers live in the human world."

This conversation just took a completely unexpected turn. "What... are you talking about?"

His brows knit together as he seemed to study her. After a long stretch of silence, he asked, "What do you know about your dad? Where he came from?"

"I have no idea who my dad is."

"Your mom never talks about him?"

"Never."

"Wow." He sat, studying her for a long while. "You really don't know what you are, do you?"

Jemma's jaw clenched. "And here I thought you were done being a jerk." She turned toward the door.

He caught her wrist and she paused.

"I didn't mean it that way." He swore under his breath. "First Tao, and then you."

"Tao? The guy from lunch?"

Joal nodded.

"So, *what* am I? Cause it really sounds like you're insulting me."

"I'd never do that."

"Then what am I?"

"You wouldn't believe me."

"What wouldn't I believe?" This back-and-forth conversation was driving her nuts.

Joal shook his head, "I shouldn't be the one to tell you."

"Tell me what?" she said, exasperated.

"You and I..."

Jemma frowned. "Yes?"

"You and I, we're... not human."

She barked a laugh. "Oh, that's rich. You know you should see someone about your mental health."

"I'm not crazy," Joal said.

Was he serious?

"Look," he continued, "fourth period is about to start. We both need to get to class. We'll finish this conversation later."

"If you can remember who I am."

He paused and said softly, "I'll remember." His eyes locked on hers. "I really do want to see you again. I shouldn't want to, but I do."

"What's that supposed to mean?"

He sighed and then pressed his lips together. Finally, he said, "We may have a lot in common, but we're also... supposed to be enemies."

Jemma was about to throw out a retort, but the way he was looking at her made her pause. Instead, she asked, "Are we enemies?"

Joal looked from her eyes to her lips and back to her eyes. If she didn't know better, she'd think he wanted to kiss her. Instead, he said, "No. At least I hope not. But that's up to you."

Jemma didn't say anything, but simply nodded.

"We need to get to class." Joal sighed and then turned to leave.

"Joal?"

He stopped, turned back toward her with his eyebrows raised.

After a long pause, Jemma finally said, "Why did you really come looking for me?"

He studied her face before he said, "I could see I hurt you.

I couldn't stand to see you suffer, especially knowing I was the cause of it."

"I don't understand you at all." She shook her head and ran her fingers through her hair.

He gave her a crooked smile. "You have no idea how right you are." He reached out. "Give me your hand."

Jemma hesitated a moment before she placed her hand in his. The electric buzz was stronger than ever, but if Joal felt it too, he wasn't giving any indication. He turned her palm up and scrawled ten digits on her skin in blue ink.

"If you find yourself in any kind of trouble and need help, give me a call."

Jemma nodded and swallowed.

"I need to go. We *will* talk again," he promised. Without hesitation, he stepped through the door and left.

Jemma looked down at her hand in awe. He'd given her his phone number. Despite everything he had said to her over the years, everything he'd done, she couldn't help but feel elated. It reminded her of a line from Shakespeare, *"I do love nothing in the world so well as you—is this not strange?"*

Being in love with Joal made absolutely no sense, but that didn't matter to her heart.

Chapter Eight – Jemma

Like a girl, a baby running after her mother,
begging to be picked up, and she tugs her skirts,
holding her back as she tries to hurry off – all tears
——*The Iliad*, Homer

CASSIE STARED at Jemma's hand as she held it tight in her grip. The wind blew gently through her hair as the leaves rustled above; the school stood stoic, a brick fortress in the background. "Wow, I knew this day would come."

"Yeah, right," Jemma said, pulling her hand from Cassie's grip.

Cassie frowned. "I did! Why does no one ever believe me? He's dated every other cheerleader, now it's your turn."

"I'm not a cheerleader anymore."

"That's beside the point. Are you going to call him?"

"No. Of course not. He said to call him if I needed help."

"Tell him you need help finding a good time on a Friday night."

"Yeah, right. Besides, like you just said. It may just be '*my turn.*' That sounds like a recipe for heartbreak."

"Okay, now don't say I said anything." Cassie looked around, as if someone might be spying on them. "But Tao said—"

"Tao? Joal's friend?"

"Yeah. He walked me to class," Cassie arched a brow. "He is pretty cute, don't you think?"

"I guess. I didn't really notice."

"That's because when Joal's around, nobody else exists for you. But anyway, like I said, Tao said that the entire swim team is talking about how much Joal is into you. They said he's never acted like this with any other girl."

"That's totally not true. He makes out with a new girl every week."

"And that's the difference. He's not making out with you, but he's still really into you. Tao said he thinks he cares a lot about you."

"Tao said that?"

"Yes. And I think he was being one hundred percent honest with me. I have a good feeling about this. I think you should go for it. Besides, when was the last time you went out on a date?"

Jemma glowered at her. "That's beside the point. I absolutely will not ask him out."

"Okay, okay. But I do think you should at least call him."

"No. I won't. Just look at me." She gestured to her voluptuous body.

"I *am* looking at you. So, what? You're beautiful."

"I've put on a *lot* of weight." Jemma looked at the ground, her previous high crashing down under the scrutiny of reality.

"Jemma?"

She didn't answer.

"Jemma! Look at me."

Jemma hesitantly raised her eyes.

"Do you know why Brooklyn is being such a jerk to you?" Cassie asked.

Jemma shook her head as a tear rolled down her cheek. Dang, she'd cried more in this past week than she's ever cried in her whole life.

"It has nothing to do with your size. It's because she's jealous. She's always been jealous of you. You're smart, you've got ambition, and you're beautiful—how much you weigh is not going to change that. She knows you've got a life to look forward to. For Brooklyn, this is it. High school is where she shines. After graduation, her life's over, and she resents you for that; She resents you because you represent everything she doesn't have."

"How do you know all this?"

"I just know things," she tapped her temple and smirked.

Jemma smiled. "You're not just saying that, are you?"

"I'll never lie to you. Besties don't lie."

Jemma nodded and wiped the tear from her face. "Okay, bestie. How are we going to celebrate the fact that Joal just gave me his number?"

Cassie smiled wide. "I got a package today."

Jemma grimaced. "Tell me it's not ghost hunting supplies."

"Oh yes, it is," Cassie confirmed. "Tonight, we're catching a ghost."

They ironed out the details on their walk home. And as hard as Jemma pushed, there was no dissuading Cassie from going to the old cemetery. Instead, she simply said, "I just know that's where I need to go."

Jemma may actually have to slash Cassie's tires.

When it came time for them to part ways, Jemma told Cassie goodbye and stepped around the corner of her street. She was so deep in thought that she didn't notice the police cruiser at her house until she was nearly home. She looked up, and it was there, parked behind her mom's car. Two police officers were leaning against the patrol car doors. Jemma approached slowly, a feeling of dread washed over her, growing stronger as she neared them.

"Jemma Ryan?" one of the officers said, looking her up and down. He was tall and slightly balding with sandy hair. His name tag read, Officer Glen.

"Yes?"

"We need to talk. Would you mind if we come in?"

"What's this about?"

"We just have a few questions we need to ask you," the other officer said. He was shorter and stockier with dark hair. His tag read Officer Haroldsen.

"Is my mom okay? Something didn't happen to her, did it?"

"Not that we know of."

"O...kay, so have *I* done something wrong?"

"I think it's best we speak inside." Officer Glen gestured toward her house.

Jemma sighed and then nodded as she looked at her mom's car. Wasn't her mom supposed to be at work?

Jemma reached for the front door and found it locked. Fishing the key out of her pocket, she unlocked it and stepped inside. The officers followed her in.

"Have a seat," Officer Haroldsen said, gesturing to the couch. Pulling a piece of paper from a manila folder, he placed it on the coffee table in front of her. It was a copy of her birth certificate.

"Do you recognize this?" Officer Glen asked.

"Yeah," she said, confused. "I ordered a copy, so I could get my social security number in order to apply for financial aid. Are you here to give it to me? You didn't have to go to so much trouble. Putting it in the mail would have been fine." She forced a smile.

"This is not a laughing matter," officer Glen said dryly and her smile vanished. "This is the copy the DMV has. Do you notice anything unusual about it?"

Jemma examined it closely and found the problem almost immediately. The font used for her name didn't match the font used in the rest of the document. Suddenly the air seemed thicker, and she took in a shaky breath. "It's a forgery."

"I'm glad you're willing to admit it. It will make things easier for you if you just come clean."

"Come clean? I didn't know about this. I can see the fonts don't match, and that would indicate a forgery. But you'll have to ask my mom or the DMV about it. I have no idea why they don't have a copy of my real birth certificate."

"Maybe because you weren't born in the United States."

"Listen, I don't know what you think about me," Jemma said, "but I was born in Washington. I've lived in Garden Grove my whole life. And last I checked Washington is part of the United States. I'm as much a citizen of this country as you are. There's obviously been a mistake, and I'm sure there's a logical explanation for this. Maybe the person at the DMV messed up." She pointed at the birth certificate. "Or why don't you just ask my mom about all this?"

The two officers looked at each other and then at her. "Is your mother here?"

"She should be. Her car is in the driveway."

"Right. Why don't you go get her? We'll wait."

Jemma stood, feeling a bit shaky. She headed straight for the kitchen and stopped in the doorway. Breakfast dishes still sat in the sink. The kitchen looked untouched from when Jemma had left that morning. This was odd. If her mom was home, she would have cleaned up. Maybe she's sick.

She turned back and headed for the stairs. As she strode

by, Officer Glen raised an eyebrow. "She's probably in her room upstairs, Jemma said and then climbed the staircase. The gazes of the police officers burned into her back.

"Mom?" she called. There was no answer. As she neared her mom's door, she could see it was ajar. She pushed it open. "Mom?" The room was in disarray. Clothes were strewn about, drawers open and empty, and closet open.

"Oh, no, no, no..." Jemma said and rushed inside the closet. She had to see if it was there. Her heart sank. No, it wasn't. Her mom's suitcase was missing, along with her favorite outfits.

She was gone.

Do you want me to go to prison? Her mother's words came back to her, and she thought about the police downstairs. "She was serious," Jemma whispered to herself.

"Do you need some help?" one of the officers said from the bottom of the steps.

Jemma quickly stepped into the hall and closed the door behind her.

"No," she said as she rushed down the stairs and stopped short at the officer standing with his hand on the stair railing. She attempted to calm her racing heart and act nonchalant as she moved past him. "It looks like she's not home." She shrugged. "She must have gone out."

"Right," he said, as he followed her back into the living room. "You know, being in the U.S. unlawfully is an arrestable offense, not to mention, fraud is a crime."

"I haven't done anything wrong."

"Do you have an original copy of your birth certificate?"

Jemma shook her head.

"How about a social security card?"

"No. I was going to get a social security card after I got my birth certificate."

"And why is that?"

"So, I can go to college." Her voice rose with panic.

"Your mom doesn't have either of those documents?" Officer Haroldsen asked calmly.

Jemma could feel tears burning in her eyes as she shrugged. "I don't know. *Are* you going to arrest me?"

"No." He paused, scrutinizing her. The silence unsettling, but then he finally spoke. "I think you're telling the truth."

Jemma's eyes widened in surprise.

Officer Haroldsen pulled out a business card and handed it to her. "When you see your mom, tell her to call us. We'll be in touch again."

On the way toward the door, officer Haroldsen paused at a bookshelf and fingered a framed photo of her and her mom at Cannon Beach. "Is this her?"

Jemma pursed her lips and then answered. "Yeah."

He took out his camera and snapped a picture of the photo.

When the officers left, Jemma should have felt relieved. She didn't.

Her birth certificate was a forgery. What did that mean? Where was she born? Was this why her mother fought so hard to keep her from getting a copy? And then if she didn't have a birth certificate, did that mean she also didn't have a social security number? What if she didn't? How would she go to college? What kind of future did she have? Where was she from?

Her mom had a lot to answer for. But her mom was gone. For how long...? She had no idea. Jemma made her way into the kitchen to see if she had left her a note.

On the fridge, held on by a pineapple magnet, was a note scrawled in red ink.

Jemma,

I'm sorry, baby. I'm sorry for everything. I only wanted someone to love. Someone who would love me too. I never meant to hurt you. But now I have to leave. I pulled together as much money as I could. I knew this day would come, and I'd hoped to take you with me, but I think now that you're almost eighteen, you'd be better off without me. I'm taking half the money, so I can escape the consequences of my actions and give you the other half so you could get a fresh start in life somewhere else. I left the money in the cookie jar.

I know you have a lot of questions. I wish I could answer them for you, but I can't. Please don't go to the police. And if the police come to you, don't tell them anything. Don't try to find me. I hope you can find all the happiness you deserve, and I hope someday you can forgive me.

Love always,

Mom

P.S. Destroy this note after you read it.

Jemma shook her head in denial. "No." She blinked back tears. "No, she didn't..." She couldn't even say it. But still, the evidence was staring her in the face—the missing suitcase, all her mom's missing clothes, the car abandoned in the driveway, and to top it off, the note.

Her mom was never coming back.

Trembling, Jemma sank into a nearby chair, propped her elbows on the table, and dropped her face into her hands. What was she going to do? How was she going to live? She had no relatives, no family to take her in. In a few weeks, she'd turn eighteen. She'd be an adult, and she was on her own.

Lifting her head and looking around, she wondered how long before the rent was due. What about the lights? Bills had to be paid. How much money did her mom leave?

Rising, she felt as if she were having an out-of-body experience. She moved to the cookie jar. Lifting the lid, she could see cash. There were bundles of hundreds. She removed them from the jar. $10,000 was printed on the straps of the hundreds—there were three of them, plus a few bundles of twenties—four containing five hundred dollars apiece.

Thirty-two thousand dollars. And this was only half of what they'd had? How was a waitress able to save so much money? And if she'd had this kind of money, why did her mom freak at the thought of paying for college?

She sighed. Jemma had no birth certificate, no social security number, and now that her mother was gone, she had no clue how to find out who she was or where she came from. How could she get into college? How would she even get a job? They might even take away her driver's license. Her mom may have left her with money, but she took away her life.

Fury rushed over Jemma. How could she have done this to her? How could she abandon her and leave her with this mess? Did her mom take her from her real family? Had Cassie been right?

Anger welled up inside as she realized what her mom had done. Rage and desperation filled her until she felt she might explode, and then she did. Jemma heaved the cookie jar at the floor, and it shattered, spreading fragments across the linoleum as shards nipped at her ankles. Then Jemma strode across the floor, her tennis shoes crunching against the broken glass. She snatched her mother's favorite mug off the counter, turned, and hurled it against the wall. "How could you do this to me!" She grabbed glass after glass and threw them as she screamed. "You ruined my life and then left me with no answers and no place to find them. Where did I come from? Who am I? Why couldn't you just tell me? Why couldn't you add that to my stupid note?"

Everything that wasn't locked down was smashed against the floors. She opened cupboard after cupboard and broke dish after dish, glass after glass, against the wall, against the floor... Tears streamed down her face as she screamed and cursed, telling her mom off like she'd never been allowed before. Clawing the note from off the fridge, she crumpled it up in her hands, and threw it on the floor amidst the shards.

Finally breaking under the weight of her sorrow, she leaned against the wall and sank down to the floor, surrounded by the broken fragments of her life. Feeling utterly destroyed, she sobbed. "Mom... why did you leave me?"

A dull pain gathered across her shoulders and into her back. The ache throbbed with her heartbeat and grew in intensity. Oh, please, not now! She couldn't take it. She couldn't handle one more pain to add to her tragedy, to add to her disappointment. Her world was crumbling beneath her feet, and she was helpless to stop it. The pain grew in intensity, ebbing and flowing as she groaned—physical pain mingling with emotional agony.

She thought of Joal. His face appeared in her mind. Reaching for the cordless phone, she cradled it in her hands. She wanted so much for him to be her knight in shining armor, just like she'd dreamed he'd been oh so many times. She truly wished her dreams were real, wished he could swoop in and save the day, carry her off to his castle. But that was a daydream, a fairy tale. Fairy tale endings didn't happen in horror stories. And that is what she was living, a horror story. The pain rose and she moaned. If only the earth could open up and swallow her whole. Finally, after a few minutes, the pain faded.

In her mind, she imagined she heard Joal's voice. "Jemma? Is that you?"

She wanted to talk to him, wanted to say something, but the room spun and then everything went dark.

Chapter Nine — Jemma

There is the heat of love,
the pulsing rush of longing,
the lover's whisper, irresistible
—magic to make the sanest man go mad.
——*The Iliad*, Homer

"JEMMA," a faint voice broke through the darkness, "please wake up."

Jemma's eyes fluttered open, and Joal's face came into view. He leaned above her. She looked around at her surroundings and found she was lying on the living room couch. He must have carried her in here.

"Jemma," he sighed. "Thank the gods. What happened?"

Jemma squeezed her eyes shut again and shook her head. She couldn't go there right now.

"Do you want me to call the police?" he asked. "Did someone break in? Did they hurt you?"

"No," she said, her voice raspy. "No police. What are you doing here?"

"You called me. Gods, what happened? It looks like the kitchen exploded."

Jemma followed his eyes. Through the doorway, she could see the damage she'd done.

"The note," she said, her voice breaking.

"Note?"

"On the floor." She nodded toward the kitchen as tears leaked from her eyes.

Joal stood and strode into the room, doing his best to avoid the broken glass. He found the note and strolled back into the living room as he uncrumpled it and read. At first, he looked sad, but not surprised. Then his eyes widened, and anger filtered in. "Did your mom abandon you?"

"Yes," Jemma sobbed. "And left me with no answers. I have nothing. I don't know who I am or where I came from."

Joal swore. Moments later, he knelt down next to her.

Jemma shook her head. "I just can't believe it."

"What are you going to do?"

"I don't know." Jemma took a shaky breath. "The police found out that the birth certificate my mom gave me to give the DMV is a forgery. I had no idea until they told me."

His brows rose. "How'd they find out?"

"My birth certificate went missing. So, I requested another copy of it for my college applications. Someone must've put two and two together, and they found a forged copy. I think they think I'm some kind of illegal alien." Jemma dragged her fingers through her hair.

"What a mess," Joal said.

"That's an understatement."

Jemma jumped when the phone rang from the end table next to her.

"Are you going to get that?" Joal said.

"Yeah. It might be my mom." Jemma put the phone to her ear. "Hello?"

"Hey, bestie. Are you okay? I was just heading out to come get you, but I thought I should call first."

Oh, right, Cassie. We're supposed to go ghost hunting, aren't we? "To tell you the truth, I'm not feeling so great right now. I'm just gonna to stay home tonight."

"I thought you might say something like that. Is there anything I can do to help?"

"No. Thanks. I'm just going to rest. I'll see you at school Monday."

"Oh... okay. Take care of yourself, we both know your mom won't do it."

"Yeah," Jemma said, choking on the word. Cassie didn't know how right she was.

"Okay, bye Bestie."

"Bye."

Jemma handed the phone back to Joal and lay back against the couch. "I probably should have told her, I just... I'm not ready." They were silent for a long time before she spoke, and when she did her voice sounded small, child-like in her own ears. "How could my mom do this to me?" She kept her eyes glued to the ceiling above her. "I mean, she wasn't the best mom in the world, but she's the only mom I know."

"Can you call your grandparents? An aunt? An uncle?"

"I've never met them. My mom said I'm better off without them."

"Do you believe her?"

Jemma shook her head. "I don't know. I don't know anything." Tears flowed down her cheeks.

"Hey, hey," Joal said as he knelt down next to the sofa and caressed her face with the back of his hand. "It's going to be okay. I know where we might find answers."

"What...? Where?"

"I know some people."

"You—" Jemma froze. What was she doing? Was she really going to trust Joal, after all he did to her? Her face heated when she realized how much she had already told him.

"I can help you, Jemma," he said, gently.

"Why do you want to help me?"

His expression fell. "Because, despite what you think of me, I care. And..." he exhaled softly, "I feel extremely protective of you."

She considered his words. Somehow, deep down inside, she believed him. Maybe she was stupid for doing so, but she did. Deciding to take a leap of faith, she said, "So, you know people who can help me?"

"Yes."

Jemma cocked her head to the side. "How can *they* give me answers?"

"You know when I said I'm not human?"

Oh, great, not that again. Maybe she trusted too quickly.

"There are others," he continued, "others with powers."

Her heart rate picked up. He believed what he was saying, she was sure of it. Funny how she'd lived her entire life with thinking her mom was nuts, and now... "Joal, I really think you should—"

"I'm not crazy, and I can prove it."

"Prove it how?" She frowned.

"Just... Listen, I know you don't trust me yet, but humor me, please."

Jemma paused for a moment, and then she nodded.

"Okay, just give me a minute." Joal closed his eyes and sighed. He remained still for several moments, and Jemma wondered at his silence. When he finally opened his eyes, she gasped and scrambled back against the arm of the couch.

Joal's irises swirled around his pupils like liquid, jade whirlpools, and even more shocking... they were glowing. He reached out and gently pulled her back toward him. "Don't be afraid."

Oh, gods! "What... are you?" she whispered, trembling in his grip.

He sighed and paused, seemingly hesitant to speak. "I'm the son of Ved-ava, a Nordic sea-goddess, and... I'm also the son of Poseidon, god of deadbeat dads."

God of deadbeat dads? How can he joke at a time like this? Jemma shook her head and looked down at his chest. She couldn't think straight looking at his eyes. "What are you talking about? There are no such things as gods and goddesses."

"Don't say that to my mom. That's the quickest way to get on her bad side. And believe me, you don't want to be on her bad side."

"So, what, *you're* a... god?"

"Yeah. Technically."

Jemma shook her head. "That doesn't make sense. You said I'm like you, but I'm ordinary. I'm so ordinary it's pathetic."

Joal shook his head. "You're far from ordinary."

"Says the guy who couldn't ever remember my name."

Joal frowned. "Yeah. I haven't figured that one out. I don't see how I didn't notice you before. I mean, you're—"

"Extremely forgettable?" Jemma interjected.

"Beautiful and completely memorable." He lifted his hand and brushed the wetness from her cheeks, his fingers trailing liquid fire along the way.

Jemma took a shaky breath as she reached up and pressed his hand against her skin, absorbing the electrical charge. It spread throughout her entire body and made her hands tingle.

She sat with his hand pressed to her face for a long time before she said in a low voice, "What am I feeling?"

He hesitated before he answered. "My power."

Looking in his eyes, Jemma found herself overcome with an insane desire. Given everything that had happened, it should be the last thing she wanted to do, but the truth was, she sooo wanted to kiss him.

He smiled weakly. "I don't know if that's a good idea."

Had she spoken out loud? Her confusion was overpowered by pain as it clenched her heart in its grip. "What's not a good idea?"

"It's not a good idea for us to kiss. At least—"

"But it's okay for you to make out with half the girls at school," she said, letting go of his hand and leaning back. "Am I that repulsive?"

His eyes flew open wide. "Of course not. That's not what I meant at all."

"So, what do you mean?"

He rang his hands and said, "I didn't really care about those other girls."

"You were just stringing them along?" She frowned.

"No. Yes. Gods! I can't think straight when I'm around you."

"Well, I'm thinking perfectly clear," she snapped.

"Jemma." The pleading tone of his voice caused her to pause. He truly did look concerned. After a brief pause, he finally spoke. "The truth is I don't want to move too fast with you. I've never felt this way before... never cared so much, so fast. Not with anyone."

She knew exactly what he meant. She remembered vividly the first time she'd taken his hand in hers. It was years ago, back in second grade. Her young, tender heart had pushed her right over the edge of an abyss, and she'd fallen in love. But she was a child then. Now she was a woman of almost eighteen.

"We barely know each other," she said. She didn't know which of them she wanted to convince more, Joal or herself.

Jemma remembered what Tao told Cassie. Could Joal truly care about her?

Light from the living room window created a halo surrounding his face—Joal's face, the face she's seen a million times in her dreams. Despite his not wanting to move too fast, he did move. He moved in closer, until his lips were a breath away from hers. Strange that in her dreams, he seemed more real, more tangible than he did at this moment. Enveloped in light, the image before her now was more ethereal, more other-worldly. Joal looked like the god he claimed to be and the protests in her mind faded as her heart shouted, *"Isn't this what we've always wanted? Always dreamed?"*

Hope sparked, a hope that this scene would play out the way she'd dreamed it would. Jemma closed her eyes. Conflicted, she both feared that he would kiss her, and yet she was desperate for it.

The touch of his lips made the fantasy real, and an inferno lit inside her as she leaned into him and kissed him back, passionately. Jemma pulled him toward her as she again laid back against the cushions. He didn't resist, but followed her down, meeting her passion with just as much fervor as his mouth moved over hers. His taste, his smell, the power of his magic surrounded her. Joal growled, and his arms came around her. He pulled her tighter against him. Then he tore his lips from hers and kissed down her neck as she sucked in quick breaths.

"Oh, gods," he mumbled against her skin. "We have to stop."

"I know we should," Jemma gasped. "But I don't want to."

"Which is why we have to."

"I don't understand."

"This isn't the time," he said, his voice trembling. "Gods. This is happening too fast." He loosened his grip. A curse escaped his lips as he leaned back.

"Too fast?" Jemma said, confused for a moment, and then the bitter sting of rejection returned. He didn't want her. He wanted every other girl, but not her. The pain grew, burning inside, then it turned to anger as it built.

"That didn't seem to matter with Brooklyn or Maddie or Lilly or... or... a million other girls you've made out with." She sat up, heat flaming in her cheeks. She noticed that his shirt was almost completely unbuttoned. The tanned muscles of his chest and stomach were impressive, but then she realized that *she* must have been the one unbuttoning his shirt. She'd borne her soul with that one action, letting him know how much she wanted him. And he'd pushed her away.

How could she forget years of being ignored? Years of disinterest. That doesn't change overnight. "How could I be so stupid?"

"Jemma," he said, pleading.

Pushing him back, she stood and turned, slamming her leg into the coffee table. "Ouch." Her shin throbbed. She'd literally thrown herself on the guy she had been crushing on with a desperation that bordered on insanity. She'd let him in, knowing who he was, knowing what a player he was, knowing he made out with a new girl every week. And yet, when it came to her, he wanted nothing from her. He may say he wanted her, but actions speak louder than words. He was playing her. Toying with her heart. He did say they were supposed to be enemies. What better way to tear down your enemy than by making them love you and then crushing their heart?

"Wait!" He stood and grabbed her before she could escape and pulled her around to face him. "It's not you—"

"Oh please, don't give me the 'it's not you, it's me' line." Cursed tears spilled from her eyes.

"You don't understand."

"Don't I?"

"No," he paused, "you don't." He sighed, seeming to gather his thoughts. "With those other girls, I was safe. I could stop anytime. I could stop before it went too far. But with you... I... I don't trust myself. I've... never wanted anyone as much as I want you. And to tell you the truth, it's not fair to you."

"What do you mean, it's not fair to me?"

"You felt overwhelmed, right? By my kiss, my touch..."

"Don't flatter yourself."

"It's not flattery, it's part of my power."

"What do you mean?"

"My mom isn't just a goddess of the sea, she's a fertility goddess."

Those words caused her to pause. "Fertility?"

"Yeah."

"So..."

"I've inherited some of that power from my mom. My touch... my kiss... even my presence has a powerful effect. It wouldn't be fair for me to take advantage of you. Right now, with what happened with your mom, you're in a fragile state. It would be wrong for me to take things further."

Wow, how could she have forgotten... her mom. Jemma began to tremble. Her life was screwed up every which way. Hades, she couldn't think of her mom right now. It was too raw, too fresh. Instead, she focused on the other thing he said, so she said, "You're a fertility god? And you think... You think that I'm like you?" She laughed nervously at the absurdity of it.

"Yes. Well, maybe not a fertility goddess. Although, seeing how powerful that kiss was...," he raked his hand through his hair. "Gods. You definitely could be."

"No." Jemma shook her head. "I can't be a goddess at all. That's impossible."

"Why not?"

"Because it's utterly, and completely ridiculous."

He gave her a disapproving look.

"Why do *you* think that I am?" she asked.

"I can feel your power."

"What power? I'm totally not powerful. I can't even open a ketchup bottle."

"When you felt my hand against your cheek, you felt my power, right?" He paused, allowing her to remember what she'd felt, moments before. Then he continued. "I felt yours too."

"You did?"

"Yes."

"But... what does that mean?"

"You're the offspring of gods. Well, at least one of your parents is a god, though I'm guessing they both are. You're giving off too much energy to be only half god."

"And my mom... the one that raised me, she's..."

"Human, one hundred percent."

"You think she's really not my mom?"

"I don't see how she could be."

"What, then? Whoever gave birth to me is a... goddess?"

"Probably, and your dad's most likely a god. Or one of them could be something else. Not human, that's for sure."

"What else is there?"

"There are many powerful beings that aren't technically gods. Sprites, Naiads, Dagonians, Kelpies... Although those are all sea creatures. I'm not as well versed on the others. But of all the mythological beings, the most powerful are the primordials—ones that emerged in the beginning, like the Titans.

"You mean, like Gaia and Uranus—the grandparents of Zeus, Hades, and Poseidon—"

"You know your Greek mythology."

"I pay attention in class." She shrugged. "So, Poseidon's your dad, right? He's really powerful?"

"Yes. The closer in relation to a primordial god, the more powerful you are. Usually."

"Does that mean you're really powerful?"

"Supposedly I will be. I do have some abilities now, which is rare, but I don't fully come into my powers until I'm twenty-one."

"Wait! Your friends at school—Kahula and Tao—are they like you?"

Joal shook his head. "Not quite. They're demigods. There are actually a lot of demigods at the school. I'm the only other full god there, well, except maybe you."

"But not *everyone* at the school is a demigod."

"No. Most are clueless humans who think we have an overinflated ego and insane athletic abilities."

"They're not wrong." Jemma smirked. "About the overinflated ego."

Joal chuckled. "Yeah. You're probably right."

Jemma grew serious and sighed. "How do I find out who my parents are?"

Joal shook his head. "That might be tricky. I'm not on good terms with many sky-gods."

"Wait, so I'm a, what did you call them, sky-gods?"

"Yes."

"How do you know?"

"Your scent. You smell like a fresh breeze. It makes sense you're here in Garden Grove, though. This town is kind of a haven for the demigod children of Olympians. Most of the swim team are sea demigods, ones who are landlocked."

"Landlocked?"

"On dry land. And then the Lacrosse team is composed of mostly underworld demigods."

"Wait, Evan is captain of the Lacrosse team. So, he's a—'

"Underworld demigod. Yeah, and a jerk. And the football players are—"

"Earth gods?"

Joal shook his head. 'The earth elemental belongs to the humans. The football players are sky-gods, mostly sons of Ares. The god of war really gets around."

"Do you think I'm a daughter of Ares?"

"Let's hope not."

"Why?"

"Because Ares is a jerk."

Jemma laughed dryly. What if she was the daughter of Ares? No. No way. She sunk back down into the couch and dropped her head into her hands. "I'm having a hard time wrapping my brain around this."

"You're not the first." Joal sat beside her.

"You've had this happen before? Found others like me? Other children of gods?"

He nodded.

"A few, and they all react the same. Complete disbelief."

"That's because it's totally unbelievable. I don't even believe in gods."

Joal raised a brow.

"Well, I *didn't* believe. But it's easier to believe that *you're* a god, rather than someone like me."

"You really don't see yourself clearly."

Jemma frowned at him. "I do have a question."

"Yeah?"

"Why are you here? Why are you the only full god at the school? Shouldn't you live in Asgard or Olympus or... where does your dad live?"

"Atlantis."

"Really?"

"Yeah." He smirked and then his smile faded. "My story's complicated. The truth is my mom didn't want her husband finding out about me, and my dad didn't want his wife finding out as well. So, Garden Grove it was—far away from my mom and my dad's pantheons."

"That stinks. Neither of them has publicly claimed you?"

Joal barked a laugh. "No."

"But if your mom is raising you here, hasn't anyone noticed? Doesn't her husband miss her?"

Joal shook his head. "No. She's not here often. I've had Denise to take care of me."

"Who's Denise?"

"She's a human who has been a much better mom to me than my real mom."

"I'm glad you had someone looking out for you."

"Yeah, Denise is great... a pain sometimes, but she's amazing. She stayed around even after I released her."

"Released her?"

"It's complicated. Basically, my mom plucked her out of her life and mind controlled her into taking care of me. When my powers started emerging, I inadvertently released the hold my mom had on her. Instead of leaving, like she probably should have, Denise stayed to protect me. She still does—as much as a human can."

Jemma cracked a smile. "I'm glad you have her. I guess I have Cassie. She's been my constant support over the years."

"Everyone needs someone constant," Joal said, "someone who cares."

"Yeah. I don't know how well she'll help me with adulting. She can't save a penny to save her life."

"From what I've seen, you'll do fine. But you've got me too. I can help you figure it all out. And then if you need me for anything... anything at all. Protection. A ride. Money. A make-out session. Give me a call."

Warmth bloomed in Jemma's face as a nervous giggle surfaced, and then a familiar fear set in, the fear of rejection.

"Are you sure you want to? Make-out, that is. Maybe what we feel isn't real. Maybe—"

"Jemma," he said in a low, sexy voice that made her tingle all over. "What I feel for you is real. I can't vouch for the way *you* feel about me. It's possible you're affected by my power of attraction."

"Maybe." It would make sense, seeing as how she wanted him even after treating her like garbage. But now... he was being so incredibly tender toward her. Should she be running away from him? She couldn't bring herself to admit she probably should.

"I'm sorry for the way I've treated you," he said.

"Can you read my thoughts?"

He shook his head. "You have an expressive face."

"I do?"

He nodded. "And I'm so sorry for treating you like you meant nothing. There's a mystery behind that and I intend to solve it. But I want you to believe me when I say, I've never felt for any other girl, what I feel for you. I want you so much, it scares me. But if you ask me to stay away, I will."

She looked down before saying softly, "I don't want you to stay away."

"Good." He gently pressed his fingers under her chin, and she looked up. "Because I really don't want to."

"You're not just saying that?"

He shook his head and said, "No. But I can't lose control with you. It would kill me if I ever hurt you." He brushed an errant strand of hair behind her ear.

"Too late. You've hurt me every day of my life." The pain in her voice was clear.

"I'm sorry," he said, sincerity in his eyes. "Believe me, I am."

He looked sincere in his words, but too many years of hurt

lay between them. "I don't know if I can believe you..., but I'll try. You'll have to be patient."

"I can do that." They sat in silence for only a few seconds when her eyelids began to feel heavy. She fought back a yawn and lost.

He chuckled. "Am I boring you?"

"No. I'm just really tired all of a sudden."

"You've had a rough day. Why don't you go to sleep, and I'll clean things up?"

"Are you kidding? That kitchen is a disaster." She started to get up.

Joal lifted his hand. "It's okay. Really. I can handle it."

"Are you sure?"

"Yeah." He stood and pulled the throw blanket off the back of the couch and draped it over her. "Let me take care of you. Bedsides, I'm pretty handy with a broom."

Jemma smiled. "I'll bet you are."

"Is that sarcasm I hear?"

Jemma chuckled as she tucked the blanket under her chin. "Maybe a little."

"Well, prepare yourself to be amazed." Joal smirked as he rose to his feet.

Jemma closed her eyes and fell asleep to the sound of broken glass scraping across the kitchen floor.

Chapter Ten – Jemma

Any moment might be our last.
Everything is more beautiful because we're doomed.
You will never be lovelier than you are now.
We will never be here again.
——*The Iliad*, Homer

JEMMA PARKED a block away from the school. She could have parked in the lot if she'd had a parking pass. Her mom never let her drive to school, so she hadn't needed one before, but her mom was gone. There would be no more asking permission, no house rules, and no more curfews. With her hands shaking, she put the keys in her pocket. She felt lost, adrift, but having Joal in her life did bring a small ray of hope.

No. She shook off the thought. She was *not* in a relationship with him. They might have shared a kiss, but he was a fertility god with an overactive libido. She knew what he said, but it was a new day. He probably now realized he could do so much better.

Jemma's heart skipped a beat when she saw Joal lift a hand in greeting from the front door of the school. All eyes were on her as she approached. She looked for Cassie but didn't see her.

"Hey, beautiful," Joal said, stepping up to her.

Jemma smiled at the endearment as she craned her neck to look up at him. Joal reached for her hand and leaned in for a kiss. Jemma was able to pull herself together enough to kiss him back. The touch of his lips made it feel like the pull of gravity had diminished.

When he ended the kiss, he kept his head low and whispered. "I hope you don't mind; I couldn't resist."

She shook her head. "I don't mind."

"Good." Joal beamed at her and then put his arm around her shoulders. "Are you feeling better today?" Jemma smiled up at him. How many times had she dreamed of this moment? Only about a thousand. And that was no exaggeration. And then her smile faded when she registered what he'd asked her about. Whether or not she felt better. Right. She'd been abandoned.

"Um, yeah. But I don't think it's completely sunken in. My mom wasn't home all that often before. So...," a sinking feeling in her stomach made it difficult to put words to her thoughts. "You know."

"What are you going to do?" he asked as he pulled open the door to the main hall.

"About what?"

He shrugged. "Everything."

"Right now, I'm going to concentrate on finishing high school."

"Sounds like a good plan," he said.

Jemma sighed and then said in a low voice, "Though, I'm going to have to tell the police the truth. They can't really deport me, right? They wouldn't know where to send me. But I guess they could lock me up."

"You'll want to hold off on telling them for now. I might know someone who can help you."

Brooklyn came into view, standing among her friends. Her eyes popped open wide before they narrowed. She looked from Jemma to Joal, her eyes lingering on his arm around her and then she rolled her eyes. Jemma couldn't help the smirk that lit her own face.

"I was hoping you'd do something for me," Joal said, drawing back her attention.

"Anything."

He chuckled. "Ooh, I'd be careful agreeing to anything. You never know what I might ask you to do." He fingered the collar of her blouse.

Jemma smiled as her heart fluttered in her chest. "What *do* you want me to do?"

"Go to homecoming with me."

Jemma stopped walking and turned to face him. "But that's in two weeks. You haven't asked anyone?"

He leaned down and whispered, his breath in her ear raised goosebumps across her skin. "I'd been hoping you would go with me."

"Oh," she said in a low voice. "Really?"

He chuckled. "Yes. So, will you?"

Jemma swallowed. "Yes, I will."

"Okay," he said. "I guess I'd better take my suit to the cleaners, then."

"A suit?"

"Yeah," he said, with a less-than-thrilled tone.

"Wow. Wait. Oh shoot, I need a dress."

"Do you need money? Did your mom leave you enough?"

"More money than I thought she ever had."

"Good. But if you need help. Let me know. My mom gives me access to basically unlimited funds."

"I'll be fine. I just need to find Cassie; we need to plan a shopping trip." Jemma started walking away purposefully.

"Jemma," Joal called.

She stopped and turned back, "Huh?"

Joal was obviously trying not to laugh. "You're going the wrong way. Our class is this way," he gestured down A hall. "We'll be late if we don't hurry."

"Oh," Jemma said, "yeah." Her cheeks warmed.

He put his arm around her and leaned down. "You're really adorable when you're embarrassed."

Jemma tried to look disapproving as she jabbed him but couldn't help the smile. "Shut up."

Joal laughed.

Jemma realized later that Joal had effectively helped her forget her troubles. The rest of the morning passed by quickly. When it was time to go to lunch, Cassie was still not around. Jemma strolled into the lunchroom, headed to her table, and stopped short. It was filled with members of the swim team—many more than yesterday.

"Hey, babe," Joal stood and motioned her over. "You've met Kahula, I don't know where Tao is, but this is Michael, Carter, Jazmin, Peter, Charles, Katie, Trevon, Jack, and Mateo." He pointed to each one. Jemma already knew the names of most of them but took note of the ones she didn't know.

"So, Jemma," said Jack, a boy with mousey, disheveled hair and striking blue eyes. "Are you coming to our swim meet on Wednesday? Though, I don't know if Joal could manage with the distraction. He might just lose a race for once in his life."

Joal swallowed and then said, "Not likely."

"Yeah, there's no way he'll lose," Carter said, with his arm around Jasmin, a pretty girl with tight, black curls framing her head like a halo. She gave Jemma a warm smile. Carter continued, "He wouldn't want to disappoint his girl."

His girl?

"Hey, Jemma," Charles, an older kid speckled with freckles and sporting an impressive physique spoke. "How did you get our boy Joal to finally settle down to one girl." *What is he talking about? They'd only been together one day.*

"Um..., I...," she stammered.

"Yeah, you're all he talks about," Trevon said.

"Trev," Joal growled.

"What?" He threw his hands up.

"Joal," Kahula said, "maybe she'd like to watch us go cliff diving."

"Cliff diving?" That got Jemma's undivided attention.

"Yeah," Charles said, his eyes on Jemma, "You want to be impressed, you need to watch Joal cliff dive."

"Can I dive too?" Jemma asked.

There was a chorus of approval all around, and Jemma got excited.

"Have you gone cliff diving before?" Joal asked.

"No, but I've always wanted to."

"It's not a good idea," Joal said, shaking his head.

"Why not?" Jemma asked.

"You could drown, or break your neck," Joal answered.

"Like you'd let that happen," Charles said.

"No, really," Jemma said. "I'm an excellent diver. I've just never dove off a cliff before."

"Come on, great ruler," Kahula said, "we'll all be watching out for her."

Joal sighed and sat for several long moments looking at Jemma's pleading eyes. Finally, he shook his head. "I know I'm going to regret this. Okay, you can jump."

"I can, huh?" Jemma said. "You do know you're not the boss of me, right?"

"Joal thinks he's the boss of everyone," Peter said.

"I am your captain." Joal said to Peter, then he turned to

her and cracked a reluctant smile. "And we're going to The Falls."

There were groans all around, and someone said, "That's for babies."

Kahula shrugged. "It's a good place to start."

Jemma arched an eyebrow and looked at Joal. "You really are bossy. So, when do we go?"

"We don't have practice tomorrow," Peter said. "How about after school? Do you have a wetsuit? The water is freaking cold at the falls."

She didn't have a wetsuit, but her mom did. It might be a little long on her, but it should work. "Yeah, I do."

"Sweet!" Carter said. "Let's do this."

"Do what?" Cassie stepped up to the table with Tao's arm around her. Jemma arched a brow. Tao was holding a tray with a ton of food—must be for both of them.

Joal looked pointedly at Michael, who sat on the other side of Jemma and said, "Move."

He scooted over immediately, and Cassie sat between them. There was still no room for Tao, but one glance from Tao had Michael standing and saying, "I think I'll sit next to Mateo."

"Good choice," Tao said, and then sat and put his arm around Cassie. Her lips looked a bit... full, and her hair had more flyaways than usual. Jemma didn't need to guess what Cassie and Tao had been doing.

Cassie turned to Jemma and asked, "What have you guys been talking about?"

"We're going cliff jumping," Jemma said excitedly.

"Cool, can I come?" Cassie asked.

"Of course!" Jemma said.

"Wow," Cassie said, looking around. "There's a lot more of you today." One by one, they each introduced themselves.

Cassie smiled, friendly, but her attention seemed divided as she grabbed a Coke. Jemma would have to quiz her friend later to make sure Cassie remembered all the names. Not surprisingly, Cassie's attention was on Tao for the rest of the lunch period. The conversation at the table was filled with talk of preparations and who will ride with whom.

As the bell rang, Jemma and Cassie broke off from the group and headed to their Language Arts class.

"Where were you today?" Jemma asked.

"My car wouldn't start, and Tao was nice enough to walk me to school."

"He was, huh? And that's why you missed all your morning classes?"

"I simply had better things to do."

"Like make out with Tao?"

"How did you...? Oh, well, I guess it's pretty obvious. But don't blame me. He is an exceptional kisser."

"I'll take your word for it."

"So, have you kissed Joal yet?"

Jemma's cheeks warmed.

"You did!" Cassie beamed. "And he asked you to homecoming, didn't he?"

"How did you—"

"Besties know these kinds of things and since you are my bestie, you probably know that Tao..." she paused as if she'd just given Jemma a cue.

"Asked you to homecoming too?" Jemma ventured a guess.

"Yes! We totally need to go dress shopping, soon."

"Well, I have a test to study for tonight, and we can't go tomorrow; we'll be cliff jumping. How about the next day, right after school?"

"Perfect!"

Λ

Jemma stood in awe. The Falls was the most beautiful place on the planet. They were surrounded by a lush, green forest speckled with wildflowers, a cascading waterfall, and clear blue skies. The cool scent of mossy pine filled the misty air.

Jemma stood at the edge of the rocky cliff, looked down, and frowned. "I thought this would be higher."

Peter smiled and leaned into Jemma. "If you ever decide to kick Joal to the curb—"

Joal cut him off with a glare.

"Hey." Peter put up his hands in surrender. "I'm just saying."

Jemma smiled and then turned to look at the surface of the water, gaging the distance.

"Remember, no diving," Joal said.

"There aren't any rocks beneath the surface, are there?" she asked.

"About twenty feet down," Joal said. "You don't need to worry about them. But at this high, you'll be entering the water at about forty miles an hour."

"Noted," she said, with a smirk. She took several steps back, so she could make her approach. One, two, three steps, and then she leaped from the cliff, piked, and then laid out into a dive. Coming up to the surface, she could hear the whoops and hollers of the swim team. Looking up, she could see Joal shaking his head and smiling. A second later he backed to the edge and then sprang, executing a backflip from a pike position, laying out to dive into the water. He surfaced inches from Jemma's face, a smug smile on his face.

"Show off," Jemma said as Joal wrapped his arms around her.

"I was going to say the same thing about you," Joal said. "How did you learn to do that?"

"Diving is not much different from what I did in cheer."

"Right, you were a flyer."

"And I told you I could dive." She smiled brightly, enjoying Joal's embrace. Leaning in, she kissed him, and he kissed her back.

When he pulled away, he said, "You should try out for the diving team. The swimming and diving teams always go to meets together, so we can hang out."

"Is that the only reason I should try out?"

Joal cracked a smile and shrugged. "It's the most important."

Jemma laughed. "Right."

"You want to go again?"

Jemma nodded, smiling.

When Jemma and Joal reached the top, she was greeted by Cassie's wide eyes. She was searching the trees around them. "Are you sure there aren't wild animals out here? I swear a pack of wolves or wild dogs are going to jump out and attack at any moment."

"I've been here a hundred times," Tao said, "there are no wolves."

"Or vicious dogs?" Cassie said.

"No. No vicious dogs either."

Cassie seemed to lose her worry over wild animals when it was replaced by a whole new fear. Her eyes widened further as she peered over the edge of the cliff.

Tao had his hand in hers. "It's really not so bad." He tugged her forward.

"I know." She hesitated just a moment before they jumped over the edge together. Her scream was loud enough to cause birds to flutter from the trees. Her wail was cut off when she submerged. Tao had her back to the surface in a heartbeat. She laughed and then shouted, "That was awesome!"

They all spent the next several hours swimming and diving, and then relaxing by the water's edge. The sun set, leaving a warm glow behind the silhouette of darkened trees. They lay in small groups lit by the light of Coleman lanterns. Joal and Jemma lay side by side away from the group with a lantern of their own, turned down low as they munched on ranch-flavored chips and sipped soda.

Joal was propped up on his elbow with his arm draped across Jemma's waist. A thick quilted blanket cushioned them against the hard ground, and Jemma was using Joal's backpack for a pillow. Cassie and Tao were on an oversized towel across a clearing, glued to one another.

"Joal," Peter said, standing in the midst of the others. "We're going to head back."

Joal nodded. "See you tomorrow."

"How much longer before we need to leave?" Jemma asked after the crowd dispersed.

Joal looked down at her and raised a brow. "Neither of us has a curfew, and Cassie is riding with Tao; we can stay as long as you'd like. But it looks like it'll just be the two of us."

"What a shame." Jemma smirked.

"Hmph." Joal cracked a smile. "What are we going to do?"

Jemma shrugged, and then her gaze dropped to his lips.

Joal groaned. "You're killing me smalls."

"What?" she said, feigning ignorance.

He just shook his head and then lowered his smiling lips to hers. His mouth was magic, it was warmth and Jemma wished the moment could last forever. Minutes later, the kissing became more fervent. She could hear the zipper of her wet suit slide down as a cool breeze brushed over her chest, which shook in nervousness. She was wearing a bikini under her wetsuit, but she knew what Joal's actions meant. How far should she let him go? Was she ready for this?

"Wait," she said. Joal froze just as his hand touched her bare stomach. He kept his knuckles against her skin. "Before we go on," Jemma continued, "I need to ask you something."

He lifted his head and raised a brow.

She paused, gathering her courage. *Should I tell him? Am I stupid for trusting him, trusting that he won't break my heart?* She'd already lost her mom, and she was surviving that. Somehow... if things turned bad with Joal, she'd survive that as well.

"You've got me worried," he said, his brows creased.

"I just..." She sat up and he mirrored her actions. Finally, she continued. "I need to know how you feel about me. I know you *want* me, but..." She took a deep breath, and said, "If this is all about lust, you need to know that..." she sighed. *Here goes.* "I've loved you since the second grade. Even when you paid no attention to me, I loved you."

His eyes widened in reaction to her words, but he didn't pull away. She took that as a good sign.

"Now I know," she continued, "it's too early in our relationship for you to love me back and after hearing this you may feel like running for the hills, but I need to know that I'm not just another girl in your long line of conquests. If I am, we need to stop. I just... I can't... handle another heartbreak right now."

Joal's brows knit together. "Why would you love me? Especially after treating you like I did."

"I don't know. It's..." she didn't continue, she didn't know how to explain.

When she hesitated, he said, "It's what?"

She sighed, gathering her thoughts. "It's like fate. The first time you touched me, I felt it. I couldn't fight it. Believe me, I've fought my feelings so many times over the years. It was like... like jumping off that cliff." She glanced toward the falls;

he kept his eyes on hers. "Once I fell, there was no undoing that, no way to stop, no way to make myself not love you. No matter how much I tried."

"I don't deserve you."

"Believe me," she huffed playfully, "I know that."

Joal smiled sadly. "But I do understand how you feel. It's how I felt my first day back. When I saw you, I... you captivated me. You still captivate me." He sighed. "As for my long line of conquests. I really don't have one."

"What are you talking about? I've seen you make-out with more girls than I can count."

"Yeah, kiss, make-out, but it didn't go any farther than what you saw. I have a rule. No serious relationships with humans or demigods, and then as you know I am not allowed near either of my pantheons, so dating a goddess is usually not an option."

"Wait, are you a... um..., I don't know if racist is the right word."

He shook his head. "No. No, of course not. It's not like that. It's just... mortal life spans are far too short for a long-term relationship. At least they are for me."

"Oh. So, the girls you made out with. You didn't..." She couldn't bring herself to ask what she really wanted. Maybe she didn't want to know, but still heat warmed her face.

Understanding warmed his cheeks as well. Gods, the great Joal Forseti was blushing.

"No, I didn't," he answered her unspoken question. "And now you know my deep, dark secret. Your fertility god boyfriend is a..." he hesitated.

She shook her head. "No, you're not."

"Yeah." He chuckled. "I am."

"You're a virgin?"

"Shhh!" he said, looking around as if someone might be

spying on them. "Don't let it get out. That would ruin my reputation."

"You're not kidding. Well, this is something we have in common."

Joal's brows rose. "You haven't...? Not with anyone?"

"Of course not. I've been in love with *you* all these years."

"In my experience, that doesn't mean anything. Both my parents supposedly love their spouses, yet here I am."

Jemma shook her head. "Well, I'm not like that."

Joal smiled and said, "Good to know. But..., while I'd eventually like to take things to the next level with you, we really do need to stop. I don't want to rush things. And I really don't want your first time to be outside, in the cold."

"I'm not that cold."

Joal chuckled. "I could feel your goosebumps under my palm." He gently squeezed her stomach.

"Those aren't from the cold."

He chuckled. "Still—"

"Can I have just one more kiss," Jemma said.

He looked torn, conflicted. "I don't think that's a good idea."

"Please? I promise not to steal your virginity from you."

He chuckled. "Very funny."

"Just one kiss."

Joal looked down at her with disapproval on his face. "I know I'm going to regret this, but okay, just one more."

His lips pressed against hers, and she kissed him back. Jemma drank in every touch, every caress, every sensation. His hand slid inside her wetsuit and around her back. He pressed her up against him. His mouth tore away from hers only for him to trail kisses down her neck, Jemma breathed his name. Joal growled low and deep, and then he froze and pulled away. "Did you hear that?"

"What?" Jemma said, her breath still coming out in gasps.

"Something growled."

"That wasn't you?" Jemma said, in barely a whisper.

He shook his head and moved away from her. Jemma felt empty without him as she curled on her side. Joal rose to his knees, searching the trees. In a tight voice, he said, "Something's out there." He paused, his eyes narrowing. "Come on, we're leaving." He turned to gather their things.

Jemma froze as her heart turned to lead in her chest. Two glowing red eyes peered at her from the darkness of the trees.

Chapter Eleven – Jemma

As a bull roars when feeding in the field,
so roared the goodly door
touched by the key and
open flew before her.
—— *The Odyssey*, Homer

JEMMA SQUEAKED, "JOAL?" She was too terrified to say more.

At her tone, Joal's head whipped around to look at her, and then he followed her gaze. As soon as his eyes met the creature, he rose to his feet, pulled Jemma up, and pushed her behind his back. Jemma peered around him. Two eyes turned to four and then six. Jemma's heart pounded as three horse-sized dogs stepped out from the shadows. No, it wasn't three dogs, it was one dog with three heads.

"Cerberus," Joal growled. "What are you doing up here?"

One of the dog's heads kept his eyes on Joal, the other two glanced at Jemma, growling and snapping their jaws.

"You stay away from her unless you want to lose a head," Joal snarled.

What could he do without a weapon? Just as Jemma thought it, a metallic snap pierced the air and Joal was no longer weaponless. He held a trident in his hand; the three shiny points looked as sharp as razor blades. "Jemma, go. Take my car. You just need to push the ignition button."

"I can't leave you," she said, her voice ringing in disbelief.

"Yes, you can," he growled. "When I say so, get out of here."

"I'm not leaving without you," she said in clipped tones.

"He can't kill me. Besides, I'm trained for this."

"But..."

"There's no time to argue. Go! Now!" he shouted, pushing her back. Jemma stumbled and fell onto the hard, rocky ground. Cerberus rushed to attack her. Joal threw himself between them and thrust his trident at the beast. "Stay away from her! It's me you want."

He glanced back at her and yelled, "Go!"

Jemma scrambled to her feet and took off running. She could hear the fight rumbling through the trees and felt the ground shake beneath her bare feet. She ran through the dark woods, her feet taking a beating as she stumbled over sharp rocks and gnarled roots. When she finally reached Joal's SUV, she pulled open the door, threw herself into the seat, and then slammed the door shut. Looking back, she could see dark trees against the starry, moonlit sky, limbs and branches thrashing and whole trees falling over. Cerberus broke through to the parking lot, one of his heads was missing, another was hanging, lifeless; it was held on by a piece of skin and was being knocked about by the creature's front legs as he ran. The third head had his eyes trained on her as it charged.

Where was Joal?

He appeared, leaping onto the creature's back and

swinging his trident. The trident was a blur as he swung, going through the neck of Cerberus like a knife through Jell-O. The final head dropped with a thud to the ground, and the body of the beast followed as Joal gracefully stepped from the falling creature's back. The animal lay still as black blood pooled beneath the three stumps at the edge of the parking lot.

Jemma sat, shaking. Her hands gripped the wheel like a vice. Joal approached the SUV and opened the door. Jemma leapt from the car and threw her arms around him.

"It's okay," he said, "it's okay. He can't hurt you now."

Jemma shook her head and looked up at him, his face blurry behind tears. "I thought he was going to kill you."

"I already told you." He smiled weakly. "I can't die."

"But you can be ripped apart, right?"

"Not by a creature as dumb as this one." His eyes narrowed in disapproval. "Why didn't you leave?"

"I didn't have time. I just barely got here."

He frowned and was quiet for several moments. "Well, we know one thing. You're no daughter of Hermes."

Jemma scowled. "Are you calling me slow?"

Joal raised a brow.

Jemma caught a wafting smell of burnt dog hair. She looked at the large, dead mound. "What are we going to do about that? We can't just leave it here."

Joal pulled out his phone. "I know just who to call."

It was only a few seconds before Joal began talking to whomever he was calling, "Jemma and I just got attacked by Cerberus."

She could only hear one side of the conversation, but it was easy enough to follow. "Yeah, he's missing three, well, almost all three heads."

"At the parking lot by the falls."

Joal hung up and put his phone back in his pocket.

"Who did you call?"

"Dante."

"Dante...? Like, *Dante's Inferno*." Jemma asked.

"He's the very same."

"Wait. Wait, he's not *the* Dante. He's just named after him, right?" she said, scrunching her brows.

"Nope. He's the one and only Dante, the man who braved the nine levels of Tartarus and lived to talk about it."

"No, it's the nine levels of hell and that's a Christian story."

"The Christians high jacked that story and bent it to fit their views."

"So is Dante a god?"

"To tell you the truth, I'm not sure *what* he is, but he's been around a long, long time and knows a lot about the Underworld."

"And Cerberus is from the Underworld, right?"

Joal nodded. "He guards the gates."

Now that the danger was over, Jemma's feet began to throb. She groaned. "Just a minute. I need to look at my feet."

Joal looked down. "Gods, you're barefoot." He lifted her up into the cab, and Jemma crossed her leg to inspect the foot that hurt the worst. Her foot was covered in dirt and blood.

Joal swore.

Jemma looked down at the floor of the cab. "I got blood all over the floor."

"I couldn't care less about the stupid car. What does your other foot look like?"

Jemma crossed the other leg over. "This one's not nearly as bad."

"We need to clean them off."

"Should we go back to the falls?"

Joal shook his head. "We don't need to." He raised his hands and spread his fingers. It looked like he was holding an imaginary ball. Droplets of water floated toward the center and gathered into a simmering ball of water. When it was about the size of a cantaloupe, he said, "Okay, lift your foot up."

Jemma did and the ball of water enveloped it making it sting, really bad. "Ouch," she cried and tried to pull her foot back.

"Don't move," Joal said. "I'm sorry it hurts, but your foot needs to be cleaned."

Jemma squeezed her eyes closed and balled her fists at her side. She could feel the water flowing over her foot, almost like it was under a facet. And dang it hurt! But then the water was gone, leaving her foot feeling cold in the night air, but at least it didn't hurt as much. Joal inspected it again.

"You're a quick healer. You had a few scrapes and one larger cut, but it's healing quickly. In fact, I can actually see it closing."

"Let me see," she said, and crossed her leg. She could see exactly what he was talking about. There was pink, fresh skin over what must have been scrapes and a larger gash that was closing right before her eyes. "I've had cuts before, but they've never healed like that."

"Looks like you're coming into your powers."

"I thought that doesn't happen until I turn twenty-one?"

"I told you you were powerful."

"Do you heal fast too?"

"I do, but not this fast." He glanced at her curiously, as if she were an anomaly.

Attempting to distract him, she said, "Okay, let's clean the other foot." Joal repeated the process again, Jemma bracing herself for the pain, but it never came. Still, she found it hard to keep her foot inside the ball of water.

"Hold still," Joal said.

"I can't. It tickles." She giggled.

"You're ticklish?" He cracked a teasing smile. "That's good to know."

"No. It's not. You just forget that bit of information, Joal Forseti."

He let the ball of water float several yards away and splash to the ground. The headlights of a vehicle appeared and shone on them as a large, black truck pulled up. A man got out.

It looked like Dante had arrived. Jemma's eyes widened in surprise. Dante looked nothing like Jemma expected. Sure, he was handsome, dark, and intimidating, but he didn't look much older than they were.

"So, this is Jemma," he said as he approached. He searched her from head to bare feet, lingering on her stomach, and raised a brow. Jemma followed his gaze and was mortified. Her suit was still unzipped down to her belly button. She quickly pulled the zipper up.

"No need for me to ask what you were doing when the creature attacked."

Joal frowned. "Like you've never—"

"So," Dante interrupted, looking around and then his eyes fell on the dead Cerberus. "This is your work, huh?"

"Yep."

"Impressive."

"Are you gonna bury him?" Jemma asked.

"He's not dead," Dante said.

"All of his heads have been cut off." Jemma said. "How can he not be dead?"

"He's a primordial creature, which means he's immortal. When his heads are reattached, they will heal."

"Is that what would happen to Joal if someone cut off his head?" Jemma asked.

"Would you like to see a demonstration?" Dante raised his brows and rubbed his chin. It seemed as if he was seriously considering it.

"No!" Jemma jumped out of the car and stumbled between Joal and Dante.

"Jemma," Joal said, reaching out to steady her, "your foot."

Jemma shrugged. "It's fine."

Dante laughed and looked at Joal. "Oh, I like her. She's already protective of you." He looked back at Jemma and his brows furrowed. "Though Jemma's power feels... different, strange."

"That's me," Jemma said, suddenly feeling awkward. "I'm pretty strange."

"Ignore him," Joal said. "Dante's the king of strange."

"With my doctorate degree," Dante said, "you could call me 'Doctor Strange'."

"You have a doctorate degree? You don't look old enough."

Joal huffed. "Oh, he's definitely old enough. And he tells the worst dad jokes to prove it, as you've already heard."

Jemma chuckled.

Dante shrugged, "I have my talents. But to answer your question, yes, severing Joal's head wouldn't kill him."

"That's both comforting and horrifying," she said.

"Huh, yeah," Joal said. "For you and me both." Joal turned to Dante. "What are you going to do about Cerberus?"

"Tell me you've gathered up his heads."

"Two of them are right here," Joal said, "but the third is somewhere between here and the falls."

Dante sighed and looked at the downed trees. "I'll take care of it. It's not like you didn't leave a clear path for me to follow." He approached the forest. "Hades, could you have tried to be more discreet?"

"I wasn't the one knocking down the trees," Joal said.

Dante sighed. "There's no way I can cover this up. But the question is, who sent Cerberus after you?"

Joal shrugged. "Gods, I don't know. I haven't gathered too many enemies."

"No, but your father has."

"Not many people know he *is* my father."

"The Dagonians do," Dante said.

"The Dagonians don't have Cerberus at their beck and call," Joal said.

"No, they don't. But word might have gotten around."

Joal swore. "Another legacy of my dad."

Dante shrugged. "We can't choose our parents."

"Unfortunately," Joal said.

"Get your girlfriend home, I'll clean this up."

Joal nodded. He turned and swept Jemma up into his arms and carried her around to the passenger side.

"I can walk, you know."

"Not until I see that your feet are completely healed."

He sat her down and inspected her feet once again.

"You don't have a foot fetish, do you?" Jemma said, jerking her foot away as he brushed his fingers over the soul of her feet.

He shrugged. "Your feet *are* exceptional."

Jemma chuckled.

"Everything about you is exceptional." His eyes widened in disbelief when he got a good look at her feet. "They're completely healed." He shook his head. "Not even a scar."

"No scar?" Jemma looked closely and confirmed what he said. Then she had a thought. She bent her arm and looked at her elbow. "Wow. I used to have a scar here." She pointed to a place on her arm. "But it's completely gone too."

"Hmm. That's unusual," Joal said, reflective. Then he looked over his shoulder toward the trees. "I need to go back and get our stuff." He turned back to her. "Will you be alright here for five minutes?"

"Sure."

"Okay," he leaned in for a kiss. Joal pulled away far too soon and said, "Hmm. You taste so good."

Jemma could feel her cheeks flush.

Joal cracked a smile. "I'll be right back."

She nodded. He stepped back, shut the door, and disappeared into the forest.

Jemma sat in the vehicle, completely alone... in the dark. Her eyes drifted to Cerberus and her breath hitched. His body was a black silhouette against the dark forest. Adrenaline spiked in her blood when she thought the shape seemed different somehow. Had he moved?

The wind blew, lifting the fur for a moment and making his body appear to shudder. But that was impossible. There's nothing he could do without his heads.

Jemma's heart slammed against her ribcage when Cerberus rose unsteadily from the ground. The one remaining head hung to the side. It was still mostly severed, but it had healed substantially—enough for him to function again. His dangling head scanned the forest.

I have to move! I have to hide! Jemma mustered all the courage she could find, slid off the seat, and tucked herself under the console. She lowered her head, hiding her face from view. *Please don't let him find me.*

She could feel his footsteps shaking the ground. They seemed to be coming closer. And then they stopped. Jemma's heart pounded out of her chest. Did he find her? Was he about to attack and bite her in half? Could *she* survive that? Maybe Joal was wrong about her. Maybe she wasn't a goddess. Maybe she was going to die. She heard deep, grating breaths. It sounded like he was sniffing her out.

Lifting her shaky head up, her eyes locked onto two red eyes peering at her through the window. Cerberus growled and then slammed into the side of the car. Glass shattered, shards flying everywhere as Jemma screamed. Cerberus's jaws opened wide as he neared the window. Jemma closed her eyes, waiting for powerful jaws to chomp down on her.

She heard a shout. *Joal?* But she felt nothing but the moist, rancid breath of the beast. And then the vehicle lurched nearly tipping over. Opening her eyes, she could see Cerberus was no longer focused on her; all his attention was on Joal hanging onto his back. The creature swung his head from side to side, attempting to dislodge him. And then something flew at an incredible speed, coming toward the creature. Joal leapt from his back, flipping midair and landing in a crouch on the ground as the thing slammed into the creature, knocking him back. Joal took off after the monster, his trident in his hand as he leapt over Cerberus. Swinging his weapon, Joal cut off the creature's remaining head. The head rolled over the compacted dirt as Joal rotated, flipping through the air and landing on his feet. The head came to rest next to another head. That must have been what she saw hit the creature.

Dante stepped into view. "Cerberus," he growled. "You never learn."

Joal sprinted to the SUV and ripped the door off its hinges as he opened it. He tossed it; it flew several yards away, crashing into a tree.

Jemma took a shaky breath, frozen in place.

"Jemma?" He pulled her from her hiding spot and then searched her, his hands brushing over her skin. "Are you okay. Did he hurt you?"

She couldn't speak. She couldn't move. She could barely breathe. All she could do was tremble.

"She's in shock," Dante said as he stepped into view. "Let's get her to my truck." Dante pulled out his keys and gave them to Joal. "Take her home."

"Shouldn't I take her to a hospital."

Dante looked at him like he thought Joal had lost his mind.

"Okay, okay, that was stupid."

"You aren't overly attached to this vehicle, are you?" Dante asked.

"Right now, I couldn't care less about it."

"You don't need anything from it, do you."

"No." Joal picked up Jemma. She tucked herself against his chest and clawed her arms around him and gripped him fiercely. Now that she was in his arms, her stupor wore off and she wept.

"Gods, Jemma, I'm sorry," he said as he carried her to Dante's truck. "This is all my fault."

Jemma shook her head. "No," she said between sobs.

"Shhh. It's okay now. You're safe."

Minutes later, Jemma was wrapped in a blanket and lying across the front bench seat with her head on Joal's lap as he drove. Her arm was a vice around his leg. Eventually, she fell asleep.

Jemma awoke when the truck came to a stop. She blinked open her eyes and sat up, swaying as sleep threatened to overtake her again.

Joal guided her out of the driver's side and scooped her up in his arms. Now that some time had passed, her fear had dissipated, and she was left feeling ashamed. She'd prided herself on her strength and independence, but tonight, she'd acted like a damsel in distress, and she hated that.

"You keep carrying me," she mumbled. "I really can walk, you know."

"You can't even keep your eyes open."

"I don't walk with my eyes."

Joal chuckled. "You have a point there." He continued to carry her.

Minutes later, he lay her down in her own bed. He left for a few minutes and came back with one of the few remaining mugs she owned. "I made you some chamomile tea. You should drink some."

Jemma nodded, took the mug, and sipped. The warmth penetrated her body, and she sighed in contentment.

"You should sleep. I'll be close by if you need me."

Jemma shook her head. "No. you need to sleep too."

"I can sleep on the couch."

"You have no idea how uncomfortable that couch is. No, we have school tomorrow. You should sleep in your own bed."

"You're not actually going to go to school tomorrow, are you?"

"Of course, I am. I can't afford to let my grades slip."

He pressed his fingers against her wrist. "Your pulse is better. You're going to be fine."

"I wasn't even hurt."

"You were in shock."

"Can gods and goddesses go into shock?" she asked.

"Apparently they can."

"What if you're wrong, and I'm really not anything special?"

"It doesn't matter what you are, you're still special. But you are supernatural."

"But—"

"Have you forgotten how fast you healed tonight."

"Oh..."

"Exactly, and now you need to sleep."

"And you should go home," Jemma said. "You need sleep too."

Joal frowned down on her.

"I'm fine, but..."

"What?" Joal said.

"Once Cerberus heals, will he come after you again?"

Joal shook his head. "I doubt it. That was more of an

annoyance to me than a real threat. But you... He could have really hurt you. I just... if I hadn't..."

"I'm fine now. It wasn't your fault."

Joal shook his head. "It was completely my fault. If you weren't with me, you wouldn't have been in danger. And then I stupidly left you alone with him. I should have known—"

"Joal, it's over, and I'm fine."

He sighed as he looked her in the eyes. "Yes, it is over," Joal kissed her on the forehead. "But are you really fine?"

"I am. I just feel super embarrassed about how I reacted. I mean, you must think I cry at everything.

"You're kidding me. You almost got eaten by a giant, three-headed dog and you think I'd look down on you for crying?"

Jemma shrugged.

He shook his head in disbelief. "I don't, not even a little bit. Now go to sleep. I'll see you tomorrow."

Chapter Twelve – Jemma

No one can hurry me down
to Hades before my time,
but if a man's hour is come,
be he brave or be he coward,
there is no escape for him.
—*The Iliad*, Homer

JEMMA LOOKED out the window of her calculus class. She thought about Cerberus and shuddered. Joal had tried so hard to take her mind off what happened. But he couldn't help her now. The teacher was lecturing about something she already knew inside and out. That was the drawback of studying ahead. It made class boring and allowed her mind to wander.

After what felt like hours, the bell rang, and she was out the door. Thank the gods school was over!

Joal met her in the hall, with a smirk on his face.

"What?" Jemma asked. "You look like you just ate a canary."

Joal's smile widened. "That expression is so strange."

"Would you like me to explain the origins of it?" She chuckled.

"Maybe later. Right now, you have diving tryouts."

Jemma's heart took off in a sprint as her smile faded. "What? Tryouts are today?"

"That they are."

"I don't have my swimsuit."

"We have time to go get it."

"I didn't sign up to tryout."

"It's an open tryout. You just need to show up."

"But I haven't even practiced."

"I'd say last night was good preparation."

"If I was diving off a cliff, maybe."

Joal shrugged. "The cliff was just a little lower than the platform."

"He's also going to ask me to perform certain dives," she said. "I don't know the names of the dives, I could probably do them if I saw them, but I don't know them by name. This is going to be a disaster."

"Actually, you choose the dives. You'll need three solid dives to make the cut."

"What if I'm not good enough?"

"I've seen the other divers compete. You're definitely good enough."

"I don't know... If I had time to prepare, I could probably do it."

He took her shoulders in his hands. "You'll do fine. I have faith in you."

"Well, at least one of us does."

"Come on." Joal tugged her arm toward the parking lot. "We've got to get your suit.

"This is going to be a disaster."

"You'll do great."

"I..." Jemma hesitated and then shrugged. "Well, I guess it can't be worse than cheerleading tryouts."

"That's the spirit. Let's go."

Λ

Jemma's heart pounded when she saw how many divers were there. What chance did she have?

"The coach always starts with the first row and goes left to right," Joal said. "So, if you sit on the last row, far left, you'll be able to see all of the other divers first."

Jemma nodded; her throat tight. She took a seat three rows up and the last place on the left. Joal, Cassie, and the entire swim team sat a few rows above her. Each time she turned to look at them they smiled and gave her an array of whoops, hollers, and supportive gestures. *That's not at all embarrassing*, she thought as she fought the urge to roll her eyes.

A middle-aged man with a clipboard stepped into the pool room. His eyes assessed the hopefuls. He paused when he saw her friends above. "Well," he said. "It's nice to see the swim team showing such enthusiastic support for the divers." He turned back to the hopefuls. "I'm Coach Baerenike, but you can call me Coach B. I'm happy to see so many at tryouts today, but I need to warn you that only a fraction of you will make the team. And we will begin weeding you out after your first dive, so don't get any stupid ideas of saving your best dive for last. I want to see your best dive first."

I don't even know what my best dive is. Please let me go last.

"You will do three different dives," Coach B continued. "Each dive you'll perform twice."

"Okay," the coach said, "let's shake things up. Instead of

starting with the first row, I want to start with the last row, far left."

Jemma felt faint. She was going first. She scowled back at Joal. He shrugged and mouthed, "Sorry. You'll do fine."

What should she do? The coach said to not save her best dive for last, but she didn't even know what her best dive was. Last night, Joal was impressed with her dive. She was sure she could do better than the dives she did last night—if she could practice. But she hadn't had time to practice, and anything more might prove disastrous.

Her legs were shaky as she approached the coach.

"Jemma, right?" Coach B said.

She nodded. "Jemma Ryan."

"Okay, Jemma, the pool is yours. Impress me."

"Can I start with a platform dive?" she asked.

His brows creased and then he relaxed and said, "You're a flyer, from the cheer squad. I've seen you perform."

"I *was*. I decided to try diving this year."

He nodded appreciatively, "Good choice. Yes, you can use the platform."

Climbing up the platform, she focused on breathing evenly. She could do this. She had no nerves last time she did this dive, and this was no more pressure than cheer competitions.

She really could do this.

Stepping to the edge, she looked down to see the rippling, aqua-blue water. Then she closed her eyes to calm her nerves and focus her mind. When she opened them, she took a three-step approach and leaped into the air. Piking her body, she then laid out into a dive. The water enclosed her like a glove. She was smiling when she surfaced. Oh, how she loved the feel of flying. It was like nothing else. Cheers rang out. She looked up and the entire swim team was on its feet.

When she approached the coach, he had his brow raised.

"Not willing to take risks?" Her previous high crashed. He was not happy with her dive. "Take a seat."

Tears burned in her eyes. She'd blown her chance.

The next fifteen minutes she watched dive after dive, and little by little, her hopes rose. The other divers, for the most part, looked unskilled, except for a few spots of talent. When the last diver completed their first dive, she felt a thousand times better. She turned to Joal.

"I told you so," he mouthed.

Five minutes later the coach approached the benches and said, "I have the first cuts. If I don't read your name, you didn't make it and your tryout is through. Just know that I appreciate your willingness to try out regardless."

He began listing off names. "Trevor Prince, Amanda Lawrence, Avery Richardson..." Jemma was happy to hear the swim team cheer at each name. "Tawney Capp, Rosey Thorn, Jemma Ryan..." Jemma didn't hear any names after that. Not only did the swim team's cheer rise to deafening levels; she was so relieved at hearing her name. Then she realized she needed to dive again.

Great. Now what am I going to do? The coach didn't seem so happy with her first dive. What kind of follow-up dive should she do? Pursing her lips, she analyzed the situation. The coach was disappointed in her for playing it safe.

Closing her eyes, she ran through her memories of different platform dives she's watched—most of them came from the Olympics. Yeah, those weren't going to work, but perhaps... She took one of the Olympic dives and scaled down the difficulty, to where she might actually pull it off. The resulting dive she pictured in her mind had her smiling. Maybe she could do it.

"Jemma," a voice shouted. She looked up and realized all eyes were on her. "Are you ready?" Coach B asked.

"Um," Jemma said. "Yeah.

She approached the platform. This dive would use skills she used in cheer and combine them with diving. Stepping up to the edge of the platform, she turned her back to the water, spread her legs in a A-frame and reached down to the floor. Putting pressure on her hands, she lifted her feet off the platform and executed a perfect handstand—something she'd done a million times. Picturing herself atop a cheer pyramid, she tipped, falling toward the water, tucking her legs to her chest, she flipped backward, the world spinning around her. When the water came into view, she layout into a dive. The slap of the water against her back felt like concrete. It was a painful and embarrassing indication that she'd laid out too soon. The dive was a complete failure, and she ruined her chances of making the team. She wished she could remain underwater until everyone had left. The last thing she wanted to do was face a crowd of laughter and jeers. But she had to. It was best to just get it over with.

When she surfaced, she couldn't have been more shocked at the deafening cheers. Searching out Joal's face, he looked concerned. "Are you okay?" he mouthed.

Jemma nodded; her face was probably as red as her back. When she got to the edge of the pool, she saw the coach's smiling face. Why was he so excited about a messed-up dive? "Jemma Ryan." He shook his head. "Now *that's* taking a chance." He reached out his hand and pulled her from the pool. "I bet that hurt like a bugger."

Jemma sighed. "Yeah."

"Don't worry," he said, "we'll work on it."

We'll work on it? Did that mean he expected her to make the team?

"Why don't you sit the next round out," Coach B said. "Your back needs a rest and I've seen enough of your skills."

"Does that mean I made it?"

He laughed. "After that last dive, there's no doubt."

"But I messed it up."

He shook his head, "No, you took a chance and let me see what you are capable of. Now sit down and relax, and then, if their cheering is any indication, I'm sure you and the men's swim team have a lot of celebrating to do tonight. Just be ready for practice on Monday."

"Yes, sir," Jemma said, smiling. What started off as the world's worst school year was now becoming better than she could have dreamed.

Chapter Thirteen – Jemma

The creations of genius always seem like miracles,
because they are, for the most part,
created far out of the reach of observation.
—— *The Odyssey*, Homer

JEMMA HAD her back pressed against the cool, brick wall of D hall while Joal warmed her with his kiss. Gods how she loved kissing him. It was magic; it was bliss. Slowly, he pulled away and pressed his forehead into hers. "I wish I didn't have to go practice."

"You love practice." She reminded him.

"It'd be better if the diving team was practicing too."

"Yeah, but this does give me and Cassie a chance to go dress shopping. *Someone* asked me to Homecoming."

Joal smirked and then frowned. "Shopping? I guess swim practice isn't so bad."

Jemma chuckled. "Go on." She pushed him back. "You're going to be late."

"When will I see you again?" he asked.

"Cassie's going to be spending the night at my house, so it won't be 'til tomorrow. Do you think you can wait that long?"

"A whole night?" He raised a brow. "Are you sure *you* can survive that long without seeing me?"

"I bet I could survive longer."

"Let's not test it."

Jemma chuckled. "I'll see you tomorrow."

"I sure hope so."

He leaned in and gave her one more sweet kiss. When he pulled away, he said, "See you in the morning."

She nodded and Joal turned to walk away. Jemma watched him saunter down the hallway and push open the door leading to the pool. He took one last look back at her, flashing her a heart-stopping smile before he disappeared through the door.

Jemma turned to see Cassie running toward her with a scowl on her face.

"Hey, Cass," Jemma said, "what's wrong?"

"I'm really sorry. My mom is making me go to some family thing tonight. Nothing like springing things on me last minute."

"So, we can't go shopping?"

Cassie shook her head." I tried to get out of it, but my mom wouldn't let me."

"No. That's okay. We can go tomorrow. Don't worry about it."

"You sure? I ruined our whole night."

"You totally didn't ruin it. And absolutely, you need to go."

"You're the best," Cassie said and gave her a hug. "Call me in the morning."

"I will."

With her afternoon suddenly free, Jemma decided now would be a good time to visit the finance office. She approached the open window and said, "Hey Mrs. Richard-son, can I get a parking pass?"

Mrs. Richardson pushed her wire-rimmed glasses higher on her upturned nose and leaned on the wide ledge that doubled as a counter. "Sure, Jemma, that'll be ten dollars."

Jemma paid the fee and collected the hanging parking tag. Heading back to her locker, she noticed the hallways were deserted. Right. It was Friday. The weekend. Everybody else had plans. Well, since Cassie bailed on her and Jemma didn't have a ride, maybe she could watch Joal practice and then he could spend the evening with her.

A tital wave of pain slammed into Jemma's back. Gasp-ing, she staggered forward, crashing into the lockers before her knees gave out. Hitting the floor, she groaned out as the agony overwhelmed her and the hallway spun. She pawed desperately at her backpack straps to pull it off. Removing the pressure on her back alleviated some the pain, but not much. *What's happening to me?* She sobbed as she crawled along the floor. It felt like her back was being ripped to shreds. The pain lessened a bit for a moment but didn't go away completely.

Reaching behind her, she brushed her fingers over where the pain originated—from her upper back. What she felt had her jerking her hand back. Glancing behind, she sucked in a breath. Her shirt stretched over her shoulder blades like a tent.

"Oh my gosh," she whispered harshly, and then the pain made her cry out. She took in heaping gasps of breath and attempted to get on top of the agony as it ebbed and flowed. At its worst, she was incapable of coherent thought, and when it ebbed, her thoughts were frantic. What if someone found her here? If they'd thought her a freak before, they'd think she was completely hideous now. Why didn't she use her money to get a cell phone so she could call for help? She had to hide. At least until the pain was gone and she could think more clearly.

The pain *would* leave, wouldn't it? It always had before. She couldn't possibly feel like this forever.

Looking up, she could see the door to the old biology lab at the end of the hall. That's where she had to go.

"I know!" a familiar voice came from down the hall.

Brooklyn.

"I can't believe she's making us practice on a Friday. I have Trent's party to go to tonight. I don't want to be all sweaty, and if I shower, it'll mess up my hair."

Jemma scrambled off the floor and limped toward the lab. She could hear Brooklyn's footsteps coming around the corner as Jemma opened the door and closed it behind her clicking the lock in place.

Did Brooklyn see her?

She sank down on all fours as she got an up-close look at the cracked, linoleum squares. Clenching her jaw tight, she held in a cry that begged to escape her lips as another wave of agony overtook her.

When it eased, she sobbed, "Please make it stop."

Crawling over to the old couch, she pulled herself up and lay down on her stomach. Whatever was growing out of her back was pressing painfully against her blouse. Unbuttoning her shirt, she pulled it off, leaving her only with her bra. She planted her tear-streaked cheek against the rough, threadbare couch. The musty smell of old furniture wafted around her as she rode wave after wave of pain, agony, and torture. "Joal," she sobbed as her body convulsed. "Where are you? What's happening to me?"

The pain was not going anywhere. Days and weeks before she'd had flashes of hurt, but those were just hints, shadows of what was happening now. This was what her body had been building up to. Maybe she was a monster. Joal said she was something mythical. He thought she was a goddess, but now... Jemma was sure she was something more hideous. Perhaps, a harpy, a gargoyle or... or... Gods, maybe she was a daughter of Echidna—the mother of all mythical monsters. There were so many hideous creatures from myth. She could morph into any number of grotesque things, and gods, morphing really hurt!

Jemma wept in agony for what seemed an eternity. Exhausted, her sobs turned to moans as she moved in and out of consciousness, always aware of her body, the feel of it changing, transforming.

Joal didn't come. He didn't answer her desperate pleas. He wouldn't. He couldn't hear her. He didn't know she was here. He expected her to be with Cassie. And then tomorrow was Saturday. They were supposed to see each other, but how would he find her? He'd never think to look at school. Not on a Saturday.

Night descended slowly, shrouding the room in darkness. Jemma didn't pay attention to the fading light. Her thoughts were in a jumble. All she could comprehend was pain and exhaustion. That was her world now. And it royally sucked!

As the moon rose in the sky, the pain soared to new heights. Her stomach churned and heaved. Looking up, she spotted a nearby sink. Dragging herself over to it just in time to throw up. Sweat dripped down her face and back. When she'd finally emptied the contents of her stomach, she sank to the floor. Cold seeped into her as she leaned against a metal cabinet. Her teeth chattered as nausea rose again. Now she was not only in pain, but she was also sick and cold.

Looking around the room, she could see what looked like a sink or tub sitting on the floor with a spout. It sat in the corner at the far end of the room with an old mop propped up against it and a bucket nearby. Two handles, on either side of the spout jetting from the sink, caught her attention—one had a blue dot and the other had a red. Hot and Cold. At the thought of a hot bath, her spirits lifted.

Maybe if she—

Pain sliced through her, severing her thoughts. It felt as if she were waging a war inside her own body. Something fought to get free. The agony was the greatest when it seemed she'd made progress. It reminded her what it might be like to give birth. The pain would be horrible, but then you'd have a child to love at the end of it.

No. This was nothing like that. This pain was pointless. It had no silver lining. It became a living embodiment that stretched and pushed out from her ravaged back. If anything were to come from this, Jemma knew it would be monstrous.

The struggle and its accompanying pain and exhaustion continued on. When it did subside, it didn't last for long. Wave after wave always returned, the pain assaulted her in an endless cycle. Through it all, she continued to dry heave. She was too weak to stand at the sink, but thankfully, there wasn't much left in her stomach. She had nothing left to give. Every bit of moisture was gone. Her parched throat screamed and begged for water. Even her lips cracked and bled. She'd tried desperately to count the minutes, count the hours, but they ran together. And with each passing moment, her thirst grew more severe. She tried to stand, hoping she could get to the spout in the sink above, but she was too weak.

As the room continued to darken, the pain finally ebbed, giving her a measure of relief. Sleep overtook her and she found respite for a time. When she awoke, the room was blanketed in moonlight. She tried again to stand but couldn't. Across the room, she could see the basin near the floor. It seemed so far away.

If only...

She was so exhausted that the thought of moving an inch, much less the twenty feet it would take to get to the basin, was unbearable. At least the pain was not as bad. The smell of her own body odor and vomit were enough to keep her stomach sick, but she simply had to get to the basin. Everyone, including Joal, would be back in school on Monday. Someone had to find her here and when they did, she didn't want to smell worse than sewage.

Her shaking hands pulled her across the floor as she dragged her legs—one and then the other—behind her in a pathetic army crawl. It took her a long time, but she finally made it. The red handle was the closest one to her. She reached for it and pulled. Water flowed, seeping into her hands. It started out cool and she spooned the liquid into her parched mouth. Soon it turned warm, and she wanted to crawl into the basin and never come out. If she was going to die anyway, at least she wouldn't be cold.

With great effort, she pulled herself in and let the hot water wash over her battered back as she used her arm as a pillow on the edge of the basin. Something drifted into her vision. It was long and pointed with webbed skin stretching between points—like a pale bat's wing with purple spider-webbed veins showing beneath translucent skin. At the sight of it, she jerked up and the thing extended.

No. *She* extended it.

It was a wing. What was she becoming? Some kind of bat thing? She really *was* hideous. Tears bloomed in her eyes. How could Joal love something so repulsive?

Moving more fully under the hot water, the near scalding heat was a welcome distraction. Exhaustion eventually over-took her, and she curled up and fell asleep.

Chapter Fourteen – Joal

For already have I suffered full much,
and much have I toiled in
perils of waves and war.
Let this be added to the tale of those.
—— *The Odyssey*, Homer

JOAL LAY in bed as he hugged his pillow and rested his head against its softness. It was Saturday. There was nothing that required him to get out of bed. Nothing but the thought of a girl. He groaned, imagining that the pillow was Jemma.

He really had it bad. He was the fertility god. People were supposed to go crazy for him, not the other way around. But Joal couldn't get Jemma out of his head—her touch, her taste, her smell. Everything about her appealed to him.

No. Appeal wasn't strong enough of a word. She captivated him. And as difficult as it was, he'd given her space last night to go dress shopping with her best friend. Today, he hoped she would want to spend the day with him. He hoped she'd spend every waking moment with him.

Gods, he was sounding like a stalker.

A flash of light so bright that he could see it from behind his eye lids filled his room. A moment later a deafening boom shook the house. He opened his eyes and looked out his window. Black clouds filled the skies. Another flash of lightning skirted across the length of the window. The wind howled and groaned, pushing against his pane, and causing the nearby tree branches to flail like an angry toddler.

Wow. Washington state has been having a lot of severe weather lately. That was something you didn't see too often.

"Joal!" his mother's voice called from downstairs.

Joal swore under his breath.

"I heard that."

Of course, she did.

"Hey, mom," he said, using his normal indoor voice.

"Come downstairs. I've got a lot to tell you."

Looks like Jemma will have to wait. "Coming."

Joal flung off his satin sheets and put his feet to the plush, grey carpet and stretched. Of all the times for his mom to come home. He sighed.

Descending the curved staircase, Joal could see his mother standing in the family room, pacing the floor. She had her blonde hair pulled back into a ponytail and she was dressed in jeans, a blue cotton jersey, and Nike tennis shoes. This was super casual for her. Usually, her clothing was silk and lined with gold trim. It looked like she was trying to pass for a human. Her perfect features and glowing skin were working against her. She needed to give herself a few flaws to complete her disguise, though her mother would never do it. She was much too conceited for that.

"Crazy weather we're having," he said.

She shook her head in annoyance. "The Greek sky-gods are having another hissy fit. Their beloved king is gone."

"What are you talking about?" Joal asked, plopping down on the couch.

"Where's the human?" she said, ignoring his question.

"You mean Denise?"

"Whatever."

"She does her grocery shopping Saturday mornings."

"Good, I don't want a human hearing this."

"Hearing what? What's the big news?"

"Sometimes I forget how isolated you are here. Well, let me give you the short version. Zeus has been imprisoned and Petros is now on the throne." His mom paced the floor. He'd never seen her this hyped up.

"Who in Hades is Petros?"

"He's Poseidon's brother. Of all the grandchildren of Gaia, he's the most powerful. His elemental is earth."

"Earth, but that's the human's element."

"I know!"

"So, why have I never heard of him?" he asked.

"Our memories were erased. Petros was the true king, but Zeus locked him up in Tartarus and then took the throne for himself. I know it sounds crazy, but that's what's happened. Now everyone remembers, and Petros is back on the Olympus throne and *Zeus* is in Tartarus."

"I don't remember Petros."

"You were born after it all happened."

"How was Zeus captured?

"He was caught by the true king and four pathetic half-breeds."

"Demigods?"

His mother's blonde curls swayed as she shook her head. "No. Gods with mixed elementals and then some beings I'd never heard of before called Aethers. Apparently, Zeus was using them to steal power from infants born of gods. And not just in his own pantheon, but in ours as well."

"You mean in *your* pantheon?"

"It's your pantheon too."

"I don't think so. I'm a god without a pantheon."

His mother's sparkling eyes darkened just a bit as she frowned. "That's only temporary."

"Right, so someday I'll just show up and say, 'I'm here! Oh, and by the way, don't ask me who my parents are.' Be realistic, mom."

"Stop your wining. It's a good thing I did keep you a secret. Zeus would have probably stolen you from me as well. It's his loss. Once you're powerful enough, you can take your place on Olympus. We could use someone on the inside. You could really help our cause."

"I'm not going to be anyone's pawn."

"You will do what needs to be done," she snapped.

This was their eternal argument. His mom had big plans for him, plans he wanted no part of. "You're getting off topic, mom. What is this about Zeus?"

His mother sighed as if the answer exhausted her. "He was siphoning power from children born of the gods. The parents' memories were erased and then the children were placed with human families. But now that Zeus has been captured, the children who were being syphoned of their powers are being released. The problem is none of these children know who or what they are, I'm helping to identify the lost sea-gods and return them to their families."

His mom suddenly had his undivided attention. "Wait. How long has Zeus been doing this? How old would these gods be?"

"He's been doing it for millennia. We're finding a few infants and children, but most are full-grown adults. The only way to find them is to mix with the humans and look for signs of their power. One thing's for certain, they are a danger to themselves and others until we can locate them and return them to the sea. We found one goddess in a massive lake where a small town used to be. She was in shock, surrounded by the drowned corpses of her adoptive family, friends, and townspeople."

"How long ago were these gods and goddesses released?"

"They were supposed to be released two months ago, but it's taking longer than expected. Many are still being syphoned, though their power is now being returned to the cosmos instead of being given to Zeus."

Jemma. She must be one of them. *That's why I didn't feel her power until now. Maybe that's why I didn't even really see her. Zeus had been hiding her from the gods.* "Why'd you wait 'til now to tell me?"

"I've been busy," she said dismissively. "I'm still busy. I only have a few minutes before I'll be missed."

"Why didn't you ask me to help?"

She sighed. "I couldn't."

"Yeah, I know. I just have to stay here and pretend I don't exist."

"I don't know how many times you want me to say I'm sorry."

Joal wished he could point out that she's never actually said she was sorry for anything, but that would just make things worse. Instead, he shrugged and said, "It's not your fault. It is what it is. So, what are you doing with the other gods you find, the ones that aren't sea-gods?"

His mother cracked a smile as her eyes sparkled. "I'll tell you, but you have to swear not to tell anyone else."

Joal's stomach sank. What was his mother up to?

"This is a prime opportunity to tip the balance of power to the sea-gods."

"Oh, mom. Please tell me you're not."

"Not me personally. I just tell Ægir and he takes care of them."

"He's killing them?"

"Don't be ridiculous. We don't have the power to kill a god. He's simply imprisoning them where they can't escape, and where no one will find them. Rea is trying to figure out a way to destroy them permanently, but who know if that's ever going to happen."

Joal scowled at the terrible confession.

"Don't act so appalled. They're not one of us. What we get rid of today, we don't have to fight tomorrow."

"It's wrong, mom."

"Don't you take that tone with me!"

Anger rose in Joal's chest, but he suppressed it. Getting his mother angrier than she already was would only make things worse.

"No one knows who they are," she said. "No one will know when they're gone. And *you* will not say a word. Do you understand me?"

Joal didn't answer.

"Do you understand me?" she asked again, her voice raising an octave.

"I understand, but I don't agree with what you are doing."

"Well, agree or not, if you tell anyone, Petros will destroy me himself, and he is one god capable of doing it. Do you want my blood on your hands?"

Joal swallowed a lump in his throat. "No, I don't." How could his mother put him in this position? For that matter, how could she be involved in something so heinous?

"Good. You need to remember where your loyalties lie."

For the first time in his life, Joal was ashamed of his fellow sea-gods.

"Now I have to continue the search," she said.

"Will you be looking in Garden Grove?"

"No. We have enough demigods here already. If a god or goddess comes into their power anywhere near here, it will not go unnoticed. There's no reason to send anyone else. I've got to go. I probably won't be able to visit you for a long time yet. These new, inexperienced sea-gods will need a lot of looking after and I've got to get back to the search."

A long time? He already sees her only every few months. "It's okay mom. You've got important things to do."

She left without giving him a hug, left without telling him she loved him, left without even saying goodbye. It wasn't her way. She'd never been an affectionate mother. Still, she gave him a large, elaborate home and all the money he wanted. And, most importantly, she'd given him Denise—a woman that cared more for him than anyone. He shouldn't resent his mom, but he did.

Joal didn't stay and wallow in self-pity, he had to find Jemma. Pulling out his phone, he called her landline. It rang five times and then he heard her mother's voice say, "You know the drill, leave a message."

"Jemma," he said as he ran up the stairs. "Call me as soon as you can. I'm coming over. Something's come up." He ended the call and quickly dressed in a pair of blue jeans and a navy-blue t-shirt. His heart sank when he realized what he needed to do. He needed to find out where she belonged and give her back to them. It was the only way to protect her from others like his mother.

He threw on a jacket and ran to his car. Minutes later he pulled up to her house. The rain pounded against the small structure as the wind blew, flinging branches across her lawn. Joal pulled his hoodie up over his head and raced to her front door. The rain drenched his clothes by the time he got there. Knocking, he said, "Jemma. Open up, I need to talk to you."

He waited for her to come to the door. A minute later, he knocked again. She didn't answer. His chest tightened as his anxiety spiked. He tried the knob. It was locked. He stepped around to the back. Leaning into the wind, he raised his arm to protect his face from being pelted. The backdoor was locked too, but then he noticed a window cracked open. He removed the screen, opened the window, and climbed in. As he pulled the window down, he shouted, "Jemma?"

Nothing.

No answer.

He took the stairs two at a time and then he saw the door to her bedroom open, her bed neatly made—and empty. He swore and looked through her window at the rain beating against the glass.

Where was she?

His heart pounded as he attempted to calm himself. She was probably with Cassie. Perhaps she slept over there last night instead of here.

The harsh ringing of the phone came from the first floor. Joal flew down the stairs and picked up the receiver.

"Hello?"

"Hello?" Cassie's surprised voice came through the phone, clearly. "Who is this?"

"This is Joal."

"Oh, um...hi. Is Jemma there? She was wanting to go dress shopping today, but I don't think we ought to go out in this storm."

Joal's anxiety spiked. "I thought you went dress shopping last night."

"She didn't tell you? I had to cancel. Can you give her the message?"

"Wait, where were you when you told her you couldn't go."

"At school. Why's that important?"

"No reason," he said through gritted teeth. "I'll give her the message."

"Oh, okay. Good. Tell her to call me when she's free."

"Yeah, okay."

Cassie hung up and Joal stood with the phone clutched tight in his hand. He swore up a streak under his breath and slammed the phone onto the receiver "Where are you, Jemma Ryan?" *Mom, so help me if you or your friends got to her...!*

He didn't want to consider the possibility. He needed to retrace her steps and go to the last place she'd been seen. Step one on his to-do-list: break into the school.

Joal parked on the street to avoid any suspicions from the neighbors. Using his power, he cloaked himself from view as he stalked up to the school. Making his way around the side of the building, he looked for a window he knew he could unlock. He'd discovered the faulty lock during practice last year when he'd been bored and messed with it before practice.

He grasped the handle and wiggled until the latch bolt slipped free. He pushed the window open and climbed into the pool room. Jogging to the hall housing Jemma's locker, he strode purposely toward it and skidded to a stop. Her back-pack lay on the floor. He knelt, picked it up, and pressed it to his nose. It smelled like a sea breeze with a hint of bee balm.

It smelled like her.

He growled as that smell invoked a wave of protectiveness. "Jemma!" he shouted as he looked up. He knew it was highly unlikely she was still here, but he had nowhere else to search. "Jemma!" he shouted again as he flung her pack on his back and rushed down the hall.

"Jemma!" Finally, he saw a door that had him running. It was the old biology lab, her hideaway. He could hear water running and his heart pounded with each step. He reached for the handle and pushed his body against the steel door. It didn't move; it was locked. Why was it locked? Thrusting his weight against the steel, he growled as he pushed with everything he had. The door gave way, flinging open and slamming against the wall. He scanned the room; his eyes landed on Jemma. His heart leaped in his chest just before it stopped, and he cursed.

Gods, he was so relieved to see her, but his joy was overshadowed by the hopelessness of their future together when he saw her.

Long, scrawny, wings with patches of white downy feathers had sprouted from her back—obviously, the wings were still growing. "She really is a flyer." He shook his head.

After the initial shock of seeing her emerging shape wore off, he looked her over and his heart froze in his chest. She was lying in a dirty mop sink with water cascading over her body. Her lips were blue, and she wasn't moving. Joal ran to her and turned off the water. It was the hot water handle that had been turned, but the water was frigid. How long had it been running?

"Jemma," he said attempting to rouse her. "Jemma wake up." She didn't stir. She lay still as death. He was shocked to see how gaunt her face looked. Where she had been healthy and rounded before, now she was thin, skeletal. Her eyes looked sunken; with circles so dark that they seemed bruised. He remembered how he'd only ever seen her eat salad at lunch and how she was so concerned about her weight gain. If only he'd known, it was her body's way of preparing for a transformation, he'd have insisted she load up on calories. Her diet had sabotaged her. Seeing her now, he could see how devastating that mistake was. Gods, he couldn't imagine what she'd been through in the last few hours!

"I'm so sorry, baby. I'm sorry I wasn't here to help you." He brushed his hand across her hollow cheekbone. Her skin was cold as ice. He had to warm her up.

Turning off the water, he lifted her from the basin and swept her up in his arms. At the touch of her skin a wave of possessiveness washed over him.

Mine.

He couldn't explain it, but having her in his arms, weak and vulnerable, drove within him a primal urge to claim and protect her. It overcame all reasoning.

She was his, despite her parentage. As if to emphasize his thoughts on their differences, one of her wings drifted into view over his shoulder. It was nearly as long as she was tall, with thin bones silhouetted through translucent skin.

He was surprised at how light she felt. Even with the added weight of her wings and being wet. He guessed her drenched jeans weighed nearly as much as she did.

Closing his eyes, he concentrated on using his power. A cloud of mist surrounded them as he vaporized the water. There wasn't a speck of moisture left on her body.

He debated what to do with her. He could take her to her house but knowing there were gods out looking for lost gods, that may not be the safest place. Evan had noticed a difference in Jemma; if he tipped the wrong person off... that could be disastrous.

Joal could take her to his house, but if his mother showed up, it would be worse. The best place for her would be with the sky-gods, but even as he thought it, his mind rebelled against that option. Holding her in his arms he realized he'd been a fool to think he could ever let her go. Though he'd have a battle ahead of him, he'd rather be thrust down to Tartarus than live without her.

Joal sat on the couch and wrestled his phone from his pocket as he kept Jemma pressed against his chest.

Kahula picked up on the first ring. "Hey, oh mighty leader," he said with a smile in his voice.

"I need your help," Joal said with no hint of amusement.

Kahula paused a moment. His tone was serious when he asked, "What do you need?"

"I need you at the high school. Enter through the window

in the pool room and come to the old biology lab at the end of D hall. And bring a warm blanket."

Minutes later, Kahula stepped through what remained of the doorway to the lab with a blanket crushed against his chest saying, "You really did a number on the steel door. Do you know how much force it had to have taken to—?" His voice cut off, and his eyes widened as he looked at Jemma. "Great gods of Olympus."

"Yeah," was all Joal said.

Kahula stepped up to Joal, his wide eyes on the girl in Joal's arms. "She's definitely not sea-born."

"Obviously."

Kahula cursed. "What are you going to do with her?"

"I need a place to keep her."

"Why don't you just give her back to her own kind?"

At Kahula's words, fury rose in Joal's pulsing heart and pumped through his veins. He growled low, menacing. The words, "she's mine," grated through his teeth.

Kahula swore. "What's wrong with you? She's not a pet. You can't just keep her. Besides, your mom would kill you!"

A low rumble shook the building as Joal tightened his grip on Jemma.

"Woah, hey man, stop." Kahula raised his hands in surrender as he looked around. "You'll bust every pipe in this building."

Joal attempted to calm his anger. If he wasn't careful, he'd cause enough damage to bring in the humans. He could not let them see Jemma in this condition. Finally, the rumbling stopped, and all was quiet.

"You really need to learn some control," Kahula said.

"No, what I really need is somewhere safe to keep Jemma."

"Man, she's completely messed you up. Do you have any idea what your mother would do if she found you with a sky-goddess?"

"Yeah, she'd be ticked."

"That's the understatement of the century. And if she knows I helped you. I'd be dead. Literally. I mean, she probably won't kill you since you're her son, but me... she'd torture me within an inch of my life and then she'd impale me on spikes to bleed out and die. And unlike you, I don't come back!"

"Listen," Joal said. "I know it's dangerous, and I'm sorry. But I have no one else I trust with this."

Kahula shook his head. "Man, this is so messed up."

Jemma's head rested under Joal's chin. Holding her this close filled him with.... It was hard to explain. He felt... complete. "Please, just please help me." The pleading tones of his voice finally seemed to reach Kahula.

"Alright." He blew out a breath. "Gods, alright, I'll help you. But where are we gonna put her?"

"That's what I'm asking you."

"Yeah, well unlike you, I don't have endless funds. I live with my mom in a two-bedroom house. I don't have any secret room or secret cabin to hide people in. And my mom would *not* be okay with keeping a sky-goddess in our house."

"Yeah," Joal said, sounding defeated.

"How long is your mom going to be gone?" Kahula asked.

"I don't know. Probably months, but then again, she could come back tomorrow."

"What are the chances of that?"

"Slim."

"Okay, so take her home for now and then we'll figure out where to put her later."

"I don't know."

Kahula shrugged. "It's the best plan we have."

Joal sighed in defeat. "Okay, bring my car around."

Kahula stepped out of the room.

No sooner had Kahula left than Jemma began to shutter

in his arms. A low keening grew sharp, agonizing. "Nooo," she cried, her voice low and hoarse and then growing in intensity. "Ow, ow, ow, please make it stop!" She thrashed around and Joal had to fight to keep her from falling onto the floor. Her eyes flew open, they were panicked, pleading. "Joal," she cried, tears filling her eyes and spilling down her cheeks. "It hurts. Please make it stop. Make it stop!"

The agony in her voice broke his heart. "Gods, Jemma," he said, feeling helpless as tears burned his own eyes. "I don't know how."

He could see a glow in her infant wings as they stretched and grew, infinitesimally. If he didn't have such keen senses, he wouldn't have seen the progress, but there was something else. As her wings grew, her face went even more gaunt, her cheekbones sharper, her eyes more sunken. These wings were literally stealing the life from her body.

He swore as he lifted his hand to her emaciated face. "Baby, I don't know what to—" As soon as his skin touched her cheek, he felt power drain from him. It was so forceful and unexpected it took his breath away.

He was about to pull his hand back when he witnessed something amazing. The wings grew more quickly, several buds of down feathers sprouted, and her face filled out, just a bit more. Forcing himself to keep his hand on her cheek, he allowed the power to flow from him. She drained him for several minutes more until it finally slowed and then she stopped. Jemma closed her eyes. With ragged breath she said, "Thank you."

Joal's own breathing was heavy as he lay his cheek on her head and breathed out a curse. "You're welcome?" he whispered and then kissed her on top of her head. He felt weak; the power he'd given her was gone. Releasing it to her went against everything he'd been taught; it went against his own nature. Gods don't give their power to other gods. It just isn't done.

But he would do it all over again. Looking down at Jemma's face he thought, *I will do it again. Even if it kills me.*

But if he were really going to help her, he needed something to replenish him.

He needed seawater.

Chapter Fifteen – Joal

We must set aside old notions
and embrace fresh ones;
and, as we learn,
we must be daily unlearning
something which it has cost us
no small labour and anxiety to acquire.
——*The Iliad*, Homer

JOAL LEANED over the jacuzzi and turned a handle on the wall to the right. Then he turned on the main faucet. Ocean water flowed into the tub. He adjusted the temperature to warm and stepped back. He loved this room, it was large, square, had plush chairs, fine art, and an ancient Greek bath tapped into a pipe that led to the ocean.

"Ooh, this girl really needs a bath," Kahula said, holding Jemma in his arms. "She's ripe."

"Shut up," Joal said, unamused. "If you'd been through what she's been through, you'd smell worse." He pulled his shirt over his head and then peeled his jeans off. "We need to take her clothes off."

"You're not going to *both* be naked in there?" Kahula said, his tone bordering between disapproval and awe.

"Of course not," Joal said as he laid a towel on the floor. "We just need skin to skin contact. Now put her down."

Kahula did what he asked. Joal knelt beside her and slipped her jeans over her hips. He took a quick breath when he noticed how prominently her hip bones were sticking out. If he hadn't found her when he did, he could only imagine what shape she'd be in. He dashed away the images in his mind. He did get to her in time. That's all that mattered.

When she was stripped down to her matching pink bra and panties, he stepped into the sea water and sat on a reclined seat. The water worked its magic as his legs tingled and fused together. In minutes, a dark gray tailfin replaced his legs. He was now in his true form. Closing his eyes, he relished the power that filled him. It replaced all that Jemma had taken from him and more. He felt "normal" again. He lay back and sighed. This jacuzzi was his favorite feature in the house. He could bask in the sea and lay back comfortably while doing it. Though the temperature was warmer than he liked, it still felt amazing, and Jemma needed the warmth.

"You know," Kahula said. "If chlorinated water changed us like the sea water did, our swim meets would be that much more interesting."

"Very funny," Joal cracked a smile. He'd heard that joke many times, but it always brought an amused smile to his face. "Okay," he said, looking at Kahula. "Now put her in the water and lay her on my chest."

Kahula did what he was asked. Joal pulled her down, the top of her head resting under his chin. Sighing contentedly, he couldn't help thinking how right it felt having her here with him. He scooped up some water in his hand and washed it over Jemma's hair and skin, washing away the grime.

Kahula barked a laugh. "Gods, look at you two. The bird and the fish—it's like the line from that one chick flick my sister made me watch with her. You know that one Cinderella story? She said that a bird and fish can fall in love, but where would they live? I guess the answer is Garden Grove."

"I've never seen that one. I don't watch chick flicks."

"Yeah, try saying that after taking that girl on a few dates," he gestured toward Jemma.

"I don't think she'll be going to many more movies," Joal said. "Not as long as she has these wings."

"Oh, yeah. The humans would surely notice something like that. Gods, where *is* she going to live?"

"I don't know. Hopefully, she has a way of hiding them."

Jemma wrapped her arms around Joal, and her grip tightened.

"It's happening again," Joal said and braced himself for the drain on his power.

He waited, but nothing happened. Then he saw it—her wings growing, still slow, but quicker than before, even more quickly than when she'd taken his power. He was in awe as he watched her feathers lengthen and gain an iridescent quality to them. Once they were fully in, he expected that they would look spectacular. Joal looked from her wings to her face. Her cheeks had also filled out a bit more.

"Woah," Kahula said. "I'd *say* that worked." He turned to Joal. "How do you feel?"

Joal sat stunned, unable to speak.

"What? She couldn't have taken that much power, you look fine."

He shook his head, still in a stupor. "I don't believe it."

"You're scaring me. What don't you believe?"

"She didn't take any power from me?"

"Then... how..."

"She took it directly from the sea water."

Kahula shook his head. "That's impossible. Sky-gods can't take power from the sea."

Joal scoffed. "You think I don't know that?"

Kahula's eyes dropped to the girl on Joal's chest. His expression filled with wonder. "What is she?"

Joal looked down on her himself. "I have no idea."

Joal held Jemma close. Hours passed and her wings continued to grow and expand. Many of the feathers, when they sprouted, looked strange, unlike any he'd seen before, they seemed more like scales than actual feathers. She wiggled, like she was uncomfortable. He turned her on her side, and she curled into his chest. Tucking her legs up, his eyes widened. Her legs were changing too. Scales were beginning to form— the same pearly iridescent color as her wings. And her knee joint had smoothed into a gentle curve. He reached down and traced his hand over her thigh. He felt just what he expected, but it shook him to the core. He adjusted her to get a better look and gasped. This flyer had a tailfin. No, not just one tail- fin, but two. Each of her legs had changed and morphed.

"Kahula," Joal whispered loudly.

"What?" Kahula stepped through the door, rubbing the sleep from his eyes. "What is it?

"I'm so stupid," Joal said. "This all makes sense."

"What makes sense?"

"I know what she is. I need you to get a book off of my bookshelf. It's about four inches thick and really old. You'll see it on the bottom shelf."

Minutes later, Kahula carried the book into the room and sat on a chair. "Okay, what am I looking for?"

"Look up siren."

"You mean mermaid?"

"No. Mermaids aren't true sirens. You'll find the ancient sirens about two thirds through the book."

Kahula thumbed through the pages. "This is in Greek."

Joal swore. "You're right. It's written in ancient Greek." He raised his hand from the water and steam rose as he dried his fingers. "Bring it close; I'll find it."

Turning the pages, he soon found the passage and read, translating as he went.

Sirens: winged, daughters of Gaia and Oceanus, born betwixt earth and sea. Named Molpê, Aglaophônos and Peisinoê for their voices. The power of three, when combined, create a melody as old as time, laced with power that creates worlds and fells kingdoms of gods and men. At the end of the Titan war, the Sirens escaped imprisonment and served Persephone until her abduction by the hands of Hades. They were given wings to help in retrieving Persephone from Hades hands but were ultimately unsuccessful in their pursuit. Out of fear of their primordial power being unleashed, Zeus separated the sirens, banishing Molpê and Aglaophônos to the hidden isle of Anthemoessa. Peisinoê, the more powerful of the three, he held fast by Prometheus's chains at the bottom of the River Acheron.

Joal stopped reading.

"Is that all it says?" Kahula asked.

"Yeah. The older the legends, the less information there is."

"What does any of this have to do with Jemma?"

"Look," Joal said nodding toward the book.

Just below the entry for Siren, there was an intricate, ancient painting of three identical women, their hair blowing in the wind and their wings spread in flight as they hovered, their glistening twin tails just above the ocean waves.

Kahula leaned down and examined the picture. "But I thought that ancient sirens were like birds with a woman's head."

Joal shook his head. "Humans are always distorting reality to fit their understanding."

"So that's what a siren really looks like?" Kahula asked.

"Yeah. Now look at Jemma."

Kahula's gaze shifted from Jemma to the picture and back to Jemma. He cursed and then said, "They look just like her. A mermaid is bad enough. These have the power to destroy worlds."

"Only when the three are combined."

"Yeah, well, my advice, let's not go looking for her sisters."

"She's not one of the three original sirens," Joal said.

"Why wouldn't she be?"

"Does she look thousands of years old?"

"No, but none of this makes sense," Kahula said.

"Either way, the two sirens banished to the island of Anthemoessa were killed by Odysseus thousands of years ago. Jemma must be the daughter of Peisinoê, the one hidden by Zeus. That would make total sense." Joal paused, caressing his fingers over the image of the siren.

"So," Kahula said, "if Jemma is her daughter, then Jemma's father is probably..."

Joal froze as he realized who the most likely suspect was. What other god slept with more women than there were stars in the sky *and* had access to a beautiful siren? He looked up and met Kahula's eyes. He could see he'd figured it out as well. They answered simultaneously, "Zeus."

"But you told me Zeus had drained Jemma's powers. Why would he do that to his own daughter?" Kahula asked.

"He's my dad's brother. I guess they're both jackasses."

"Wait. Ugh! So, you've been making out with your cousin?"

"Yeah, probably."

"Oh, man!"

"What?"

"You don't think that's gross?"

"No. It's different with the gods. Zeus is married to his sister. Hades is married to his niece. All the gods in the Olympus Pantheon are related to each other somehow—and most of them are married. It's just... not the same as it is with humans."

"I'll take your word for it, but I still think it's disgusting."

"Kissing Jemma is anything but disgusting."

Chapter Sixteen – Jemma

And, oh! whate'er heaven's destined to betide,
let neither flattery soothe, nor pity hide.
—*The Odyssey*, Homer

JEMMA AWOKE HUGGING her pillow tightly in her arms. Her blanket rose and fell against her back, surrounding her with warmth. *Wait. What?*

Jemma's eyes flew open as she raised her head, cracking it against something hard.

She opened her mouth.

"Ouch."

She froze as the word she was about to say was spoken by someone else—someone with a deep voice.

She looked up and saw Joal's face. He smiled hesitantly at her as he rubbed his chin. Then she looked down and realized she'd been sleeping sprawled across his chest. And they were in the water?

"How did I...?"

"Do you remember much?" he asked.

Memories flooded her mind—horrible, painful memories. Jemma nodded and whispered, "Yes." She turned to look behind her and gasped. She couldn't believe what she was seeing. She had wings—large, expansive wings with strange feathers, feathers that were milky and shimmered like stained glass.

"What am I?" she asked, partly in awe and partly horrified.

"A siren."

"Mermaids don't have wings, but—" she was in a panic as she pushed against Joal's chest and examined her hands. Thank the gods they were still there.

Joal must have known what she was afraid of because he said, "No, you're not some weird bird thing with a woman's head. The humans were really off on their portrayal of winged sirens. Their pictures and drawings look more like a harpy than a siren."

"That's... that's good to know," Jemma said, her voice strained. "How long was I asleep?"

"It's Tuesday afternoon, so it took a while, but I think your wings and tails have finally finished coming in."

Tails?

Jemma slid off Joal's chest, resting on a seat in the oversized jacuzzi. She looked down to see she was only wearing her pink laced bra and panties. She slapped her arms across her chest. Her legs brushed up against something rough and she looked down into the water and jerked back. There were two clear shapes of tailfins, pearly white. But then beside the white tails was another tail, dark and much larger. "Am I dreaming...?"

"No, it feels like it though. Right?"

"Yeah," Jemma breathed. "Um, this is a lot to take in."

"For both of us," Joal said. "Do you know how rare your

kind is?" He shook his head. "And I thought you were a sky-goddess."

"I'm not?"

"No, sirens get their power from the sea. That makes you a sea goddess. But no one has seen a true siren in thousands of years, not since Odysseus's time."

Jemma's stomach growled, much to her chagrin.

"I guess that's our cue to get out of the tub, "Joal said. "You sound hungry."

"Yeah," Jemma breathed.

Joal turned to pull the plug and then pushed himself up and out of the tub. His legs formed as they left the water.

That's not all that formed. Joal was completely nude. Jemma slapped her hand over her eyes as her face burned.

"Sorry," she heard Joal mutter. "Give me a minute." She heard him rummaging and then he said, "Okay, I'm relatively decent."

Jemma hesitantly removed her hand from in front of her eyes and peeked around her fingers. He was still shirtless, but he now had a towel wrapped around his waist. Steam rose off him in a cloud. Man, he was beyond hot—tanned and muscled.

"Is that better?" he asked.

Jemma dragged her eyes away from his chest and nodded. And then she remembered she was in her bra. Grabbing her wing, she pulled it in front of her, blocking her body from Joal's view.

"So, exactly what are you?" she asked.

Joal frowned. "You already know I'm a sea-god and son of Poseidon. The tailfin just goes along with it. I didn't tell you?"

Jemma frowned, "No. You forgot to tell me that part."

"I guess, I should have explained better."

"Wait! You didn't have a tail at the falls."

"I'm only affected by sea water."

"Oh. Is it rude for me to even ask what you are?" Her cheeks warmed.

"Not at all. People used to call us Tritons. I know there's a god *called* Triton—he's technically my brother, but I've never met him. All the sons of Poseidon that have tailfins were once called Tritons by the humans. *King* Triton was simply the first, so his name stuck. I don't know what you'd call the rest of us now. I guess the humans would simply call us mermen, but that's not right either. Mermen are the sons of Triton."

"Will my tailfin disappear when I come out of the water too?"

"Why don't we get you out and see what we're dealing with."

Jemma frowned at him.

"See if your tailfins turn back to legs," Joal clarified, and Jemma relaxed her scowl.

Joal easily lifted her from the tub and Jemma felt her fins tingle. Gently, he placed her on the floor. She looked down. Her feet were back!

"Well, your legs changed back, but your wings are still there." He shook his head and looked at her face. His scowl melted into concern. "We'll figure it out."

Jemma stood on shaky legs, her mind swirling with emotions and jumbled thoughts. "How?"

"I don't know. But I swear we will. You're going to be fine," he said. Jemma didn't know whether she believed him. How could all of this be okay? Her entire life plans might be derailed. How could she graduate and go to college looking like this? Crimson red dripping down Joal's arm made her heart stop.

"You're hurt," she croaked.

He looked down and raised an eyebrow. "Well, look at that." He fingered the wound. "It's a clean slice." He turned his eyes to her wings. His brow raised as admiration warmed his gaze as a hint of a smile formed. What was he admiring?

She followed his line of sight and saw red on the tip of one of her feathers. Joal stepped toward her. "Do you mind?"

She wasn't exactly sure what he was asking her, but said, "No."

He reached out and gently pinched a feather with one hand and with the other, brushed his finger over the edge, coming away with a smear of blood on his fingertip. "These are sharper than razors, quite a formidable weapon."

Jemma was horrified. She was a walking porcupine with razors for quills. How on earth would she be able to navigate her world? How would she— Her thoughts derailed as she gasped, quick gulps of air. Her heart pounded against her chest wall.

"Woah, hey," Joal said, interrupting her thoughts. He took her by the shoulders. "Look at me."

Jemma raised her eyes to his and her beating heart slowed.

"Everything's going to be okay. Let's just take this one day at a time, okay?"

Jemma nodded, blinking away tears. "It's just a lot to process."

"I know, but I'll be here every step of the way."

She nodded, grateful. She was about to thank him when her stomach interrupted her by growling again.

Joal smirked. "You've got to be starving; I know I am."

"Yeah, I'm famished." A thought struck her. "Wait, have you had anything to eat?"

"Oh, yeah. I felt bad about eating while you couldn't, but Kahula insisted. He said I couldn't protect you if I was half-starved."

"Why would you need to protect me?"

"Oh, um, I wouldn't." He shrugged. "It's just in case."

Something about the way he said it, gave her doubts. *Was Joal lying? Could I really be in danger?*

"How about you shower to wash away the salt water while I get Denise to fix us breakfast?" he said, interrupting her thoughts.

"Is it okay for Denise to see me?"

"She's already seen you. You can trust her."

"Oh, okay."

"I'll be close by if you need me. Your clothes are in the spare room, on the bed." he gestured toward a door. "I can't guarantee any of your clothes match. Kahula got them for you while you were... out of it."

Kahula touched her clothes? Did he touch her underwear? Jemma was mortified to even think the thought—though she guessed it couldn't be worse than having Joal *see* her in her underwear. But he's Joal, Kahula, he's... well, that's just different.

"I'll go talk to Denise," he said. "She's an amazing cook; you need to build up your strength. And we have a lot to talk about."

"Okay."

Joal turned his back and Jemma blurted, "Joal?"

He turned back around, his eyes curious. "Yeah."

"Thank you, for... everything."

He paused and smiled. "Anytime." That word, as simple as it was, seemed to hold infinite weight. Seconds later, he left through a door adjacent from the guest room.

Jemma looked around and spotted the shower immediately. Her feet padded across the wet stone tile, past the granite countertop. When she turned to pull the shower door open, she heard a high-pitched screeching sound and then the shatter of broken glass. She turned back. *Shoot.* Her wings just wiped the counter clean of toiletry items. She picked up the items that weren't broken and replaced them on the counter.

The broken pieces, she threw in the trash. She'd have to come back with a broom and mop. She wondered just how much more trouble her wings would cause. She couldn't possibly go to school with them. She couldn't go to the grocery store either, or the movie theater, or homecoming... for that matter. And how would she drive? She couldn't even fit in a car!

Feeling tears building in her eyes, Jemma tried to drag her hand through her hair. It got caught in tangles. Wow. She really did need a shower. Maybe it would help calm her. Stripping out of her underwear, she squeezed herself into the large shower. *I'll never fit in my tiny shower at home.* How in the world could she deal with this?

She shook her head. No. No more negativity. Like always, she'd find a way past it. Joal said he would help her. The image of Joal's bare, muscled chest and the memory of snuggling against it brought an immediate smile to her face. He was waiting downstairs for her.

As she showered, she examined her wings, focusing on the plumage. The feathers closest to her body were soft and felt like a feather should. The long ones on the wing tips, though, they were razor sharp. But the color, that was the most stunning thing. They appeared white, yet when the light hit them right, they displayed a rainbow of colors. She'd never seen anything so beautiful—and so inconvenient. No. She'd told herself she'd focus on the positives. She could have transformed into a bat-thing. This was much better than that possibility.

She brushed her finger over one of the longer feathers to see how sharp it really was. It felt sharp, but it didn't cut her finger like it did Joal's. Even when she increased the pressure and tried to slice, it wouldn't break the skin. Hmm. Well, at least she wouldn't be slicing off her own digits. Other peoples...? She wasn't so sure about.

She showered thoroughly, turned off the water, and then

dried herself off—at least she dried her skin. The wings were too sharp to dry with a towel, she'd just end up shredding it. Instead, she shook her wings and let the droplets of water splash against the walls and floor of the stall. She wrapped the towel around her and exited the shower. She located a drawer with new toothbrushes still in the packaging, opened one, and brushed her teeth. Then she found a clean brush and worked out the tangles in her hair. Once she was done, she felt human once again.

Stepping into the bedroom, she located a mound of clothing on the bed—shirts, jeans, bras, and underwear. *Kahula did touch my underwear!* Jemma grimaced at the thought. She searched for clothes and found her favorite pink blouse and a pair of jeans. She was able to put on her underwear and jeans with no problem. But there was a major problem with not only her blouse, but all her shirts. They wouldn't fit over her wings!

Finally, she found a stretchy, pale pink tank top. Putting her legs through and pulling it up over her hips, she was able to get her arms through it. The back was stretched to its limit, but at least she was clothed. *Looks like backless shirts will be a necessity.*

She returned to the bathroom and stepped in front of the mirror. She was surprised as she studied her reflection. She used to have splotches on her skin and small pimples on her forehead. Now her skin was flawless, perfect. Even her hazel eyes were brighter, greener than brown. And her body shape... she still wasn't rail-thin like she was before, but everything was smooth, with sloping curves and a small waist—like an honest to goodness hourglass. And then she looked at the wings on her back. She spread them out wide. She could touch the walls on either side of the bathroom. Her wingspan must be over fifteen feet wide!

I might feel more human, but who am I fooling? I'm not

human. But at least I'm not a harpy. She'd heard Joal and his friend joke enough about them, that they must be repulsive. Still, she didn't know how to feel about her new look. She might be beautiful, but she was also... Well, she looked like she belonged in a fairytale book.

Jemma sighed. That was the only place she belonged. She certainly couldn't be seen in public like this. And then there was a question she still hadn't had the courage to form, even in her mind. But finally, she thought it.

I wonder if I could fly.

Chapter Seventeen – Joal

This is the truth: and oh, ye powers on high!
Forbid that want should sink me to a lie."
—*The Odyssey*, Homer

JOAL SAT on the great room couch as Denise stood over the stove, frying bacon, and grilling French toast. He hoped Jemma wasn't a vegetarian. What do sirens eat after all? Maybe she should be cooking fish. Yeah right. He shook his head. He was as much of a sea creature as Jemma was. And he loved nothing better than a steak, medium rare.

The doorbell rang, and Joal looked up. It was probably Kahula. His eyes opened wide when he saw Cassie through the peep hole, standing with her hands on her hips.

She narrowed her eyes, glaring at him through the lens. "Joal, I know you're there. I can feel your eyes boring into me."

How can she see me? She has to be bluffing.

"I'm not bluffing."

He swore under his breath. Hesitantly, he cracked open the door.

Cassie shoved the door open wide and stomped past him. "Where is she?"

"Jemma?" he asked.

"Of course, Jemma! I know you're hiding her. You answered her phone while she's AWOL, so I know you know where she is. If you've done anything to hurt her, I swear, I'll kill you."

"I don't know where she is," he said. "I saw her on Saturday, but I haven't seen her since. Did you talk to her mom?"

"She's missing too."

"Well, there you go. They probably went somewhere together, and Jemma forgot to call you before she left. It's got to be difficult not having a cell phone."

"Yeah, I'm sure it is, and that's what I was thinking too, until Monday. She missed school, not just one day, but two! Jemma is never absent. And then when I saw that you were gone too, I knew she had to be with you."

Joal shook his head. "She's not here. I guess we just happened to miss school on the same days."

"You are totally lying; I can smell a lie a mile away."

Joal's temper flared. "What do you think I did? Murdered her in her sleep?"

"No. But I do think you slept with her."

"And if I did? That sounds like none of your business."

"She's my best friend. It is my business, and you'd better not be playing some game. I was all for her dating you, but then you pull this."

"Missing two days of school?"

"Yes," she said with her chin out. "Jemma and I have been best friends since kindergarten. And like I said, she never... misses... school."

A loud crash came from the kitchen. Joal turned toward

the sound and Cassie brushed past him and ran into the house. Joal swore and then chased after her. He skidded to a stop before he could plow her over. Cassie stared wide-eyed, with her mouth gaping open as she looked at Jemma who was standing near Denise. Bacon sizzled and popped in a frying pan on the stove. Joal was shocked into silence as well. Denise stood blinking, her brows raised, but she'd given no other indication that anything was amiss.

Joal had to school his features when he saw that Jemma's wings were gone.

"Did I see..." Cassie stammered. "I thought I saw..." *Did she see?* Cassie shook her head and pressed her hands to either side of her face. "I must have been hallucinating."

Jemma looked behind her, from one side to the other. She looked just as surprised as the rest of them. *How did she make her wings disappear?*

"People are always telling me I'm crazy. Maybe they're right."

Jemma recovered her own shock and said, "You're not crazy, you're just stressed."

"I... oh wow." Cassie was stunned, then she composed herself as she looked up at Jemma. "Where have you been?"

"I've been sick, but I'm feeling much better now."

Cassie scratched her cheek. "You look so... healthy."

Jemma shrugged.

"And Joal's taking care of you?" Cassie asked, turning and looking at him.

"Yeah, and he's done a pretty good job of it," Jemma said.

Cassie turned a sharp glare at him. "Why didn't you just tell me?"

"She's had a really bad weekend." Joal said. "I didn't think she was up for visitors."

"You just lied to me." She jabbed her finger at his chest.

"You said you hadn't seen her, and here she is." She glared at him.

"Breakfast is ready," Denise said behind them. He turned to see her loading serving plates filled with food on the table.

"Oh, um," Cassie stammered. "I'm sorry I interrupted."

"You didn't interrupt anything," Denise said, giving Joal a quick *"you be nice"* glare before she gave Cassie her sweet, undivided attention. "There's plenty of food. You're welcome to join us."

"Uh, thank you," Cassie said, her voice brightening. They all sat and ate.

Denise went to clean up the dishes. She seemed to ignore them, but Joal knew better. She may play the role of unassuming housemaid well, but she'd be grilling him later, though he'd already given her the rundown of what had happened.

"So, what happened?" Cassie said, drawing back his attention. She was looking at Jemma.

"My mom left," Jemma said.

"What? No"

"Yeah. It came as a real shock."

"I'm so sorry," Cassie said. "I take it you don't know where your mom is."

"I have no idea. She... I guess she had a past that caught up with her."

"Oh, I'm so sorry." Cassie rose from her chair and surrounded Jemma in a hug. "Your mom is the worst mom ever. I always knew there was something wrong with her. She just wasn't right in the head."

Jemma leaned back and frowned.

"I mean she was always more concerned with her... self..." Cassie's words dropped away as she looked Jemma in the eye. "I'm not helping, am I?"

"No, it's okay. I'm just still feeling pretty raw about it."

"I'm sorry, I just..." Cassie bit down on her bottom lip and sighed. "Do you need a place to stay?"

"No, I'm fine."

Cassie looked from Jemma to Joal and back to Jemma. "Have you been staying here this whole time?"

"Um, yeah, I have."

Cassie's narrow eyes turned to him. "You better not be taking advantage of her in this emotionally fragile state."

Right. If I did that, Denise would flay me alive. "It's not like that," he said. "She really has been sick."

"Why didn't you take her to the doctor?" Cassie reprimanded him and then turned to Jemma. "You didn't let him, did you? Are you still worried about what your mom—" Cassie stopped mid-sentence. "I'm sorry. We should just talk about something else. Oh, I almost forgot, homecoming is Saturday, and you still need a dress. I got mine yesterday, and it was a nightmare trying to find the right one. They've all been picked over. If you don't go soon, it'll be impossible."

"I don't know if she's up for a shopping trip," Joal said.

"Oh, yeah, Einstein?" Cassie said. "And what do you expect her to wear? I don't even think she owns a dress."

"I can help with that," he said.

"Oh really?" Cassie frowned.

"Yes, really. My mom and Jemma look like they're about the same size—same build, same height."

"So, what? Are you going to have her wear one of your mom's dresses?" Cassie sounded appalled.

"Come with me," Joal smirked. "I want to show you two something."

Joal trotted up the stairs and Jemma and Cassie padded along behind him. He didn't hesitate when he got to his mother's door but went inside. His mom's room looked like it always did—spacious, luxurious, massive, and rarely slept in.

"Is this..." Cassie's voice rang with awe.

"My mom's room," Joal said as he pulled his mother's closet door open.

"Wow," Cassie said. "Your house is bigger than it looks, and it already looks pretty massive."

If she only knew.

Jemma stepped in front of him, and his eyes caught the sight of her back. On either side of her spine, the places where her wings had sprouted from, there were iridescent, faint intricate designs mirroring one another—like two halves of a snowflake separated by her spine. He had an insane urge to touch the designs. He resisted, and instead brushed her arm as he reached for the light switch, the familiar tingle spread across his skin. Her touch had a powerful effect on him. Cassie's gasp sounded behind him as he saw Jemma's eyes fly open wide.

As massive as his mother's bedroom was, her closet was even more impressive. At a whopping five hundred square feet, every wall was covered with glass cupboards containing handbags, shoes, and fine clothes stitched by Rhapso, the patroness goddess of seamstresses herself. And Rhapso didn't design for just anyone. Among her list of clients, were not only his mother, but Frigga, Hera, Aphrodite, and even the fates who have her create the threads of life for every man woman and child on the planet.

"Holy fashion, Batman," Cassie said.

"Yeah," Joal said. "My mom's kind of a fashion freak."

He turned to Jemma. "You're welcome to pick out anything that might work. Just make sure you remember where everything belongs and put them back in place before you leave. My mom has all these sorted by color, fabric, and the gods know what else. She'll notice if anything's not in its exact spot and I really don't want to cover your butts by telling her I've started crossdressing."

Cassie gave a nervous chuckle. "Wait. What about the dress she chooses? Won't your mom know it's missing?"

Joal shook his head. "She's out of the country for a while. Homecoming will be over long before she comes home. Just mark where you pull it from."

"Oh, okay," Cassie said and then turned. "But what about pictures. Your mom will see her dress on Jemma."

Joal shook his head. "No. She won't. She doesn't care about that kind of thing."

"Really?" Cassie asked.

"Oh, yeah."

"Are you sure about this?" Jemma asked, even as her eyes seemed to drink in the sight of so many elegant dresses.

"Absolutely," Joal said. He smiled at the sparkle in Jemma's eyes.

Cassie lay her hand on her arm and said, "This is going to be awesome."

Joal looked at Cassie. "Does this make up for me being a jackass?"

"It's a good start," she said still scowling at him.

"I guess that will have to do for now. I'll leave you two to it," Joal said. "Shopping for clothes is among the top ten things I hate to do most."

"But you're always dressed so well," Jemma said

Joal raised a confused eyebrow. "Uh, yeah." He glanced up at the clothes surrounding them. "My mom stocks my closet too."

He smiled back at her, his heart swelling in his chest. "Don't take long, we need to leave for school in about a half an hour."

"That's not near enough time," Cassie said. "We may have to resume the search after school."

"My mom's closet is your closet—at least for today."

Cassie didn't answer, she was already sifting through the dresses.

Jemma looked him in the eyes and said, "Thank you."

Chapter Eighteen – Jemma

CHAPTER 18

> But listen to me first and swear an oath
> to use all your eloquence and strength
> to look after me and protect me.
> —*The Iliad*, Homer

JEMMA STROLLED through the glass doors of Olympus High and the first person she saw was April, "Jemma, is that you?" she asked, her eyes wide.

Jemma's face heated. She knew she'd get some attention. The changes in her appearance were so striking to herself, she didn't know how anyone else would not notice. Joal was so wrong. He said no one would see a difference, but the first person that saw her today had noticed, and Jemma was sure April wouldn't be the last. How could people not see it?

Jemma looked like she lost ten pounds and gained perfect skin over the past few days.

"Um, yeah," Jemma said, "it's just me."

"You look... different. Good, but different."

Jemma was beyond uncomfortable with April gawking at her. "Uh, thanks." She spun around and paced down the hall — in the opposite direction she needed to go. Thank heavens this hall looped around. If she hurried, she wouldn't be late to class. If only Joal hadn't had early morning practice. He was going to skip it, but she insisted that she'd be okay. And truthfully, she was. A few gaping stares never hurt anyone. At least that was what she was trying to tell herself.

Joal rushed into their first period class seconds before the bell rang. The smell of chlorine wafted to her as he gave her a peck on the lips, and he was in his seat before her heart had a chance to skip a beat. Today's lecture was a continuation of the Greek underworld. Jemma had read ahead, which allowed her mind to wander.

She glanced around the room. People were staring at her. Well, not everyone. It was mostly the guys, and Joal was glaring at them in response. The ones who made eye contact with Joal looked away quickly and turned their attention back to the front of the class.

A young student Jemma didn't recognize strolled in the room with a note and handed it to the teacher.

"Jemma?"

Jemma's eyes widened. She got up and took the note. It was from the devil. Well, this person was not exactly the devil, she was close. Ms. Richards, the cheer coach, was Brooklyn's biggest supporter, and she wanted to see Jemma in room D21. What in the world did she want from Jemma? Jemma was not a cheerleader anymore and thank the gods she didn't have a class with her.

Joal gave her a confused look as she stood. She shrugged in response. Looking at the clock, she decided it was too close to the bell to leave her things there, so she picked them up and left. As she wandered down D hall, her stomach tied itself into knots. She approached the door and knocked. She waited a few seconds and then pushed it. The room was dark and empty. Chairs were perched on tables as Jemma stepped inside and moved forward.

"Ms. Richards?"

The sound of the door shutting came from behind her. Jemma turned to see Brooklyn locking it.

"Brooklyn?" Jemma said confused.

"I'd heard from April that you were sporting a whole new look—and I'm not talking about your clothes, even though those could definitely use an update." She stalked forward. Jemma stepped back away from her, stopping only when she backed into a table.

"And I must say," Brooklyn continued. "I'm surprised to see you looking like this, but I really shouldn't be. Evan told me to keep an eye on you. And you know what?"

Jemma swallowed, attempting not to be intimidated by Brooklyn. "What? What is it Brooklyn? What do you want?"

She narrowed her eyes. "I saw you."

Jemma's heart skipped a beat. "What do you think you saw?"

"I saw you sneaking into the old bio lab on Friday. You locked yourself in."

Jemma could feel the blood drain from her face.

"Because you didn't want people knowing what a freak you are."

"I don't have time for this," Jemma said, her voice shaking. She started toward the door. "I should be in class."

"And do you know what I heard?" Brooklyn said, ignoring Jemma's words and stepping in her way. "The school was broken into this weekend. I heard it was vandals. But it wasn't, was it? First you stole Joal from me, and now you're moving on to Evan."

"What?" Jemma's voice rose in surprise. "I have no idea what you're talking about. You and Joal broke up at the start of summer break, and I am sooo not interested in Evan."

"Right," she said, drawing out the word. "I stole the surveillance footage from this weekend and watched every last second of it."

Surveillance footage?

"You... going into the old biology lab," Brooklyn said, "and... you coming out." She narrowed her eyes and smirked. "I saw it all."

Jemma felt as if she'd been punched.

"When I told Evan what I saw, do you know what he did? He took the tape from me and then told me I saw nothing."

"When I disagreed with him, he said I was crazy. But I did see. I saw Joal carry you out. I saw what you are. You're a freak. Some kind of science experiment gone wrong. I talked to the principal, and he wouldn't even look into it. He told me to drop it. He even offered to help me find a therapist! But I'm not crazy. They're *all* keeping your secret. I don't know why, but it doesn't matter. Screw them! I already know what I saw."

Jemma attempted to step around Brooklyn, but she followed suit and blocked her path.

"Turn around," Brooklyn growled. "I want to see your back."

"Now who's being the freak?"

"Do it now," Brooklyn growled.

"No."

"Do it, or I'll tell the school what I saw."

"Like anyone would believe you. You've lost it, Brooklyn. You really have gone crazy."

"Just do it!" Brooklyn shouted.

"No. You're insane."

"I'm. Not. Crazy! I've seen the footage. I saw you crawling into the old bio lab, and when you came out... I saw them, your hideous bat wings. Evan saw them too, and then he covered for you. Even Principal Angelo is acting strange, I confronted him about not calling the police about the steel door being smashed in, the door you hid behind. He just said he was handling it."

"You sure get around, don't you," Jemma said, her throat dry.

"You have no idea. How do you hide them?"

"Hide what?" Her heart raced. Brooklyn had seen her. She'd seen...

"Don't act dumb. Where do you hide your freaky wings?"

"You are crazy."

"I'm not! And by the end of the day, everyone will know what you are."

"No one will believe you."

"Oh, they'll believe me. You might think you've gotten away with all this, but you haven't."

"Brooklyn, you really don't want to do this."

"Oh, I think I do." Brooklyn stood, her hands clenched, her eyes narrowed.

"I don't have time for this," Jemma said, pushing past Brooklyn as she headed toward the door. "And if you try and spread any rumor about me, you'll regret it."

"Is that a threat?"

Jemma narrowed her eyes. "It's a promise." She unlocked the door and made her way into the hall just as the bell rang.

Λ

Jemma approached her second period class when Joal intercepted her. "Hey, babe," he said. He gave her a quick kiss and then frowned at her. "So, who called you out of class?"

"Brooklyn."

He looked genuinely surprised. "What?"

"I think you left out a few things that happened when I was... out of it. Evan—"

Joal shushed her and pressed a finger against her lips. Looking around, he pulled her down the hall. "Careful what you say. There are ears everywhere.".

"You're telling me," she said, thinking about Brooklyn. He backed her into a corner, and she put her arms around his waist. His arms came around her in response. "Brooklyn knows," she whispered against his chest.

"Knows what?" he whispered back.

"She saw the surveillance tapes. She knows I have wings. She threatened—"

"Mr. Forsetti, Miss Ryan. Don't you have somewhere to be?" a deep, stern voice came from behind Joal and Jemma jumped as her face heated. She looked around Joal's figure and her eyes landed on the principal scowling at them.

"Yeah," Joal said as he kept his arms firmly around her shoulders. "But it's nowhere near as enjoyable as this."

The principal cleared his throat. Was he trying not to laugh? "I'm not even going to try and argue that, but while Miss Ryan is here, I'd like a few words with her in my office."

Jemma's mouth went dry. She'd never been asked to go the principal's office before. Was this about the surveillance? Her absent mother? The police? She turned a desperate glance at Joal. What would the principal say if she asked him to come? Before she got the words out, the principal said, "Mr. Forsetti can come too."

Her relief was palpable. Joal took her hand in his as they strode to the front office and entered a pristine room with a wide, mahogany desk. Jemma was surprised at the decor. Ancient Greek paintings hung on the walls and a shadow box contained what looked like old, gold coins. They looked like drachmas and if they were real, the gold ones were worth tens of thousands of dollars. *How much do principals make?*

"Have a seat," the principal said and then sat down himself.

Jemma and Joal sat, but he kept her hand in his. "Well, Miss. Ryan, from the sounds of it you've had a big week."

Jemma's eyes widened and she looked at Joal.

Joal didn't look bothered at all. "Principal Angelo knows all about our kind. He's the son of——"

"My parentage doesn't matter," he interrupted. He turned to Jemma with understanding in his eyes. "What matters is Jemma no longer needs to worry about the police or other authorities."

Jemma breathed, the air filling her lungs. "Thank you."

"And though I cannot say I support public displays of affection within the walls of my school," he continued, "I have nothing against your relationship with Mr. Forsetti. However, others may *not* agree," his eyes flickered to Joal's, "and I would hate for either of you to face retribution from certain parties. There are eyes everywhere within the walls of this school."

"I'm well aware of the risk. Jemma will be safer if we don't hide our relationship. If anyone tries anything, they'll have to contend with me."

"Does that go for your mother as well?"

Joal hesitated a moment before saying, "Yes."

"I hope you understand what you may face. Prejudices run deep, especially ancient ones, like your parents. If you do wish to be public with your relationship, you'll need to surround yourself with allies."

"I'm already ahead of you," Joal said.

Jemma's wide eyes turned to Joal. Is that why Joal's teammates have become so... present in their lives? They've been like one big, happy family. Joal pressed his lips together in a fine line. Jemma hadn't even thought about the risk Joal was taking being with her. What would his mother do if she discovered their relationship?

"Good," Principal Angelo said.

"And I think you should know," Joal said, "that Brooklyn—"

"I'm already aware of what she saw," the principle interrupted. "I'll handle it. Now, you two hurry on to class. Mrs. Benedict will get you both notes to excuse your tardiness."

Λ

Joal could feel the tension coming from Jemma as they stepped into the hallway. Jemma spun to face him. "What was the principal talking about? He sounded serious. What kind of danger are you in?"

"It's fine."

"Oh really," Jemma said. "What would your mother do if she found out we were together."

Joal shook his head and said, "Nothing I can't handle. It's not like she'd kill us or anything."

"That's where you went to?" Jemma squeaked. "I thought you were going to say something like she'd ground you, or at the worst, disown you."

She'd definitely disown him if he chose to be with a sky-goddess. But Jemma wasn't a sky-goddess, she was a sea-goddess (who could fly). "Once she understands what you are, she'll probably be fine with it."

"Probably? Well, then why don't you just tell her? Tell her all about me."

"That's not a good idea."

"Why?" Jemma said, jerking her head back and scrunching her eyebrows.

"I just..."

"What?"

"I don't trust her."

"Don't trust your own mom?"

"Definitely not."

"What do you need to trust her with?"

"With you. My mother is... a bit ruthless. In fact, she can be downright cruel—and exploitive."

"You think she'll exploit you."

"Me, probably. You, absolutely. I just wish..." he hesitated, not wanting to hurt her.

"What?"

He sighed. "I wish you had a protector."

"I have you."

"Until I reach my twenty-first birthday, I'm not powerful enough to be much protection against more powerful gods and goddesses. Your father would have—" Hades. This was not the time to tell her about her father.

"Wait. What?" Jemma said, catching his blunder. Her hand clutched his arm, desperation in her grip. "You know who my father is?"

He frowned. This was *so* not the time for this conversation.

"You *do* know. Tell me," she said.

"I'm not certain, but it's possible your father is, well, was... Zeus."

"Zeus? The king of the gods?"

"He *was* the king of the gods. I don't think he's still alive."

"I thought you said gods can't die."

"We don't die easily."

"Well then, who killed him? And why?"

"It's kind of a long story."

"Give me the short version."

Joal sighed, "I can't. The whole story is too complicated to explain right now. But I will tell you." He looked around at the seemingly empty hallway. "You need to get to class. Since we've been together, your perfect attendance record has really taken a hit."

Jemma frowned and hesitated. Finally, she relented. "Alright. After practice. And Joal," she looked at him, her eyes pleading, "you need to tell me everything. No more keeping things from me. It may be a lot for me to handle, but I *can* handle it."

Joal nodded sadly. She has already handled more than most other people her age. Her mother, the only family she knew, abandoned her, and she'd handled that surprisingly well. Still, he wanted to protect Jemma from further heartache. But she was right, he couldn't protect Jemma from the truth; she needed to know.

Regardless, this couldn't be a short conversation. She would have to process a lot and finding out your own father stole your powers and then stole you away from your mother..., well, that would be a lot to handle.

Chapter Nineteen – Jemma

Let me not then die ingloriously
and without a struggle,
but let me first do some great thing
that shall be told among men hereafter.
—— *The Iliad*, Homer

JEMMA SAT ON THE MAT, thirty feet from the pool side with her legs in a V and stretched one side and then another. She laid her body against her leg and embraced the burn of the stretch, her nose touching the fabric of her gray sweatpants. Her muscles were tight and a bit sore. She just might have overdone practice the previous day. She just didn't want to make a fool of herself at her first meet. Sitting up, she then pulled one arm and then the other over her head and then behind her back. Her arms were even more sore. Not surprising, given that she'd done about a million handstands in the last week, or rather armstands—as divers call them. More than she'd ever done in such a short amount of time.

Coach B. had been so impressed with her ability to hold an armstand, he'd insisted she do a dive showing off that ability. Looking into the bleachers, she was surprised to see so many seated, waiting for the meet to start. Goosebumps broke out across her skin when she saw *her* and then her heart took a stuttering beat. Brooklyn was high in the stands. The glare she gave Jemma was unmistakable. What was she doing here? Then she noticed more of the cheer squad sprinkled throughout the crowd. What in the world—?

"Hey, sexy." Joal's voice interrupted her thoughts and had Jemma nearly jumping out of her skin.

"Woah," he said, "I didn't mean to scare you."

"Sorry," Jemma said, not taking her eyes off rows of spectators.

"You nervous?" Joal seemed surprised.

"No," Jemma said, shaking her head. "Brooklyn's here, along with most of the cheer squad."

Joal looked up, surprised. "Oh, really? That's strange."

"Why? Have they never come to the swim meets before?"

"Not that I can remember," he said. "Brooklyn hates sports. Even when she was chasing me, she didn't go to my swim meets. She said that she wouldn't be going to *any* games if she weren't a cheerleader."

"Some others from the squad are here too," Jemma nodded toward them. "What do you think they're doing?"

"I don't know." He narrowed his eyes at the crowd. "Maybe they're here to support Olympus High." His statement sounded more like a question.

"Something's fishy," Jemma said, "and I don't mean the swim team."

"Ha, ha," he frowned. And then sighed, serious once again. "It may be as simple as they are hoping you belly flop and they want to be here to witness it, maybe catch a viral video." He shrugged.

Jemma huffed a laugh. "Yeah, that's probably it. I really hope I don't give them the satisfaction."

"You won't," Joal said, sounding way more confident than she felt.

A garbled voice floated through the rafters. *"Heats one through ten, gather to the bullpen."* Jemma looked up to see the ancient, rusted speakers above. This place needed updating in a major way.

"Looks like I'm up," Joal said.

"Break a fin," Jemma said, smiling.

Joal chuckled, leaned down, and gave her a kiss. "Oh, I'm going to break more than a fin."

Hours later, Joal's name was listed in first place in four events. He never used his god powers in a competition, but his natural abilities were close to unbeatable. The coach, who Jemma found out was the demigod son of Oceanus, told him not to hold back. As long as he didn't use his powers, the coach considered it fair. Besides, the rest of the team would be better off if they attempted to out-swim Joal at his best. And today, Joal broke not just one, but two regional records (both of which had been previously set by himself). When the swimming portion of the meet was over, the divers gathered, waiting for their turn to shine.

"Hey Jemma," the coach said as he approached. "Are you ready to wow the crowd?"

"I'm just hoping not to make a fool of myself," she said.

"Just do what you practiced, and you'll do fine. You'll do better than fine. Just remember, tuck in tight and unfold like a flower opening in the sunlight."

"You're so poetic," Jemma chuckled.

He barked a laugh. "Yeah, I guess I should have been an English teacher. But seriously, it's all in the imagery. You see it first, then let it happen."

"I will," she promised. She looked for Joal and found him

watching her from the stands--along with all the other swimmers on the team. Joal gave her a thumbs-up.

The first three rounds had the competitors all performing the same dive. By the time the individual choice dives were up, Jemma had a solid lead.

"The last dives are coming up soon. It's time to make me look good," the coach teased.

"Jemma?" Cassie's voice caught her attention.

Jemma turned and smiled. "Hey, Cass."

"Um," Cassie said, her voice shaky.

"What's wrong?"

"I... I don't know. Promise me you'll be careful?" Cassie asked.

Jemma frowned. "Of course. What's this about? I've practiced this dive so much I could do it in my sleep."

"I know, it's just..." she hesitated, "I feel like something bad is about to happen."

Jemma mirrored her frown. "Nothing bad is going to happen..., well, I might mess up the dive, but I'll survive even if I do."

Cassie's expression didn't soften.

"You worry too much. Seriously, I'll be fine."

Cassie attempted a weak smile. "You're probably right."

A minute later Jemma was climbing up on the platform. Her heart pounded out of her chest. She'd never been so nervous. Maybe she was about to make a complete fool of herself. She looked for Cassie, but she wasn't in her seat. Maybe she couldn't take the pressure. Maybe—no. No more negative thinking. The dive was going to go fine. In fact, it would be perfect. Cassie was just being a worry wart and her worry was rubbing off on Jemma. She had nothing to be afraid of.

Jemma backed up spreading her stance three feet apart. She backed toward the edge of the platform until her heels hovered over the open air—her back to the pool. She leaned down and pressed her palms to the deck between her feet. The sand-like texture bit into her skin. With controlled grace she lifted her feet from off the edge and got into a piked position and then straightened her body into an armstand. Her arms quivered slightly under the weight of her body, but she held steady. A clap of thunder had her nearly losing her balance. Still, she held it.

Pain exploded in her hip as the world tilted to the side. Her hands lifted off the platform and the pool room spun. Somewhere in the recesses of her mind, she heard Joal's shout, but she didn't give it a second thought as her leg cracked against the side of the platform and then there was nothing... nothing at all between herself and the glistening water and harsh pool edge that flashed past her vision as she fell.

Adrenaline flooded her veins, and she felt her wings explode from her back. Then everything froze, like literally in place. Jemma hung in the air, one foot hovering over the water, and the other hovering above the edge of the pool.

"Gods how I really wish I could have let this play out," she heard a deep voice say behind her back. "Sometimes I wish I hadn't developed a sense of responsibility."

Jemma felt a tug on her suit as she floated away from the pool's edge and over the water. "Who are you?" she gasped.

"The name's Loki, little one," said a tall lanky man with cropped red hair and a crooked smile.

"Jemma!" Joal shouted close by. She turned to see him skidding to a stop at the pool's edge.

"Hello, cousin," Loki said to Joal.

Joal turned, looking shocked at who was there. "You know who I am?"

He scoffed. "Don't tell your mom, but a lot of us know," he said as he winked. "Your mom's under the delusion that she's clever." He turned back to Jemma, dangling in the air.

"Well, little goddess, it's a good thing I was here to watch my son."

Joal's eyes widened. "Which one—?"

"Don't ask." Loki shot him a glance and waved him off. "He doesn't even know." He looked at Jemma. "It looks like someone has it in for you. That," he looked up at a light fixture dangling from the ceiling, "was no accident."

"Are you sure," Joal asked.

Loki scowled. "I know sabotage when I see it."

Loki looked at Jemma, "I'd suggest you put your wings away before I restart things."

"Did you stop time?" Jemma asked.

Loki chuckled. "Not exactly."

Jemma willed her wings to disappear. She didn't feel anything happening.

"Any time now," Loki said, his brow raised as the corners of his mouth pressed down.

"I'm trying," Jemma said. "I don't know how to do it."

"Just got your powers, did you?" Loki said.

"Yeah," she said.

He shook his head. "I can hide them until you get out of sight. Then I'd suggest you learn real fast how to make those things disappear."

"I'll try."

"The doctors are going to want to check you out," Loki said. "You hit the platform pretty hard." At his words, her leg throbbed. Too bad he mentioned it. She'd felt fine until then.

"The crowd has already forgotten the wings," he continued, "things that defy logic are easier to erase from memory, I can hide your wings for a few minutes more. But your fall... yep, I'm not erasing that. It would take too much power."

"What do we do about the doctor?" Joal said.

"There's a tall man with long dark hair," Loki said, "He's a demigod son of Apollo and a doctor. Ask him to check in on

189

Jemma. We wouldn't want a human doctor to think he's gone crazy."

At those words, the water slapped across her leg. It felt like she slammed into a brick wall. Why couldn't Loki have slowed her fall? Or at least warned her he was going to restart time... or whatever trick he used to make it look like time stopped. At least she didn't hit the edge of the pool.

Jemma tried to swim her way to the surface, but her arms and legs weren't strong enough to drag her wing-laden body up through the water. A thought struck her. Perhaps her wings could— before she even finished her thought, they moved, almost of their own volition, and like a sail caught by the wind, they drove her forward. A flash of gray streaked down as she shot up and out of the water. She landed in a pile of limbs canopied by wings, her bones cracking against the cement surface. "Ouch," she groaned, and looked up to see Joal surface at the pool's edge. In a moment, he too was out of the water.

A thunder of voices from the crowd told her the spectators saw something amiss. Hopefully it wasn't something undeniably supernatural.

"*You couldn't make things easy.*" This time Loki's voice came from inside her head. It was beyond strange, and he seemed amused. The voices from the spectators died down immediately.

"Jemma," Joal said as he rushed to her side. Her coach was there too.

She took a deep breath desperately wishing her wings would disappear, and then they were gone.

"Jemma," the coach said, "are you hurt?"

She shook her head. "Just a little sore. I'm mostly embarrassed."

"You could have been killed!" her coach said.

Jemma looked up to the stands and saw Brooklyn's face as

their eyes met. *Did she cause this?* Even as her mind formed the question, she knew the answer. Her gut was telling her Brooklyn *had* done it. Jemma had a feeling that Brooklyn wouldn't rest until Jemma was exposed.

"Do you think you can stand?" Joal asked.

Jemma nodded and he helped her to her feet. A sharp pain in her thigh had her limping.

"You need the doctor to take a look at you," the coach said.

"I'd be happy to," a melodious voice rang out. Jemma looked up to see a stunning young woman with golden curls and amber eyes shadowed with concern.

"You're a doctor?" Coach B asked.

"I sure am. Don't let my appearance fool you, I'm older than I look." She turned to Jemma and said, "Do you want Joal to come with you?"

"You know Joal?" Jemma said.

"Oh, yeah. His father and I go way back." She winked.

"Oh," Jemma said, surprised. This was not the doctor Loki suggested, but if she knew Joal's father, she would know of the supernatural world. Jemma looked at Joal, he shrugged, his brows raised. "Um, yeah," Jemma said. "That would be nice."

They made their way to an office off the side of the pool. A large glass window was shuttered, giving them some privacy. Inside, there was a small room with several lockers and a wooden locker-room bench. "Have a seat," the woman gestured.

"Are you a doctor?" Joal asked, his brows scrunched.

"Not exactly," the woman said. "The Greek gods don't really need doctors, though I am a healer. You can call me Aspen."

"Aspen?" Joal asked. "That doesn't sound Greek."

Aspen chuckled. "My Greek name doesn't go over so well

for those speaking English. My Greek name is spelled *A C E S O*, pronounced *ass-o*." She shook her head. "Yeah, I'd rather people not call me an ass."

Jemma smiled. "I can understand that."

"Okay, so..." Aspen said, looking her over and homing in on the purple bruise, "it looks like your leg is bruised, but not broken. Your wings didn't seem to sustain any injury, though since you put them away, I can't examine them."

"You saw my wings?" Jemma asked.

"I saw everything. Loki's tricks don't work on me. I also saw the accident was no accident. And you could have been seriously injured, if you were human. Someone has it out for you little goddess. Do you know who could have done such a thing?"

"I have a pretty good guess," Jemma said.

"Well, you'll need to deal with them before they deal with you. Do you know if they are human?"

"Yeah, I'm pretty sure she is."

"You think Brooklyn did this to you?" Joal asked.

"Of course."

"I could heal the bruise..." she looked down. "But it's already fading. You're an exceptionally fast healer, Jemma. In fact," she sighed, "I'll need to halt the fading of that bruise." Aspen held her hand above the bruise and Jemma felt a tingle of power. "I'll let the tissues heal underneath, but the humans might notice if the bruise disappears quickly."

"Okay," Jemma said.

A small knock on the door had them all turning toward it. It was the coach. "How is my favorite diver doing?"

Jemma smiled.

"She is doing fine," Aspen said. "Just a bit bruised. I'd say she dodged a bullet on this one."

"Can I still dive?" Jemma asked. She'd practiced so much she didn't want to just throw that all away. Besides, she didn't want to give Brooklyn the satisfaction of messing up things for her.

"If it's okay with the doc," her coach said.

"It's okay with me, as long as there are no more freak accidents."

"They're just finishing cleaning up the mess," he said, and then he turned to Jemma. "You can go up next, if you're ready."

Jemma jumped up off the bench. "I'm ready." Her leg was feeling so much better, it barely hurt now.

"Okay," the coach said. "I'll let them know."

"Good luck," Aspen said as she stood and sauntered toward the door. Both the coach and Aspen left. When Jemma started toward the door too, Joal pulled her gently back.

"Are you sure you're ready? You're not still freaked out?"

Jemma shook her head. "No. I'm mad, and I'm not going to let Brooklyn take this away from me. I've worked too hard."

Minutes later, Jemma was once again climbing the platform, her heart thumping at a steady rhythm. Confidence welled up in her. She could do this. She could totally, absolutely, positively do this.

A minute later, she was preparing for her armstand. She pictured the dive in her head and was surprised at the dive she imagined. She'd never performed this dive; she vaguely remembered seeing it on TV. Either way, it seemed to call to her. It felt like an old friend. Was she insane? No. This was the right dive. She could feel it.

This time she started with her back to the water, feet together. Her coach was probably wondering what in the world she was doing. She moved back to balance on the edge of her toes. Leaning forward, she pressed her palms to the platform, her hands straddling her feet. Leaning forward she took the pressure off her feet and raised her legs in a pike position, moving slowly and fluidly until she was completely straightened out over her hands. She held her armstand steady, still as a statue for a full five seconds before she bent her legs and arms to spring and tuck into a pike position. She rotated and then flipped not just once, but twice, twisting as she unfolded into a dive, she pierced the water's surface.

When she came up, she was met with a roar of applause. Her coach was shouting, pumping his fist in the air. She swam to the water's edge and exited onto the deck. Her coach wrapped her in a big hug as he swung her around. "I knew you'd make me famous!"

Famous? She thought as he put her down on her feet. She was just steadying herself when Joal wrapped her in another hug. "Gods," he said, laughing, "hold back, why don't you?"

She was startled. Was it too much? Would she expose herself for what she was?

"I probably should have stuck to the dive I'd planned."

"Yeah," the coach said, "the dive you just performed was disqualified. They don't count it if it's not the dive you declared you'd do."

Jemma's heart sank. Right. She'd forgotten that rule. Still, the coach's smile was wider than the Grand Canyon. "Then why do you look so happy?"

"That dive, my young Padawan, is never seen in a high school meet. That's a dive you see in the Olympics."

Her eyes were wide when she turned to Joal and mouthed, *Oops.*

He simply laughed and shrugged. "You're a natural."

Yeah, a *super*natural. She'd need to be more careful. Jemma looked up to see Brooklyn's scowling face, but this time she wasn't looking at her.

"Ignore her," Joal said. "The cheer squad's loss is the swim team's gain."

Even with the disqualification of her platform dive and losing out on placing in the top three, Joal and the rest of the swim team insisted they go celebrate her dive. She tried to remind them they were the ones who'd actually won, but it seemed the focus was all on her.

Minutes later, she found herself sitting at a burger joint with a double cheeseburger in her hands. She never felt so happy to not be on a diet anymore. She wasn't going to go crazy or anything but having a burger when she wanted one was something she would never take for granted again.

Cassie nudged her right side. Jemma turned to her and swallowed.

"I'm really glad you're okay," Cassie said, her voice low.

"Where were you?" Jemma asked. "I didn't see you in the stands."

"I just..." Cassie hesitated, like she was measuring her words. And then she gave up completely and told what sounded like a lie to Jemma. "I had to go to the bathroom."

"Right," Jemma said. "Were you with Tao?"

"What? No... I mean. It wasn't like that."

"Cassie, calm down. You're not in trouble. I'm not demanding you see all my dives. But you're acting pretty weird. Like you're hiding something."

"You wouldn't understand." Right. Jemma doubted it was worse than what *she* was keeping from Cassie.

Jemma sighed. "I won't understand if you won't talk to me about it."

Cassie's eyes darted to the group surrounding them, and then they landed on Jemma. "Later," she whispered.

Chapter Twenty – Jemma

Beauty! Terrible Beauty!
A deathless Goddess—
so she strikes our eyes!
—*The Iliad*, Homer

"CLOSE YOUR EYES AND RELAX."

Jemma could feel soft bristles glide over her eyelids. Cassie's cousin, Sonja, had been at it for what seemed like forever and Jemma had no idea what she looked like. Every minute that ticked by added another butterfly to her stomach. Though Jemma had to admit, Sonja had made Cassie look like she belonged on a New York runway rather than at a high school homecoming dance. With her deep, red dress with inlaid pearls in the bodice and curls framing her face and draped over her shoulder, Cassie looked stunning. It'd be a miracle if Jemma looked even half as good.

"You look amazing," Cassie said as her hand rested against Jemma's shoulder.

"I can't take all the credit," Sonja said. "Jemma's skin is flawless. Really, it's completely flawless. I don't know what kind of skin care regiment you use but keep it up."

Ivory Soap, you're a miracle worker! Jemma smiled.

"Okay," Sonja said, "you're done in record time. You can open your eyes and see the results.

Jemma opened her eyes and turned to look in Cassie's wide bureau mirror. She almost didn't recognize herself. Her eyes were fringed with sweeping lashes. Her cheekbones glowed pink and rounded. Her lips looked plump and crimson. "Wow," was all she could say.

"Wow is right," Sonja said. "You and Jessica Alba could be sisters."

"Who's Jessica Alba?" Cassie said.

"Isn't she an actress?" Jemma said.

"You girls are making me feel old." Sonja pulled a picture up on her cell and showed Jemma.

Jemma shook her head and said, "No way."

Cassie chuckled. "Yes way. I can totally see it."

"Ooh, that gives me an idea for your hair," Sonja said.

An hour later, Jemma and Cassie were living masterpieces. Jemma wore a white, silk A-line dress with a low back crisscrossed with straps tied together at the base. Her hair was a perfect mixture of braided updo with cascading curls.

Jemma looked at the clock. Joal and Tao were late.

Cassie followed her gaze and said, "We're the ones who are supposed to make them wait, not the other way around."

The doorbell rang.

Jemma started to stand, and Cassie pushed her back. "Let Sonja get it."

"I'm guessing ten minutes," Sonja said.

"You know me so well." Cassie smirked.

A full ten minutes later, Cassie was pushing Jemma toward the stairs. "You go first. You've been waiting for this moment since grade school. Besides," she took out her phone, "I want to capture Joal's face when he sees you."

Jemma stepped down the stairs, careful not to twist her ankle in the ridiculously high heels she was perched on. Seconds later, she found Joal. His wide eyes were locked on hers as she descended the stairs. He opened his mouth and then closed it and swallowed. Reaching out his hand, he smiled when Jemma took it. She relished the mingling of power she felt at his touch. She also felt a measure of relief to be holding onto something; maybe she wouldn't fall and embarrass herself. Joal pulled her into his side and whispered in her ear. "No one is going to be able to deny you're a goddess tonight."

"Is that a problem?" she asked, anxious.

"Oh, yeah."

"Maybe I should—" she pulled back.

"No," Joal held her fast. "You shouldn't. Don't change a thing. It's only a problem for me."

"I don't understand."

He closed his eyes and inhaled. "Gods you smell just as good as you look," he said under his breath. Opening his eyes, he said, "It's a matter of self-control."

"Self-control?" Jemma asked, confused. "I don't understand."

"That's because you don't see yourself the way I see you. You're irresistible."

Jemma looked into Joal's eyes. Her gaze dropped to his mouth and her heart literally skipped a beat as she remembered what it felt like to kiss him. Her eyes snapped back to his. "I think I know what you mean."

"Maybe," he chuckled. "We'd better get going. We have reservations. And a restaurant full of people may be just what we need."

"Yeah." Jemma looked over to Cassie, who was already wrapped in Tao's arms.

"Come on, you two," Joal said. "Kahula and his date are waiting in the limo."

Jemma turned to Joal. "You have a limo for homecoming?"

Joal shrugged. "I didn't want to have to concentrate on driving when I've got you to pay attention to. I'd say that was a good call."

Jemma cracked a smile. They climbed into the spacious limousine. It smelled like leather and money—well maybe not money exactly. But it smelled expensive.

Jemma's eyes widened when she saw Kahula's date. It was Attie, the shyest girl in the senior class. Jemma had attended school with her since kindergarten, but she was hard-pressed to think of any shared memories they'd had together. It was like they lived completely parallel lives—never intersecting paths with each other.

"Hey, Attie, is it?" Jemma smiled.

Attie nodded but didn't look up. She was wearing a blue satin dress that was as beautiful as it was simple.

"You look nice," Jemma said.

Attie's face burned bright red. *I'll have to take getting to know her slowly.*

"I hope you like sea food," Joal asked.

Jemma turned to him and wrinkled her nose.

"You don't?"

"I hate it. Well... I do like sushi."

"So, you like your fish raw, but not cooked."

Jemma shrugged. "I guess so."

"That's the best way to eat it," Tao said.

"Ewe," Cassie said. "I'll take my fish cooked over raw any day."

"Awe," Tao said smiling at Cassie. "And you were so close to being perfect."

Cassie chuckled and shrugged. "Nobody's perfect."

Joal leaned over and pressed a warm kiss to Jemma's neck, just below her ear, making her breath quicken and her body tremble in response. He then whispered, "I couldn't disagree more."

Jemma couldn't imagine a better start to homecoming.

Chapter Twenty-one – Kronos

A wondrous net he labours, to betray
The wanton lovers, as entwined they lay,
Indissolubly strong; Then instant bears
To his immortal dome the finish'd snares
—— *The Odyssey*, Homer

DEEP in the pit of Tartarus, the king of the Titans swirled his fingers in an alabaster pool of waters infused with Phoebe's power of sight and watched the image take shape before him. *The young girl has finally come fully into her powers. And the fates have practically laid her at his feet.* Freedom stood so close he could feel its warmth.

"Show me the sea-goddess from the North," he said as he swirled the water again. The image broke apart and another took its place. This face was just as beautiful as the previous, but he could see the cruelty etched into its perfect planes. "It's time for your payment, Ved-ava."

She shook at hearing his voice. His tone had that effect on others. "Who are you?"

"You know who I am."

She hesitated before breathing, "Kronos." Fear laced her voice. "Wh... what do you mean by payment?"

"You didn't think we would house your prisoners without compensation, did you?"

"I... I. didn't know. Ægir is usually the one who sends them to you."

Kronos growled.

"But of course, I'll do anything you ask."

"I thought you might. Look here and I'll show you the payment I require."

He swirled the waters once more, but this time he would think the words. He needed a bit of deception to get what he wanted. *Show me the young siren in all her glory.* The face of the beautiful goddess with kind eyes shimmered back to his view. Her glowing wings spread wide at her back.

"I... I think I've seen her face before." Ved-ava's voice rose in surprise. "At my son's school. You want me to send this sky-goddess to you?" She practically spat the words out. Her hatred truly ran deep—much to his advantage.

He avoided answering the question, but instead said, "You will follow our instructions exactly."

"Of course."

As he explained, her eyes lit up with amusement.

"Now you know what you must do," he said.

"Yes."

"Oh, and Ved-ava?"

Kronos could hear her heart skip a beat.

"Yes?"

"Don't fail me. I have a pit of vipers prepared for you if you do. And believe me, once locked inside, you will... never... be... found... Do you understand?"

Her eyes flew open wide as she vigorously nodded her head. "Yes, yes... I understand."

Λ

Jemma took Joal's hand as he helped her out of the limo. Loud music filled the air as thunder rumbled from a grey sky. Looks like they may be in for rain.

She must have been scowling, because Joal said, "Don't worry about the rain. I won't let you get wet. "Cassie and Attie too?"

He cracked a smile and huffed, "Sure. Are you ready for this?"

"I guess," she said, standing in place as she watched Cassie and Tao approach the entrance to what looked like a large, clean warehouse lined with hedges and flowers.

Cassie turned back and rushed toward her, her eyes frantic.

Jemma put her hand on her shoulder. "You look worried."

When Cassie didn't say anything, Jemma said, "What's wrong?"

"I don't know. I just have a funny feeling something bad is going to happen."

"Like what?"

She shook her head and looked Jemma over, "I don't know, it... just... be careful."

Jemma frowned. "You worry too much."

"Did I worry too much when that light crashed into you and nearly killed you?"

"That was just a fluke accident. Seriously, you need to relax. Everything will be fine."

Joal looked at Cassie. "Don't worry about Jemma. I'll make sure nothing happens to her."

Cassie sighed. "You'd better."

Tao pulled Cassie into his side, and said, "Come on, let's get in line. We need to get our pictures taken. I want documented proof I took the most beautiful girl in school to homecoming."

"That's impossible," Joal said, "I'm with the most beautiful girl in school."

"We're going to have to agree to disagree."

Cassie and Tao went on ahead, but Cassie kept casting worried glances over her shoulder. *Cassie and her paranoia.*

Jemma stopped before they reached the line. She'd caught a glimpse of hundreds of chaotic dancers and flashing lights through the door. Her nerves caused her to tremble. Maybe Cassie was right to worry. Joal took two steps before he realized she wasn't next to him. He turned back.

"Do you think there's anything for us to be worried about?" Jemma asked him. "I mean if Brooklyn does something—"

Joal stepped up to her as he took her face gently in his hands. "If Brooklyn does anything to hurt or embarrass you tonight, I'll make her sorry."

Jemma chuckled nervously, endeared at his protectiveness. "And what could you do?"

He shrugged. "I could make her pee herself."

Jemma's eyes widened. "Can you do that?"

Joal laughed. "I may not be able to do a lot with my powers yet, but that's one thing I can do. It would make for a memorable homecoming for her, don't you think?"

Smirking, she said, "Uh-huh." She paused. "Okay, okay." She took a deep breath. "Let's go in."

"Together." Joal offered his arm and Jemma took it.

As they joined the line, the song ended, and another started. This tune was beautiful, but strange. Jemma felt a bit off-balance. The music thrummed in her head, in time with her heartbeat, and made her feel... odd.

"Is something wrong?" Joal asked.

"Does the music seem off to you?"

"It's a bit loud, but then it always is at these dances."

It was loud, but there was something else. Something she couldn't put her finger on.

A student council member stood at the front door collecting tickets. Joal gave him theirs and they were ushered through the door to a picture line.

"Pictures already?" Jemma said.

"This is homecoming. I guess they don't want anyone to miss out." Joal shrugged.

They stepped up to an elaborate backdrop—a replica of the Parthenon. Jemma shook her head. "This school takes their Greek mythology seriously."

"Well, we are the home of the demigods."

"Literally," Jemma said.

Minutes later, they snagged a table and sipped their drinks —something called a Greek Lantern. It was delicious, made with lime and club soda. Joal took her hand and said, "Dance with me."

Jemma smiled as she kicked off her shoes.

"No shoes?" Joal chuckled.

"They'll just slow me down. Try to keep up."

Joal's smile widened. "That won't be a problem."

They entered the dancefloor just as a song began.

"Awe," Jemma said. "This song is slow. I can't show off my amazing dancing skills."

"No," Joal said, "but we get to do this." He pulled her up against him, and Jemma could feel the familiar current passing between them. It was amazing; she felt tingly all over. She'd never get used the way Joal made her feel.

They danced for over an hour. The fast songs were fun, and Joal really was a great dancer, but Jemma decided the slow songs were now her favorite. She loved being wrapped in Joal's arms.

Jemma glanced around and saw Cassie dancing with Tao, a contented smile on her face as they swayed to the music. She could also see Kahula dancing with Attie who was smiling wide. Jemma frowned when she saw Brooklyn dancing with Evan. Brooklyn seemed to feel Jemma's eyes on her because her eyes darted over and landed directly on Jemma. They widened for a heartbeat and then narrowed. Jemma looked away. She froze when a thought struck her.

"Brooklyn isn't a demigod, is she?" Jemma asked Joal.

"Not unless she's really weak," he said.

"Then why is she dating someone like Evan? He's an under-worlder, right? I mean, he is captain of the Lacrosse team."

"It's not always demigods who are captains of the teams, but yeah, Evan is. And he probably dates Brooklyn because she puts out."

"Yeah, well, Evan really creeps me out."

"He has that effect on people," Joal said.

"But wait, so are any of the cheerleaders demigods?"

"A few. Most of them are human. But there's a mix of demigods with different elemental powers. I'm surprised they get along so well, but then they still tend to gravitate to their own kind."

Jemma sighed. "Why do you think Brooklyn hates me so much?"

"It's Evan."

"Evan?"

"Haven't you noticed how much he watches you?"

"He knows I have a secret."

"Yeah, I know."

Jemma pulled away. "How did you know?"

Joal looked away and shrugged. "I might have spied on you a bit."

"What?"

"It was right after I came back to school. I didn't know who or what you were, I just knew you were powerful. It's only natural I'd want to find out more about you."

Jemma scowled at him. "But then if Evan's only gathering intel."

"Intel?" Joal smirked.

"What?" Jemma smacked his shoulder. "So, I watch spy movies sometimes. But like I was saying, if he's only gathering intel, why is Brooklyn so upset?"

"I think his attention goes beyond that. You are exceptionally beautiful."

"I am now."

Joal shook his head. "You've always been beautiful."

"He called me a pig." Jemma scowled at the memory.

"Was that in front of Brooklyn?"

"Well, yeah."

"There you go." He frowned. "I still may have to punch him in the face for saying that to you."

"No. You do not."

Another slow song began, Jemma didn't recognize it, but somehow it felt familiar. A wave of power washed over her and nearly took her breath away. "What's that?"

"What is what?"

"The song." It gave her a rush like nothing she'd ever felt. She had the insane urge to sing. In fact, she literally couldn't stop herself from singing. The words built up in her throat and demanded release. Finally, she gave in and opened her mouth. A sound escaped from her lips. It was a haunted song with no words, but Jemma could feel the power of her voice.

Joal's grip tightened around her, his fingers digging into

her flesh as he leaned down and buried his face into her shoulder. Someone else pressed against her back and then her side, seconds later she found herself being squeezed from all sides. Unable to take a breath, her voice faded, and she looked up at her surroundings. The entire hall of students and teachers were moving in, pressing in toward her. Gasping, she said, "Joal."

He kept his face in the crook of her neck. "Joal!" she gasped. Pushing his head off her shoulder, her heart stopped. He looked dazed, his eyes looking at her, but not really seeing her. The bodies pressed harder. Looking around, all of them had the same look as Joal—glazed, mesmerized.

"Tao!" Cassie's voice shouted. "What in the world are you doing?"

"Cass?" Jemma said.

"Jemma? What's going on?"

"It's hard to explain, but if I don't get out of here. I'm going to be crushed to death." Jemma stepped back, shoving into the people behind her and the entire group stepped with her.

"It looks like they're all hypnotized. Was that you? I heard you singing that weird song."

"Yeah, I think so."

"How did you do it?" Cassie asked. "And why didn't it affect me?"

"Can we," Jemma gasped, "talk about it... later. I... can't breathe."

"See if you can make it to the door," Cassie said. "It started raining outside, maybe the water will snap them out of it.

"Okay, I'll try." Jemma pushed away from Joal and rammed against bodies as she tried to get to the door. She found if she pressed hard enough between people, they would give way. A minute later, she broke free and ran to an emergency exit and raced out the door. Her feet sliding in the mud and rain pelting her in the face. Looking back, she could see the crowd following, also at a run. Adrenalin spiked and her wings burst from her back, slicing through a couple of straps on her dress. Thankfully there were enough intact to keep it from falling off of her.

Jemma had never flown before. But now, with hundreds chasing her down, it didn't seem so frightening. She flapped her wings and her weight lifted off her feet, mud dripping from her toes. She looked back to see the crowd following her, running, stumbling, and scrambling to keep up with her. *What have I done?*

She flew on instinct, as if she'd flown her whole life. Circling around, she spotted Cassie and then Joal just behind her.

"I knew it," Cassie shouted up at her. "I was totally not hallucinating." Joal bumped into Cassie, causing her to stumble. She turned toward him and growled. "Joal Forseti! You need to snap out of it." She slapped him across the face.

Λ

Joal stopped, stunned at the pain. Did someone strike him? Shaking his head, he pressed his hands to his temples as he fought off dizziness. "What? What in the Hades happened?"

"Look around you, genius," Cassie said.

He looked up and rain poured down his face. Squinting through the downpour, he could see the entire senior student body running, leaving circular, muddy tracks as they chased... Jemma. Gods, she was flying!

"Joal," Jemma shouted as she flew near and then banked away, keeping the crowd from trampling them.

On her next pass, she said, "I'm sorry. I didn't mean to."

He turned to Cassie. "How did this all happen?"

"She sang some creepy song, and everyone started acting

crazy trying to get to her. It was like some movie where the students all turned into zombies, and Jemma was the only human with a juicy brain. You know how that works out."

"A siren's song."

"What?" Cassie said. "A siren?"

Joal sighed. It wasn't like he could keep the secret from Cassie anymore.

"Yes, Jemma's a siren."

"I knew it! I knew Jemma was a siren."

Joal scoffed. "There's no way you could have known that."

"Don't believe me, I don't care," she growled.

"But what I don't understand, why weren't you affected?"

"*I* don't know. I just wasn't."

Joal felt a wave of power wash over him. He looked in the direction it came from, and his heart dropped. His mother was there, along with two men he didn't recognize. One of the men lifted his fingers toward the crowd of students in rain-soaked homecoming dresses and suits. A black pulse of energy passed over them and they all stiffened and then crumpled unconscious to the muddy ground.

Joal looked up to Jemma and shouted. "Jemma, go. Fly away as fast as you can!"

Before she could change direction, his mother raised her hand toward Jemma and shot out tendrils of rope. Joal recognized the green cords, made from fibers of a substance called holdfast. It was stronger than any ropes found in the human world. The cords did several things simultaneously, they wrapped around Jemma's mouth and ankles. More attempted to wrap up her wings, but the sharp feathers sliced them to shreds. Still, Jemma was tethered by her ankles to his mother.

"No!" Joal shouted as his mom pulled her down, hand over hand, as Jemma's wings flapped. His mom's feet slid through the mud as Jemma fought her. The men held his mother fast as she pulled Jemma in.

Joal sprinted toward them.

His mother shot an annoyed glance at him. She shouted to one of the men with her and he sent waves of ropes toward Joal that tied around his mouth, filling it with the bitter taste of the holdfast. His hands were pulled behind his back and his legs snapped together as they too were tied. He crashed to the wet, grassy ground and came face to face with Cassie who was in the same state as he was.

Straining with his might, he attempted to break free from the ropes. He struggled for several moments, making no progress. They must be infused with magic. He looked up at the scene, horror filling him as his mother and the other two approached Jemma who was now near ground-level.

"What are you wearing?" his mother asked Jemma and then shot a furious look at Joal.

Jemma whipped her wings, slicing through the air and the men jumped back.

His mom turned to the man at her right and said, "Stun her."

Joal roared through the thick rope as a heavy pulse, concentrated directly at Jemma, hit her. She slammed into the ground seconds later, Joal shook at the impact. He continued to struggle against his bindings. He had to get to her. He couldn't let them take her. Jemma lay as still as death.

The glimmer of a knife caught his attention. It was in the hands of the taller man who approached Jemma.

"Stop," his mother said. Joal was filled with relief. His mother had to have seen how much he cared for her. Perhaps his mom wouldn't let the man harm her. His hope was dashed when she said, "Give me the knife. I'll do it." Her narrowed eyes flickered to him with an expression of such stark rage that it sent waves of horror over him. His feelings did not protect Jemma from his mother, they only made things worse. His mother intended to punish him by hurting her.

The rain turned into a torrential downpour and lightning flashed as his mother knelt beside Jemma and did something so horrific Joal couldn't form a coherent thought, his mind and voice roared against the act.

She gripped the base of Jemma's wings, inches from her back and then sliced through tendons and sinews, severing one wing in a single swipe. Awakened by the pain, an agonized shriek tore from Jemma's throat. Blood spurted from the wound as his mom tossed the limb aside like discarded trash. Then she repeated the action with the other wing as Jemma's muted cry escaped through her bindings, a mixture of pain and horror in the sound.

One of the men carefully gathered up Jemma's wings and disappeared. The woman he had called mother looked triumphant as she fisted Jemma's hair in her hands and stood, lifting her as blood flowed red down the white fabric of Jemma's dress. With her eyes closed, she continued to cry mournfully. Joal met his mother's gaze. Fury burned within him as his mother held a smug look on her face. There was no hint of remorse. Jemma's cries lowered to a moan but peaked again when his mom roughly handed her over to the other man.

In a flash of light, he disappeared with Jemma, taking with him Joal's heart.

Joal would never forgive his mother for this. She had never loved him. She loved none but herself, and now she had taken the one person he cared for the most. His mother would pay for what she'd done.

Chapter Twenty-two – Joal

That was all gods' work,
weaving ruin there
So, it should make a song
for men to come!
—— *The Odyssey*, Homer

"I CAN'T BELIEVE you were dating a sky-goddess!" his mother shouted, her voice reverberating off the walls of his living room. "How could you do this to me? Are you insane? Have you gone mad?"

Lying on the floor, still tied up with the ropes, Joal didn't move. He simply glared at his mother. Despite who she was, despite the fact he'd spent his childhood desperate for her love and approval, at this moment, he hated her.

The front door opened, and Denise cried out when she saw him, dropped her bags, and ran forward.

"Go away!" his mother snarled as she flung her hand out and Denise disappeared.

Joal's heart stopped. Where had his mother sent her?

"What do you have to say for yourself?" she asked, not giving Denise another thought. She must have realized he couldn't answer with his mouth still bound because a moment later the ropes disappeared.

Joal remained silent as he rose; loathing filled him. The image of his mother dismembering Jemma's wings from her back filled his head and then the worry over Denise, the woman who raised him followed. If either of them suffered permanent harm, he would never forgive her.

"Say something!" she shouted.

Joal didn't answer her. There were no words capable of causing his mother enough pain, so he remained silent.

Turning to look at him, doubt filled her expression. "Joal?"

"You should have kept me tied up, mother."

Shock flashed over her face. "Why?"

"At this moment, I would like nothing more than to destroy you myself."

"You can't be serious." She sneered as her eyes narrowed and then they widened. "You *are* serious."

"I am. And though I might come to regret my actions one day, it would not be today."

"All of this over some sky-goddess?"

"That goddess has a name!" he roared as he stepped toward her, his mother stepped back. "Her name is Jemma. And she's not a sky-goddess—though I couldn't care less if she were."

"She has wings; she's a sky-goddess."

"No, mother. She's born of the sea."

"Sea-gods don't have wings."

"There were three who did."

His mother looked confused until the moment she realized the truth. "No." She shook her head. "Odysseus killed them."

"He didn't kill them all. There was one left. Jemma is the daughter of that siren."

"But then... No, no, no, that can't be."

"What is it mother? Where have you sent her?"

"But..." She stepped back, her expression frantic. "He would have locked me in a pit of vipers if I didn't do it."

He took another step forward. "Who? Who would have? Where is Jemma?"

She froze and then slowly, she shook her head, refusing to answer his questions.

"Mother, where is she?" He stepped toward her and again she stepped back.

"You have to swear you'll tell no one," she said.

"No," he said, his voice low, menacing. "I don't."

"At least promise that you won't tell anyone that I did it."

Thunder boomed outside, making her jump, he could hear the rain beat against the house. His mother turned, and his gaze followed hers. Hurricane force winds were pounding against the broad window. He looked back at his mom. Her attention was divided as she looked back and forth between Joal and the severe weather outside. Surprise shone in the flashes of lightning .

"If you tell me where to find her," he stepped forward, "I'll think about keeping your secret."

Still, she hesitated. And then she finally straightened her spine, jutted out her chin, and said, "Tartarus."

Tartarus. His mother had sent Jemma to Tartarus, the most feared place in existence. He spoke through clenched teeth. "Who was it that told you to send her there?"

"Kronos."

"Kronos? King of the Titans?" Joal's volume rose as he

spoke. "He cannot leave Tartarus. How did you speak to him? Did you go to him?"

"No," she spat. "Don't be ridiculous. I didn't go there personally. We communicated through—"

"You're a traitor!"

She shook her head vigorously. "No, no I'm not. It was on Ægir's orders. I didn't know what their plans were."

"And you never thought to ask?" he shouted.

"He said she was just some sky-goddess. I thought Kronos was doing it to spite Zeus."

"The Titans are not petty, mom. To them the war is not over. We need to report this."

"To whom? Odin doesn't care about the Greek squabbles, and Zeus is no longer in power."

"Not Zeus, Petros."

"No," his mother shook her head vigorously. "No. You don't know him. I do."

"We can't just stand here and do nothing!"

His mother studied him, her expression contemplative as she paused then finally said, "You love her, don't you? The siren."

Joal had never said it, hadn't even thought the words, but at that moment, his feelings were undeniable. "Yes. More than anything."

"And does she love you too?"

"Yes."

"Are you sure?"

Joal nodded.

"A siren is powerful." Her gaze wandered as her eyes narrowed. "More powerful than any one god, more than many gods. That's why the gods feared them so. This alone could shift the balance of power in—"

"No!" Joal bellowed. "You and your stupid balance of

power. You nor anyone else will use her in a power play. I will not allow it."

"You?" His mother shouted. "You will not allow it? Who do you think you are? You insolent son of mine." She raised her hand to strike him.

"Petros!" Joal shouted, putting the power of a summons into his words.

"No." His mother gasped; her hand frozen above him. She let her arm drop at her side. "Not him. You think *he'll* allow your girlfriend to live? He'll destroy her himself to protect this world."

His mother's words made him pause. *What have I done? I know nothing about the character of the new king of the gods.* If Joal could take back his rash summons, he would. *Please don't let Jemma suffer any more than she has.*

Power like he'd never felt before slammed into him. Joal dropped to his knees, not because he wanted to kneel before the king, but because the force of his power had rendered him unable to stand. He chanced a glance up and saw a mountain of a man towering above him, his eyebrows raised.

"You called, young son of Poseidon?" Petros's voice rolled from his mouth like a landslide.

"You know who my father is?" Joal asked.

"*I* know who your father is," the tinkling voice of wind-chimes spoke softly. The power of her words cut through him like a celestial bronze dagger. A stunning goddess stepped out from behind Petros. Her power washed over him. This goddess felt even more powerful than Petros. *How was that possible?*

She placed her hand on Petros's arm. Her white hair hung around a young face and then cascaded in waves over her shoulder and past her narrow waist.

"Who are you?" he said in awe.

"This is Sara," Petros's voice rumbled deep. "My grand-daughter, the goddess of fate."

"...and time," she supplied as she raised an eyebrow, looking pointedly at Joal.

Joal considered his words carefully before he spoke. "I need your help. Jemma, my girlfriend. She's in trouble."

When Joal hesitated, Petros asked, "What kind of trouble?"

"She's been kidnapped and taken to Tartarus."

"By whom?" Petros asked, his voice rumbled.

Despite his current anger with his mother, he left her part out of it. "Kronos is the one who orchestrated it." He noticed Sara glanced at his mother. *Could she already know the part his mother played in Jemma's abduction?*

Petros shook his head and paced the floor. The floorboards creaked under his weight. "They just cannot let this war end, can they?" He looked up at Joal. "Why would they want your girlfriend?"

"Before I answer, you must swear not to harm her."

Petros stopped short. "Why would *I* harm her? Does she wish me or those in my kingdom ill will?"

"No," Joal said. "She's good and kind and would never hurt anyone—intentionally."

"Intentionally?"

Joal remembered his mother's words about the newly released gods and goddesses. Perhaps he could mislead the king of the gods, just a little. As long as it protected Jemma, he could handle any repercussions. "She's only recently discovered what she is. She doesn't always have complete control over her powers."

Understanding relaxed Petros's expression as he said, "I see." Then he surprised Joal when he continued. "I promise as long as she does not mean me or those in my kingdom harm, I will not harm her in return."

"Will you swear on the River Styx?"

"My word alone is not enough?" Anger rumbled in his voice.

"Forgive him, majesty," Joal's mother surprised him by speaking. "He was raised among the humans. He does not trust easily."

Petros turned his glance at her. "Humans are not trustworthy." He turned back to Joal. "I swear on the River Styx, I will not harm Jemma as long as she does not wish me, nor my kingdom ill will."

"Thank you."

"So, why does Kronos want her?"

"She's a winged siren."

"Gah!" Petros shouted, making the entire house shake. He leaned down until his nose was nearly touching Joal's, and growled, his voice rumbling when he said, "You tricked me."

"I told you only the truth," Joal said, holding his ground despite the fact that this king of the gods terrified him.

"A winged siren is good and kind?" He sounded doubtful as he paced again.

"Yes. I swear on the River Styx that she is."

Petros froze and turned his head to Joal. "You're a fool, boy. If that girl had been lying to you about her motives, you would not still be standing here."

"No, I wouldn't, but then you wouldn't be sure of her character, either."

Petros turned and glanced quickly at Sara and then back to Joal. "Perhaps." He paused for a moment. "So, what do you want from me?"

"Obviously," Sara said, "he wants Jemma back. And, young god, there is another who needs to be rescued."

"Who?" Joal asked.

"The one who is immune to Jemma's voice."

Joal's brows pressed together and then his eyes widened. "You mean Cassie?"

Sara nodded.

"Why would they want Cassie?"

Petros took a step toward them. Ignoring the question, he said, "If Kronos has them, I cannot help. Upon the imprisonment of Kronos and his Titans, I swore an oath to leave them alone in the pit of Tartarus. If I break that oath and enter their realm, the hundred-handed guards will leave, allowing the Titans to escape."

"Hundred-handed guards?" Joal asked.

"Yes." Petros said. "They are the ones who keep the Titans in Tartarus."

Joal shot a quick glance at his mom, and then looked Petros in the eyes. "Could you sneak in?"

He shook his head. "My presence would not go unnoticed."

"Could I sneak in?" Joal asked.

"Getting in is not the problem," Petros said. "Getting out... would be impossible."

"There is one who has accomplished the impossible." Sara said and then turned to look at Joal. "And you know him."

"Dante?"

Sara nodded. "But it will still be a difficult, if not impossible journey. It takes a powerful god to escape Tartarus, and Dante cannot do it for you."

"But how can I?" Joal asked. "The Titans are powerful beings, much more powerful than me. I'm willing to trade my life for Jemma's, but if I fail trying to save her... she'll still be left unsaved."

"You do have the power to save her," Sara said to Joal. "It's locked inside you."

He shook his head. "I can't access that power until I turn

twenty-one. That's three years away. I can't leave her there for three years!"

"And that's why I've come," Sara said.

Joal was confused, and then understanding washed over him as his eyes flew open wide. "Goddess of fate and *time...*"

She nodded and then turned to Petros. "Grandfather, you might want to transport us somewhere safer."

"Safe from whom?" Joal said, looking around at the house. It was empty, except for he, his mother, and the two other powerful gods.

Sara turned back to Joal and raised a brow. "Safe from you."

In a blink, all of them were standing on the shore of a deserted beach. The turquoise waves crashed against the pale, sandy shore. Sara looked out over the water and said, "Father? We're going to need your help."

Joal felt another wave of immense power wash over him. A muscled man with a bare chest, unruly blonde hair, and striking blue eyes stood before him. His expression warmed when he looked at his daughter. "Anything for you, baby girl."

Joal had never met him in person, but he knew who this man was. It was Triton, beloved son of Poseidon—his brother.

Between the king of the gods, the goddess of fate, and King Triton, Joal had never been in the presence of so much unadulterated, raw power. He'd thought Tyr was powerful. The power of these three dwarfed the Nordic god of war. Joal had never felt so inadequate.

"Hello, brother," Triton said with a crooked grin.

"You know me?" Joal's brows raised in shock.

Triton barked a laugh. "Yes. I'd know a brother of mine anywhere. And don't judge me harshly because of our father. It was wrong of him not to claim you. Though, you should count yourself lucky he leaves you alone."

"So, he wasn't a good father to you either?" Joal asked.

"That's the understatement of the millennium. My father murdered my beloved children."

"What?" Joal gasped.

"It's a long story."

"That's best left for another time, dad," Sara said, resting her hand on his shoulder. Then she turned and reached out her hand toward Joal. Hesitantly, he took it. The power he felt at her touch nearly brought him to his knees. He stumbled forward as Sara led him into the encroaching surf.

"So, you're going to make me older?" Joal asked.

Sara nodded, "Just in body, not in mind." She sighed. "Are you ready?"

Joal nodded, bracing himself for whatever was to come. Regardless of what he faced by embracing his power now, he had no choice but to follow through. Right at this moment, Jemma was lying somewhere. Broken. Bleeding. He had to save her, and he couldn't wait a heartbeat more.

"Yes," he said, "I'm ready." *Gods, I hope this doesn't hurt.*

"Okay, close your eyes," Sara said.

Pain wasn't exactly what Joal experienced. At first it felt odd, like his body was going through life on fast forward—hunger, fullness, sleepiness, wakefulness, growing pains, exhaustion, energy, time turning over and over like a spinning wheel... and then it hit him.

Power.

So much power.

There was no way he could have understood, no way he could have prepared for it. Power exploded inside him. It flowed through him. Every cell, every particle of his being was pure power. He felt as if he could gather all the elements into the palms of his hands and obliterate them. He roared as the immense power continued to rush over him.

No, this experience didn't hurt. It was so much worse than any pain he'd felt before; it was beyond words. He roared, unable to contain the force flowing through him. Somewhere in his tortured mind, he knew it wasn't only himself shouting. His eyes cracked open. Through a haze of white, he saw Triton on his knees, his hands raised against a towering ocean vortex surrounding them. A funnel of water loomed miles above and around them as winds battered them and then lightning flashed slamming into him. And then the agony was gone. A thundering crash of waves shook the ground and deafened him. Finally, the sea calmed, water lapping against his body as Joal lay prostrate, losing consciousness, utterly exhausted.

Chapter Twenty-three –
Jemma

CHAPTER 23

In the middle of the journey of our life
I found myself within a dark woods
where the straight way was lost.
—— _Inferno,_ Dante Alighieri

MUSIC BRUSHED over Jemma's skin and caressed her soul. It was faint, not even audible to her ears, but she could feel it. Its warmth blanketed her, called to her. As the music faded, other sensations came, frigid hardness of the ground beneath her cheek and stomach, and pain— gods! The pain!

Jemma's eyes flew open as her back screamed in agony. Memories like phantom nightmares flooded her mind. Pushing herself off the ground, everything around her spun. She spread out her fingers, her nails clawing into the cold dirt floor. The rocks bit into her knees as she braced herself on all fours.

Jemma raised her head and searched the darkness. All around her were slashes of black, and greenish gray, like a wicked forest grinning with long, jagged teeth. Above her there was a faint, mottled light.

She looked down. The beautiful homecoming dress was tattered and covered in dirt and blood. Pushing herself off the ground, she staggered to her feet. She stood on trembling legs. Her bare feet burned from the cold emanating from the ground, rendering them numb in minutes.

Jemma gasped in breaths of air; puffs of moisture billowed with each exhale. The stench was strange, yet familiar, it reminded her of the lake she and Cassie had once camped nearby—a lake that had contained layer upon layer of algae bloom.

Looking up, Jemma trembled when the familiarity of this place struck her and had her gaping in horror. Above her was a frozen lake, a faint, green glow outlined the shards of ice.

She'd read about this place in *Dante's Inferno*. It mentioned a vast frozen lake in which the devil is trapped. Despite her desperation to be wrong about this, she knew she wasn't. This was the Underworld. And not even the lowest part of the Underworld—Tartarus was above her. She was trapped *beneath* Tartarus. There wasn't supposed to be anything below. Tartarus was it, it was the pit, the lowest part of hell. But somehow, she was lower than the lowest.

Tears leaked from her eyes, the wetness trailed down her cheeks, stopping when the cold air froze them to her skin. She brushed away the frozen tears from off her face. Turning around; the ominous darkness loomed before her as she stumbled away. Pain like a knife exploded in her back as she brushed against something, every exposed nerve ending screaming, as a cry escaped her lungs, a chorus of agony echoing in the monstrous chamber. The ground shuttered beneath her feet.

What was that? An earthquake?

The ground stilled. Jemma reached behind her, gingerly touching her throbbing back. Wetness coated her fingertips. Was she still bleeding? Why hadn't her back healed? Had she lost that ability?

"Joal!" Jemma shouted into the darkness. "Where are you? What are they going to do with me?"

He didn't answer. Of course, he didn't. He couldn't hear her.

She looked around. What had she bumped into? She saw what looked to be a pillar and reached out to touch it. The biting cold stung her fingers as she came in contact with it. It was another ice pillar, or perhaps simply a shard that reached the ground. Did these shards keep the frozen lake aloof? She shook her head as she thought, there's no way an entire lake was being held up by a few shards of ice. This place defied the laws of physics.

"Beloved child of Peisinoë," a light, feminine voice spoke to her mind, interrupting her thoughts. *Pea-sin-oi*? Who in the world is that? She'd never heard that name before. It didn't sound the least bit familiar. Was it a Greek name? She didn't know.

"Who are you? What do you want?" she said.

"You will free the old ones, or you will never see the glowing light of Olympus again."

"Glowing light of Olympus? What are you talking about? Who am I supposed to free? I'm below the deepest pit of the underworld. I can't even free myself."

The voice didn't answer. Maybe she realized how stupid she was being. Besides, Jemma had no idea who wanted to be free. What kind of beings were they? Maybe they were trapped for a good reason. She needed to know who she was dealing with. "Are you still there?"

There was no answer. Jemma's stomach grumbled. She wasn't sure if it was from hunger or sickness. Probably both.

How long had she been unconscious?

"Who is Peisinoê?" she decided to ask again.

"She is your mother." Jemma's heart pounded as she realized the significance of that information. She was being told who her birth mother was.

"Is she a goddess?"

"She's more powerful than a goddess."

"More powerful? What do you mean?"

"The son of Poseidon left you in darkness. I wonder why. Perhaps he's no ally to you."

"I trust Joal a million times more than I trust you." The bite of her words was sharp. Who could blame her? This entity was telling her if she didn't free "the old ones" she would never leave. And now she was telling her not to trust Joal. This woman was the one she didn't trust. She may very well be the woman who'd cut off her wings and dragged her down here.

"Joal is your natural-born enemy."

"I choose who my enemies are, not you. Besides, I thought I was a sea-goddess."

"You are so much more."

"So, who am I? Do you know who my father is?"

"Your father is nothing now." There was a bitter bite to her words.

"What does that mean?"

"He is being punished for taking the power of the gods, stealing the Aether's mates, and nearly destroying the world."

Her father did all that? "My father is Zeus, isn't he?"

The voice hissed. "Do not speak that foul name!"

Jemma frowned. From what Joal had said about Zeus, Joal didn't seem to like him much either. "And my mother...?"

"Your father, fearing her, turned her to stone and hid her away. And then because he could not kill you and your sisters, he stripped you of your powers and sent you to live among the humans."

Jemma's heart plunged in her chest. Not only had she lost her human mother, but her biological mother was gone too. And to make things even worse, her own father had murdered her and wanted to kill Jemma as well. Talk about a dysfunctional family. But there was one spark of hope. She had a sister. No, not one sister. Sisters. That means at least two.

"Where are my sisters? Who are they?"

"The three of you were too much of a risk for the former king of Olympus. There had never been three born of three in all the history of the gods."

"Three born of three. What does that mean?"

"Your mother shared her mother's womb with two others, as did you."

"I'm a triplet?" The shock of that bit of knowledge rendered her speechless. Finally, she recovered her senses and said, "But where are my sisters? How can I find them?"

"They have been close to you your entire life, but barriers have been placed between you three, as well as between you and any other god or goddess. The former king of the gods did not want you to garner any powerful allies."

"Wait a minute. I know what kind of barrier was between Joal and me. Is this the same kind of barrier with my sisters? Do we keep forgetting each other?"

"I'm not sure of the nature of the barriers, only that they exist."

"How do you know all this? And by the way, who are you?"

"I'm of no consequence."

"You're the only being I've met who knows who I am. The

only one who knows my story. I think that's pretty important."

"I'm the being who stole your powers and left you weak and ignorant."

"I... I don't understand. I thought Zeus stripped me of my powers." She couldn't bring herself to call him her father. "Why did he do it? And you helped him? Why?"

Silence.

Jemma didn't know her father, but it sounded like he had done terrible things to her, her sisters, and her mother. "You said my father hid my mother's statue? Why? If she's dead, why would he need to?

"She was the most powerful of the three. Zeus did not have the power to destroy her."

"So, she's alive?"

No answer.

"Where is she?"

"How can I find her?"

"Do not seek her out alone. You will need the power of three to release your mother."

"Three? What, me and my sisters?"

The voice didn't answer. Jemma tried, again and again, to speak to the being, but it seemed the conversation was over. No matter how hard she tried, she couldn't elicit a response. Finally, she gave up and was left alone with her thoughts.

I have sisters, she thought, still not quite believing it. She'd always thought she was an only child. It was beyond strange to think she was a triplet. *And they're close.* Considering where she was now, in this dark, dank pit, she hoped they weren't too close. Jemma wrapped her arms around her body as the chilled air seeped into her skin and caused her to shiver.

Why was she here? Who brought her here? What did they want from her? She couldn't bring herself to consider how difficult it would be to escape or how difficult it would be for

Joal to find her. Nope. She totally couldn't go there. This was the last place she'd want Joal anyway. If there was one thing she'd learned about the Underworld—it's nearly impossible to escape from. If Joal tried to retrieve her, he'd just get himself stuck here as well. But... Jemma's eyes flew open wide when she realized who Joal's protector was, Dante, one of the few beings in existence who had escaped Tartarus. Perhaps, with his help, Joal could get her out. But she wasn't about to sit here and wait for help. If she was so powerful even Zeus feared her, perhaps she could escape here herself.

Jemma stood and stumbled forward. If she could just find the edge of this pit, maybe she could find a way to climb out. Hours later, she growled in frustration. No matter how far she walked, it all looked the same. It seemed as if she passed the same shards of ice over and over. She had to be walking in circles. Finally, her legs refused to take another step. She was utterly exhausted. Finding a spot of relatively even ground, she lay on her side and closed her eyes.

Despite the fatigue, her mind continued to race. Perhaps sleep was still a way off. Left with her own thoughts, Joal came to her mind and tears leaked from her eyes, once again freezing on her cheeks. Hades this place was cold! And people thought hell was a burning pit. No, it was the opposite, it was a frigid nightmare.

She couldn't think about Joal right now, instead she focused on trying to figure out who her sisters could be. If they were close, they must be somewhere in Garden Grove. She made a mental list. Cassie? Nope, she couldn't be. Jemma had known Cassie and her family her whole life. They all looked alike. Cassie and her sister could almost be twins, except for the fact her sister was seven years old. Besides, there was apparently a barrier between herself and her sisters, so it couldn't possibly be her best friend.

The barrier... That was likely the clue she was looking for.

This barrier worked well on Joal, but it didn't seem to work on her. But maybe it was different between her and her sisters somehow. It was unlikely to be physical, given her experience with Joal. It was strange how she seemed unaffected by it, or perhaps immune to it. It only affected Joal. But what about her sisters? Did they have the same type of barriers? Perhaps. Joal had continuously forgotten her. Maybe she and her sisters forget each other. Are there two girls at school she always forgets? Jemma breathed a laugh. If there were, she would have forgotten them. How could she remember someone she's forgotten? Perhaps... A thought struck her. Her picture-perfect memory may be just the thing to solve this mystery.

Her sisters' situations were likely similar to her own. They were in Garden Grove, probably lived there all their lives. If that were so, there was something she could do. She could mentally recreate all her classes, remembering where the other students sat. Then, maybe she could see a difference between an empty chair and an occupied chair without an accompanying face to go with the person sitting there.

The picture would be clearer if she worked her way through her classes. It should work... if her sisters go to the same high school as her. If they were homeschooled, this wouldn't work. History class would be the first one she'd tackle. She started with the first row going left to right: Gina, Emily, Cameron, Bobby and ...?

And...

Seriously?

She closed her eyes and thought hard. Someone did sit there, next to Bobby. She was sure of it. Maybe her memory wasn't as good as she'd thought. She couldn't have possibly located one of her sisters so quickly. She mentally put a red circle around that desk. She'll come back to it later. Next to the nameless person was Victor at the end. In the next row on the left, there was Ally, Irene, Grace, Arianna, Rafael, and

Connor. On the third row sat Joal... her heart clenched as she pictured his wind-blown hair as he sat at his desk, his back toward her. Shaking her head, she thought, *No. Focus.* Then came Brittney, Alex, Will, Summer, and an empty seat. On the fourth row sat Francine, Mia, Jemma herself, and then two empty seats and then... someone sat in that seat. But...

This was crazy. Both of her sisters couldn't be in her same history class. What were the odds they were in the first class she'd mapped out? Actually, Jemma could easily figure out the odds.

There were sixteen different classes at any one time and approximately twenty-five students in each class. The odds that one of her sisters was in her class would be approximately one in sixteen. But the odds that both of her sisters were in her class would be about one in two-hundred and fifty-six, give or take.

Jemma shook her head. It was more likely her memory was faulty. Besides, there was no point to this mental exercise if she couldn't then figure out *who* was sitting at those desks.

Perhaps she could prove her memory was faulty. If she forgot other students, forgetting three in one class for instance, that should prove her memory was inaccurate. It would take her a long while to go through all the seating charts of the rest of her classes. But it wasn't like she had anything better to do right now. Half an hour later, she was feeling more hopeful. She remembered all the students in all of her other classes save one. There was one student who sat directly to her right in her Latin class. How could she not remember someone who was sitting two feet away from her? There had to be a reason. It had to be one of her sisters.

She hoped.

If she could ever get out of this prison, she would find out who that person was, and if that person matched one of the two in her first-period history class, then that would be further evidence.

Jemma's jaw shook, chattering as she yawned and felt her eyes droop. Gods she was tired, cold, and beyond uncomfortable. If only she had a bed, a pillow, and a blanket. Gods she was so desperate for a warm blanket. She tucked her arm under her head. The uneven, cold ground faded from her mind as exhaustion finally lulled her to sleep.

Chapter Twenty-four – Joal

For this I hold no other responsible
but my own father and mother,
and I wish they never had got me.
—*The Odyssey,* Homer

POWER FLOWED through and around Joal. He could feel exactly where the ocean touched the shore—five yards from his current location and then beyond that, the flow of the waves and currents. He could even detect each particle of moisture in the clouds and their movement in the skies as they billowed above him. He instinctively knew that each of those particles would respond to his commands. They moved, vibrating with warmth, brimming with energy. They eagerly awaited his command.

Petros scowled as he turned to Sara, "You had to do it didn't you?"

"It was his destiny." She shrugged.

Petros turned back to Joal. "You are powerful, young one.

More powerful than... well, never mind." He turned to Sara. "I hope you know what you're doing."

"He won't be the last," she said.

Petros grunted, clearly unhappy about something.

"These are not the ones you should be worried about," Sara said.

"Very well," Petros said with reluctant acceptance.

Joal only half listened to the conversation. He was too mesmerized by his new-found powers. "I need to try something," he said, half to himself.

Joal gathered the charged particles of moisture around him. The particles brushed against his skin and pushed at him as if hungry for his attention. Then he had another thought.

Directing the water vapor beneath his arms, he told them to move up, cradling him. As soon as his feet left the ground, he had the particles beneath them join the others in raising himself. Within seconds, he was several feet above the group.

"I told you he would amaze you," Sara said, looking at her father whose eyes were wide with wonder.

"You can fly," his mother gasped. "How can you fly? You're not a sky-god."

"He's using the water in the air," Petros said. "Can you not see?"

As the water particles rubbed against each other, Joal could feel something strange. Another kind of power—a power he'd only felt once before. Years ago, when he had found himself in the presence of Zeus.

"I don't understand," he said as bursts of electrical currents danced over his hands and across his fingertips. He lowered himself so his feet were once again touching the ground.

Sara stepped toward him. "You have rare powers, powers that need a new master. The balance must be maintained, and the fates have gifted you with Zeus's abilities." The current increased as they spoke. "I would ground yourself before you generate too much energy."

"How...?"

"Touch my grandfather."

Petros reached out and Joal pressed his fingertip to his hand. Petros jerked as he absorbed the shock.

"I forget how powerful the bolt can be," Petros shuddered.

"I don't understand," Joal said. "Why do I have Zeus's powers?"

Sara stepped forward. "Now that the betrayer has been sent to Tartarus, his powers need to go somewhere. Fate has chosen you."

"This is impossible," his mom spat. "My son is a sea-god. He couldn't possibly have anything to do with sky-god powers."

Sara turned to her and asked, "And why is that so terrible? The powers of the sky-gods aren't inherently bad or good; they are pure elements, and Joal is now the caretaker of two elemental types—sea and sky."

"You've corrupted him," his mom snarled.

"Sea-god, sky-god," Petros growled. "I hate those terms. They are meant to divide the gods."

"Tell me. Is he now a sky-god?" His mother spoke in clipped tones, ignoring Petros's words.

Sara's expression saddened as she glanced at Joal and then hardened when she turned back to Ved-ava. "The majority of his powers do come from the sky, yes."

Rage bloomed on his mom's face. "You, take them back. My son wants nothing from Zeus or any other sky-god."

"The powers are now a part of Joal," Sara said. "You would rob him of his essence?"

"Why do you despise these powers?" Petros asked, taking a step toward her. "Zeus was powerful, the most powerful besides myself."

"I disagree," she spat, "you're only an earth-god. You don't understand. There is nothing more powerful than the sea, the currents, the force of the waves... nothing stands against it. The air, the earth, and fire all succumb to its power. And now you've turned my son into one of them!" she shouted. Then she turned to glare at Sara. "You, you did this! His mother glared daggers at her. You've stolen my son from me by turning him into a sky-god!" The anger laced in his mother's voice whipped out as she stepped toward Sara.

"No one has taken him from you," Sara said, standing her ground. "It is you who rejects him because of your ignorance."

Joal's eyes widened as he could feel his mother's power building. His mother was going into a rage, against the goddess of fate, not to mention in the presence of Petros, this was possibly the most idiotic thing his mother had ever done. Actually, she had a list of ludicrous things she'd perpetrated today alone. Petros and Triton moved to step between his mother and Sara, but before they could, there was another hulking presence in the house.

This god was not as large as Petros, but he still had to be at least seven feet tall and well-muscled. His power was unmistakable, yet strange—similar to Joal's own elemental powers. But the most important thing, he was lethal. Joal could not imagine even Ares himself could present a more deadly aura. And this god had his blade at his mom's throat. "Measure your next words carefully," he said, his eyes glowing with rage. "They may be your last."

Sara frowned. "I told you not to watch. I'm truly in no danger."

"Xanthus," Petros's voice rumbled. "I appreciate you wanting to protect your wife, but Triton and I can handle this."

Joal's brows were raised. This was Sara's husband?

Sara turned to him, answering his unspoken question.

"Yes, this is my husband. You and he have something in common. He is a Dagonian, *and* he has been given Ares powers."

"We've met before, Nightmare of the Deep," his mother said to Xanthus. Her eyes narrowed. "Or should I call you traitor?"

Xanthus's eyes burned with rage, but he held still.

Joal's mom turned to the others. "It looks like the war has already begun, and it appears the sky-gods are on the offensive. They're taking our most powerful sea-creatures as their own."

"Enough!" Petros's voice rumbled, his own anger high. "Sky-god, sea-god... It does not matter! There is nothing inherently different between the two. They are both born of the same elemental source controlling the universe. My brothers, sisters, and I control different elements, but we are still siblings—sons and daughters of the same mother and father. Power in and of itself cannot act alone, it's the one who wields it that is important."

"Lies," she muttered. His mother had no sense of self-preservation at all.

"Are you so blinded by your hatred you would reject your own son?" Triton asked.

She turned to Joal, her eyes pleading. "Tell them. Tell them you don't want these powers."

Joal stood silent. The powers he felt flowing through him, they were a part of him; he could feel it. To reject them would be to reject himself. Besides, he needed to be powerful to save Jemma. There was nothing more important than her life. She was everything to him.

His silence told his mother more than any words could say. And his new powers had put him at odds with everything she stood for, everything she believed. And even though his powers were derived from the same source that drove the powers of both the sea and the sky, she couldn't see it. The balance between sea, sky, fire, and earth was important and all elements were necessary. But then a thought struck him.

"When I told you what she was, you were willing to accept Jemma. She was born of the sky and sea. So then, why can't you accept me?"

She pursed her lips. "I don't accept her," she spat. "She's a weapon. A siren's song is the most powerful force on Olympus, and her wings are a weapon to wield against sky-gods, her voice is most potent when sung in the underworld. Sirens are built to destroy sky-gods and underworlders alike."

"Again, you speak of war," Petros said, his eyes narrowing.

Joal took a step forward. "Jemma would never use her powers to destroy other gods. But that's what you have planned, don't you? That's why you were so excited about her existence, why you were so happy to hear she loved me. You wanted me to manipulate her. You wanted me to help ignite a war, a war between the sea-gods and all others. And that's why you have been working with the Titans, stealing the newly released sky-gods away and hiding them."

"She has done much more than that," Sara said. "I cannot say what, but her treachery and that of the others risks the survival of all—humans and gods alike. The balance must be maintained. Zeus didn't understand that." She looked at Vedava. "And neither do you. Because of your blindness, *you* are the traitor and you've betrayed us all."

"What?" His mom's eyes widened. "No, I didn't. I don't want this war. It's you who wants it."

Joal could feel the lies spilling from his mother's lips as plainly as he could feel the sea in the distance. He'd never before seen her clearly. His mom, he sighed, she truly was... evil. His stomach sickened when he thought of the glee in his mother's eyes as she cut the wings from Jemma's back. She had enjoyed it, reveled in it. "And Jemma is a part of this plan, isn't she?" he asked her.

She looked at Joal, desperation in her eyes. "Baby, please."

"That might have worked," Joal said, stepping toward her and narrowing his eyes, "if you'd ever once in your life called me baby or shown me any kind of real motherly affection. You might have given birth to me, but you've never been a real mother."

The facade of his mom's affection melded into rage. "I've given you everything you've ever wanted. I gave you—"

"A credit card with no limit, hired help to care for me, and a house over my head. None of which truly cost you anything." His voice rose with his indignation. "You kept me hidden away. You never introduced me to my grandmother, grandfather, aunts, uncles, cousins, none but Tyr had even known I existed. I'm not even worthy of a place in your life. Why would I have any loyalty to you, when you have no loyalty to me?"

His mother absorbed his wrath and turned it back on him as she said, "You're placing yourself on the wrong side of this, Joal."

"No." He stepped back, standing between Triton and Sara. "I'm not. I finally know exactly where I belong."

Ved-ava narrowed her eyes, her rage now focused on him. "I wish you'd never been born."

"And you finally speak the truth," Joal said. He breathed in deeply for the first time in his life. He'd never realized how stifling it had been keeping his mother's secrets and even more damning was living in denial about how unimportant he was to her. But no longer. Jemma had taught him what true love and acceptance felt like. "Even if I could save you from the consequences of your actions, mother. I wouldn't. Unlike you, Jemma truly does love me, and *you* have done your best to destroy her."

"I never tried to kill her."

"Death is only one way to destroy someone," he said.

"You really are just like them, weak and pathetic," she growled. "And like them, you will die."

"No, mother. Thanks to Sara, I now have the power to save Jemma, and I will. But I need to ask you one more question, where is Denise?"

"Denise? It's pathetic you care about a human so much. I should have destroyed her."

Sara took a step forward. "Denise is safe and will remain so. And Jemma," she sighed, "is not actually in Tartarus, but beneath it."

This got Petros's attention. His fists clenched. "Who did you give her to? What do they want from her?"

His mother smirked. "Wouldn't you like to know. I'll tell you this, your days on the throne are numbered, majesty," she said in a mocking tone. "And your rule—" And then she was gone.

"Did she just leave while I was questioning her?" The ground shook at Petros's booming voice. "Xanthus! Find out where she went. She must be stopped! Triton, come with me, I must speak with your father, find out what he knows about this treacherous leech." With those words, Triton and the king of the gods were gone.

Joal stood alone with Sara and Xanthus. With Petros and Triton gone, Xanthus's strange but familiar power was even more striking.

Joal turned to face him. "Who are you? I mean what are you the god of?"

"I'm the god of peace," Xanthus answered.

"So, you're Ares's enemy?"

Sara smiled disapprovingly at Xanthus. "I told you that title would cause confusion."

Sara turned to Joal and said, "You have Zeus's power, Xanthus has Ares's."

"What happened to Ares?"

"He was destroyed by my father, your brother," Sara said.

"I thought gods couldn't die," Joal asked.

"They are difficult to kill," Sara said, "but it is possible. And now they are somewhere even Hades will not venture."

Joal looked at Xanthus. "You're not going to kill my mother, are you?" Joal couldn't help but ask. He may have thought she deserved to be punished, but that didn't mean he wanted her dead.

"No, I will not permanently harm her," Xanthus said, his expression softened, "but she does have a lot to answer for."

Joal pursed his lips and nodded. Any consequences his mother faced would be because of her actions. He could not protect her, but he could save and protect Jemma. He straightened his spine and said, "Okay, so how do I get to the underworld?"

Xanthus raised a brow and turned to Sara. "I really like this boy."

"Technically," Sara said, "he's not a boy anymore."

"Right."

Joal's impatience grew, he didn't have time for them to debate his adulthood. Just before he spoke, Sara turned to him.

"You'll need to contact Dante. He can instruct you."

"Will he be coming with me?"

"Yes. He is also the only god who has ventured where you need to go. He'll have the knowledge you need to get there. You'll find him at home. You should go now. Jemma is alone, afraid, and in pain, and things will only get worse for her." His heart broke on her words, but before he could question her further, Sara said, "We shouldn't keep you. Time is short. If you do not move quickly, you'll find you and your friends in great peril."

"Greater peril than Tartarus?" he asked, but they were gone, and he was once again standing in his living room.

"Wait," he said to the empty air. "There's more I need to know!"

There was no answer.

Joal swore.

Dante. That was who he needed now.

Chapter Twenty-five – Joal

No man will hurl me down to Death, against my fate.
And fate? No one alive has ever escaped it,
neither brave man nor coward.
——*The Iliad*, Homer

DESPERATION DROVE Joal as he raced outside. He had to get to her. Jemma was alone and afraid, and soon, according to Sara, things would get worse for her. In Tartarus...? He couldn't even fathom what that could mean. He had to get to her fast.

Skidding to a stop in front of his car, he froze. Wait a minute. Driving to Dante's house was not nearly as fast as transporting there. He had his full powers; he should be able to do it. But how does it work? Searching his surroundings, he didn't see or feel anyone watching. He closed his eyes and pictured Dante in his mind. Then he let his power wash over him.

He could feel the difference before he opened his eyes. The air felt damp, warm, and steamy.

"Joal, what the Hades are you doing here?" Dante's deep voice was mixed with surprise and amusement.

Joal opened his eyes to see he was standing in a familiar bathroom, in front of a shower door. Dante stepped out of the shower, buck-naked.

"Uh, sorry," Joal said and stumbled out of the bathroom.

Dante was laughing when he strolled into the living room, wrapped in a towel. "Your first-time transporting is always tricky. Next time think of my house, or better yet, my doorstep so you can knock and wait for me to invite you in like a normal person. So, when did that power...?" His voice trailed off as his eyes widened. A moment later, Dante appeared across the room and had Joal by the throat. Flames erupted over his skin. *Oh, yeah Dante had powers.* This was beyond the abilities of a normal demigod. How could he have not seen it before?

"It's been over a hundred years, Zeus. What are you doing here?" Dante growled. "And in this form?"

Joal clawed at Dante's hand, desperate to get a breath of air in his lungs. The moisture in the air stirred around them and electricity crackled over Joal's skin. Dante let go and swore. Joal felt a blast of hot air as the fire swelled, engulfing Dante completely. The curtains caught fire as the carpet charred and melted. Smoke filled the air. Joal collapsed to the ground coughing and sucking air into his lungs. "Stop!" Joal gasped. "It's me. Joal."

"You look like him," Dante growled. "But your disguise is not perfect. The real Joal is younger and slighter in build. I don't know why you were so stupid to come here. You cannot hide your powers from me. Tell me, how did you get away from the Aethers? And why have you come here? We had an agreement—"

"I'm not Zeus!" Joal shouted and climbed to his feet. "It really is me. Sara changed me, so that I could access my full powers. And the fates have given me Zeus's abilities."

A moment later, the fire and smoke retreated, leaving a charred room. Dante strode forward, his eyes narrowed. He stood, studying Joal for a long moment. Finally, his expression softened. He swore. "You are Joal."

"That's what I've been trying to tell you." He coughed.

Dante stepped closer. "Sara did this, huh? The granddaughter of Petros and goddess of fate?"

"You've heard of her?"

"Everyone has heard of her. Well..., obviously not everyone since you hadn't."

"Now I have. And she's not just goddess of fate, she's also goddess of time."

Dante's confusion melted into understanding as he barked a quiet laugh. "Looks like Kronos has competition, though he's not much of a competitor being trapped in Tartarus. But the bigger question is, why would she do that?"

"My mother... cut off Jemma's wings and sent her to the underworld, beneath Tartarus. I need to go there and get her back."

Dante swore. "Why would your mother do that? What do they want with Jemma? I mean she's powerful, to be sure, but—"

"She's a siren."

"A daughter of Triton?" He raised a brow.

Joal shook his head. "Wrong kind of siren."

Understanding had Dante's eyes flashing orange flames. "She's the daughter of an ancient one."

"Yes."

"By the gods." Dante swore and then strode across the room and sank down into his couch. He ran his fingers through his damp hair. "I know what they want with her." He looked up to Joal expectantly. "Did Sara enlighten you?"

"Not really."

Dante shook his head. "I swore I'd never go back to the Underworld."

"Tell me you didn't swear on Styx."

"No," Dante scoffed, "only an idiot swears on that."

Joal cleared his throat. "Well, I'm going to Tartarus and you're going with me," Joal said in a tone that gave no room for argument.

Dante must not have heard the tone, though, because argue is exactly what he did. "You couldn't pay me a trillion dollars or offer me Petros's throne to get me to go back to that place. I'd rather be hung up by my own entrails and fed to the buzzards for all eternity."

Joal looked up; his eyes narrowed. "Are you finished? Because we need to leave."

"I am not coming," he said in clipped tones.

"If I have to go by myself, I will. Sara said Jemma is alone and afraid." He paused, emotion squeezing his chest. "If you had seen her... what my mom did to her..." Joal choked on the words, fear and regret threatening to reduce him to tears.

Dante sighed. "Hades Joal." He paused for several long seconds. "You don't know what you're asking of me."

"I'm desperate." Tears leaked from his eyes. "I have to save her. She's all I have. She's my world. I don't care what happens to me. My life is worth nothing. Jemma's life... it's worth everything."

Dante sighed. "Awe, Hades Joal. Of all things you could ask of me..."

"I'm going whether you come or not."

"Without me, you'll never make it back," Dante said, his face in his hands. "And that's not me bragging. That is a cold, hard fact."

"I'm not going to make you come, but I am going."

"This trip is not worth saving one girl."

Joal tried to interrupt, but Dante put up his hand. "But there may be more at stake." Dante's brows furrowed. "What I don't understand is what they are planning. If they leave, they will just be sent back...Perhaps..." Dante's brows shot up as a thought struck him. "*That's* where they're going."

"The Titans?"

"No."

"You lost me. Where who's going?"

"The Syphers. They are being freed from the gods, but many of them are not returning to their mates." Dante stood and paced. "That has to be it."

"What are you talking about?" Joal said.

Dante stopped pacing and faced Joal. "Okay, let me explain. You understand Zeus was stealing powers from the new-born gods and hiding them among the humans, right?"

"Yes."

"Well, those gods were being siphoned by Syphers. The Syphers were trapped within the host's own body—almost like the god was possessed, only the Sypher couldn't influence or control the god. Except for the one inside of Nicoletta, she could speak to her. Um, Nicoletta is Petros's daughter and Triton's wife—."

"Triton has a wife?"

Dante waved him off. "Yes, but that's a whole other story we don't have time for. Anyway, the Syphers drained the gods of their powers to feed them to Zeus. It was all against their will, and now they are being released one by one. The Aethers are furious it's taking so long, but to release them all at once could cause untold destruction. But the problem is, despite the Syphers being released, there are only a few returning to their mates."

"Where are they going?"

"We're not sure. Zeus has been stripped of his powers and banished to Tartarus, so we thought it couldn't be him."

"Maybe the Syphers just don't want to go back to their mates," Joal said.

"You don't understand. If they don't return, they die."

"*Are* they dying?"

"Not necessarily. They can be kept in stasis."

"You think Zeus has something to do with this?" Joal asked. "But what does this have to do with Jemma?"

"I think they're planning to use her to free the Titans. Do you know who guards Tartarus?"

"The hundred-handed men."

"Exactly. And if Jemma were to lure hundreds of gods, demigods, and other creatures with her song. What do you think will happen?"

"That would keep the hundred-handed men busy. Allowing the Titans to escape."

"You're missing the whole picture. A hundred gods and goddesses brought to Tartarus, to where *Zeus* is being held.... If the Syphers are also being brought there to Zeus, the one god who knows how to steal power from the gods..."

Joal swore.

"Exactly. And Zeus would escape along with the Titans with more power than any one of them."

"Do you think the Titans know this?"

"It's possible. They'd be willing to submit to him in order to escape Tartarus."

"But with that many gods at full power, the hundred-handed men would not be strong enough to capture them."

"Have you forgotten what it was like being under Jemma's power?"

Joal shook his head as he breathed, "No. But... wouldn't the hundred handed giants be under her power as well."

"No." Dante shook his head. "They are impervious to the

powers of the gods, which is why they were able to overthrow the Titans in the first place, and why they are the ones who guard them in Tartarus."

Joal swore.

"Then you understand."

"How long do you think they've been planning this?"

"I don't know." Dante shrugged, and then it seemed a thought occurred to him as his brows raised and his eyes cut over to Joal. "Once Zeus escapes, he'll be coming for you first."

"What do you—" Joal realized the answer to the question before he'd asked it. He swore under his breath. "I have his powers, his original powers."

"Exactly."

Joal swore. "Just what I'd never wanted to do, take on the king of the gods"

"Former king of the gods, and yeah. This'll really suck for you. He'll know exactly what you can and can't do. He'll be able to use his knowledge against you. And he'll have hundreds of stolen powers."

"So, how do I beat him?"

"By not facing him," Dante said.

"Thanks for the vote of confidence."

"I'm just being realistic," Dante said. "You'll likely be no match for Zeus. My advice... stay far away from him. And if he comes for you..."

"What?" Joal asked when Dante hesitated.

"Run."

Joal shook his head and swore. Then he turned to Dante. "Now you know what's at stake. Will you help me?"

"How I found myself in the middle of this, I'll never know."

"Does that mean yes?"

Dante shook his head. "I know I'm going to regret this."

Joal stepped over to his friend and put a hand on his shoulder. "We have to do this."

Dante shoved his fingers through his hair and then clutched the strands as he bowed his head and sighed deeply. "I know."

Chapter Twenty-six – Jemma

He is a liar and the father of lies.
——*Inferno,* Dante Alighieri

JEMMA AWOKE WITH A START. The stagnant air greeted her as she shuddered. The darkness was oppressive with an eerie green light coming from the frozen lake above. Panic rose in her chest as she breathed out a whimper. The pain in her back screamed as she stirred.

"Oh, gods," she moaned. Nothing had changed.

Her stomach grumbled; hunger gnawed. It felt like her stomach was trying to eat itself. But that wasn't nearly as bad as the pain in her back. Still, she really wanted something to eat. Was there food down here?

No. No! She can't eat anything here. If she did, she wouldn't be able to leave. At least that's what the myths say. If Joal was right, she couldn't starve to death. But she could suffer... from hunger, from pain, from cold, from loneliness...

The thought of her mother crossed her mind. She

wondered what her mom, the human mom who raised her, was going through. Likely it was nothing compared to what she herself was experiencing down in this pit. She wondered if her mom ever thought of her. Maybe, but she didn't miss her enough to come back. In fact, if it weren't for Joal and Cassie, no one would miss her at all while she was down here.

A faint voice called through the cavern, floating like a phantom to her. She couldn't quite catch what it said, but the voice sounded familiar.

"Jemma," it said again, this time she could hear her name and it sounded like... Cassie? That couldn't be right. Why would Cassie be here?

"Hello?" Jemma answered.

"Jemma!" Cassie's voice was unmistakable as Jemma heard faltering steps coming closer.

"I'm here," Jemma said.

"Oh, fudge, you are here. I mean, I knew you were, but I hoped I was wrong." Cassie stumbled into view from behind a thick pillar of ice.

"What are you doing down here?" Jemma asked, tears stinging her eyes as a thought struck her. They were both in the Underworld—a place people go when they're dead. "Please tell me you're alive."

"Of course, I'm alive. I'm not going to let some crazed hag kill me."

"How did you find me?"

"How many times do I have to tell you I have a sixth sense?"

"Sorry, I guess I should believe you."

"Heck yeah, you should. But I didn't get down here by myself." Cassie's voice faded as concern blanketed her features. "How are you feeling?"

"I'm in constant pain, but considering where I am, I'm not too bad."

"I'm so sorry."

Jemma could see the sparkle of tears in Cassie's eyes through the darkness.

"I knew something really bad was going to happen," Cassie said, her voice low. "I just hoped I was wrong. I should have done something to stop it. I'm always doubting myself. When Joal's mom... hurt you—"

"Wait. That... that was Joal's mom?" Jemma asked.

"You didn't know?" Cassie asked.

Jemma shook her head as her stomach sank. "How did *you* know?"

"Um... I don't know. I just knew."

Jemma narrowed her eyes, studying her best friend. There were so many coincidences... It seemed like every time something bad was about to happen, Cassie always knew... and no one ever believed her. Something sparked in her memory. "Cassandra... Troy..." she said quietly to herself.

"Yep. That's my name," Cassie said, her eyes narrowed, and her brow pressed together.

"Cassandra of Troy."

"When you say it that way," Cassie raised a brow, "it does sound pretty cool."

"No, Cassandra of Troy was a prophetess. Apollo was hot for her, so he gave her the gift of prophecy. But then she rejected him, so he cursed her so no one would believe her prophecies."

"What are you saying?"

"You're Greek, right?"

"Yeah, but so are a lot of other people."

"But Troy is not a common Greek last name."

"We didn't start out with the name Troy. According to my mom, my great-grandmother changed the family name to Troy when they immigrated. They had lived in Thessaloniki in Greece, but my grandma insisted her ancestors were from Troy

—which was supposedly in Turkey. My mother hasn't traced our roots far back enough to link them to Troy. She probably never will. The city was destroyed thousands of years ago, so there's no surviving records."

"Wow, you know a lot about your family."

"You know my mom's a genealogy nut." Cassie shrugged. "So, what? You believe me now? Do you think I'm some kind of prophetess?"

"Oracle is the word they used in ancient Greece."

Cassie pressed her brows together. "You can't really think I'm some kind of an oracle."

"I'm a siren, Joal's a god, and your boyfriend, Tao is a demigod—"

"Wait! Tao is a what?" Cassie's jaw literally dropped.

"A demigod."

"No wonder he's so hot. But I... there's no way I can be an oracle."

"Of course, you can. I mean, look at all the stuff you know that you shouldn't know."

"Yeah, but no one ever believes me."

"That's the curse of Cassandra. I bet you're descended from her."

"Woah. That's insane... but maybe you're right."

Jemma smiled. "I'm pretty sure I am. So, great oracle, how do we get out?"

Cassie pressed her lips into a half smile, half frown. "You're going to think it's a stupid idea."

"What idea?"

"We need to get lost."

"We are lost."

"No, we need to try to not find the way out."

"What in the world are you talking about? That's crazy."

"See! I knew you'd say that."

"I'm sorry." Jemma took a breath. "You're right. I need to trust you. So..., we try to get lost."

"It's how I found you."

"I do trust you, but I have to say... this makes no sense."

Cassie huffed. "I know it makes no sense, but... I just know it's the right way to get out of here. We need to look for a way to get even more lost."

"You haven't seen a white rabbit, have you?" Jemma asked.

"What are you talking about?"

"I feel like I've fallen down a rabbit hole, Alice."

Cassie stopped and frowned at her. "You're such a geek."

Jemma stumbled her way in darkness. She had no idea how to lose her way when she was already as lost as could be. Five minutes later, she skidded to a stop at an unexpected sight—stairs leading up. Cassie bumped into her back and pain flared as Jemma shrieked, "Ouch!"

"Oh sorry, sorry..." Cassie said as she stepped back. "I forgot about your back." She shook her head. "I still can't believe my best friend has wings."

"...had wings." She breathed, attempting to get on top of the pain.

Cassie's expression fell. "Joal's mom is the worst."

"Yeah. I feel bad for Joal."

"Totally."

"So, do we take the stairs?" Jemma asked. "Or do you think it's a trap?"

Cassie threw back her head and sighed deeply. "Hades, I don't know. Just because I know some things, doesn't mean I know everything."

"Hades?"

"Tao's rubbing off on me," Cassie shrugged.

"*Gods*, I know what you mean."

They both rolled their eyes and chuckled.

Cassie looked up and said, "Well, we do know one thing.

The outside world is up." She pointed toward the black abyss above them.

"I wonder if my wings are up there, or down here."

"Do you want to bury them or something?" Cassie asked.

"I want them back."

"Back, as in *on* your back."

"Yes."

"You can do that?"

"According to Joal and Dante."

"Gods, that's... crazy," Cassie said.

"I just don't know how I'm going to find them."

"I bet Joal's mom still has them."

"Why do you think that?"

"You didn't see the expression on her face when she cut them off. I'll never forget that look. You know, it's a wonder Joal turned out so well with a mom like that."

"Yeah, well, he had Denise."

"Yeah, she's really nice." Cassie nodded and said, "And look at you, your mom wasn't the best, and you turned out amazing."

"I don't feel amazing."

"Well, you are."

Jemma felt too miserable to take her words to heart.

"Okay," Cassie continued, "first things first. We need to get out of the Underworld, and then we'll find your wings."

"What if Joal's coming down here? I bet he does, especially knowing Dante is his friend."

"What does that have to do with anything?" Cassie asked.

"Dante...? As in *Dante's Inferno*."

"Doesn't ring a bell."

"You really need to read more," Jemma said. "Dante is a legendary figure who braved all the levels of the Underworld and lived to talk about it."

"Wait a minute. How many levels are we talking about?"

"Nine."

"Nine? I wonder which level we're in now?" Cassie said.

"Well, I don't know if the stories are completely accurate. *Dante's Inferno* was a Christian story and we're living in the world of Greek mythology."

"Okay, but... how does that help us now?"

"There's probably some cross-over. I'd say, we're below the lowest level."

"How can we be below the lowest? That would mean the lowest isn't the lowest, this is the lowest." Cassie looked down at the dirt floor. "But then what's below this? There has to be something lower than the level below the lowest. And then lower than the lower level below the lowest."

Jemma shook her head. "You're so confusing."

"It's a gift. So, what other kinds of things did Dante see?"

"You don't want to know."

"Oh, yes. I absolutely do want to know."

"There are raging storms, rivers of feces—"

"Wait, are you saying there's rivers of poo?"

"Yeah, and rivers of boiling blood, rivers of fire, mental torture—" a chilled breeze brushed over her skin.

"Like best friends ruining the lives of the person they said they care about?"

Jemma froze at a tone of voice she'd never heard come from her best friend—at least not a tone directed at her. "What?" Jemma's eyes widened as she turned to look into Cassie's livid face. Something was wrong, she looked different. It was dark, so she couldn't be sure, but it seemed like Cassie's eyes had lost their softness.

"You're the reason I'm here," Cassie snarled.

"No... I...."

"If it weren't for you, I'd be home in bed, safe. Do you deny it?"

"I never wanted anything bad to happen to you."

"And yet, here we are," Cassie gestured to the darkness, "in a place where there are boiling rivers of blood, fire, and poo."

"I'm sorry. I'm so sorry." Jemma said, her voice catching.

"Sorry doesn't change anything. I'm probably going to die… all because of you." Cassie's eyes narrowed.

Jemma examined Cassie's face, she had a mole just above her left eyebrow, a spray of freckles across her nose, a small scar on her forehead where her brother hit her with a picture frame. The image before her was the perfect rendition of Cassie, but the tone of her voice screamed, *not Cassie!*

"Why are you saying things like this?" Jemma said. "This isn't you."

"This isn't me? You don't know anything about me. Everything's only ever been about you. Jemma this, Jemma that, Jemma the talented, Jemma the beautiful, Jemma the girl who makes me want to puke…"

"Stop. Just stop it."

"Stop it," Cassie said in a singsong, mocking voice. "You want me to stop?"

"Yes." Jemma's eyes burned with tears.

"Tough, I'm not going to." She propped her hands on her hips. "Do you know what I hate about you most? Everything's all about you, your love life, your oh so special powers, and even now, *your* captivity. Well, I'm a captive too! If you're really sorry, you'll sing."

The word was so unexpected that Jemma wasn't sure she heard her right. "Sing? You want me to sing?"

"Yes, as loud as you can. And then maybe we could get out of this godsforsaken place."

Jemma thought about it. Could her voice save them? Maybe. But she'd be crazy to listen to this Cassie. Not when there was something seriously wrong with her. "No."

Cassie's expression hardened. "After all you did to me, you won't sing?"

"Not when you're acting like this."

"You selfish, horrible witch. I wish I'd never met you. I wish Joal's mom had killed you. You deserve to be dead." Before Jemma had time to react, a fist flew toward her, slamming into her nose with a loud crack and an explosion of pain. She gasped, blinded by the agony.

Her friend had struck her. Cassie struck her! As much as her nose hurt, it had to be broken. She cradled her injury, careful not to touch it. And then another blow crashed into her temple. She dropped down hard, her knees cracking against the dirt floor. "Stop," she cried, "stop, Cassie. Please. What's wrong with you?"

"What's wrong with me? You're the one who is the worst friend in history."

Cassie threw another strike, but missed, hitting Jemma's hand as it blocked her face. Cassie followed with her other hand which landed on Jemma's left cheek, spinning her around. She reached out, catching herself before she landed face-first on the hard ground.

"Why are you doing this to me?" Jemma shrieked.

Another blow smashed against the open wound on her back. Jemma howled in pain. A hard blow to the back of her skull had Jemma collapsing to the ground. *Did Cassie use a rock?* Jemma sobbed curling into a ball on the cold ground, her back away from her livid friend as pain radiated. "Please, stop," Jemma said, her voice raspy. "I'm sorry. I'm so,, so sorry."

Cassie didn't answer. Jemma saw flashes of something grey in Cassie's hand as hard blows rained down on her, her arm, her shoulder, her back, the open wound screaming in pain as Cassie lashed out at Jemma's injury. Jemma's cries were cut short by her sobs. Finally, the attack ceased. Jemma lay there weeping, lying in a heap for a long time. She couldn't believe what had happened. Cassie had always been the constant in her life. No matter what happened around her—her mom's erratic behavior, the friends at school turning their back on her, her own internal struggles—Cassie had always been there, encouraging her, supporting her, letting Jemma cry on her shoulder. Though, Cassie was right, right about this all being her fault. Cassie had every right to be angry at her. Still, Jemma felt this couldn't be real. Never in a million years, had Jemma thought Cassie capable of an attack like this. But then she'd never imagined them trapped in Tartarus.

After a long time and many tears shed, Jemma was finally able to open her eyes and raise her head. Cassie was gone, but that wasn't the most shocking thing.... She looked around. The stairs were gone, and a fragment of ice lay beside her. It looked like the shard she'd broken off when she first got here. She hadn't moved an inch from her original spot. Had it all been a dream? Yes..., it probably was. She was grateful for that much. At least Cassie hadn't turned her back on her too.

Despite the relief she felt, Jemma lay her face back down to the cold, hard ground and cried. *I'm never getting out of here.*

Chapter Twenty-seven – *Joal*

⌚

"All hope abandon, Ye who enter here."
These words in somber color I beheld
Written upon the summit of a gate.
——*Inferno,* Dante Alighieri

JOAL'S MOUTH gaped open at the menacing gate in front of him. He should be asking a flood of questions, but Dante's words had rendered him speechless.

"You're surprisingly calm," Dante said, his back to the swirling black vortex framed by an old, stone doorway—words of despair etched on either side of the capstone.

"Not calm."

Dante studied him for a moment before he said, "Good. Because if you were, I'd say you're an idiot."

Joal gave a curt nod.

"Before we go through there," Dante said, "there are some things you need to know. You're a god, and a powerful one, but your chance of escaping is negligible at best. If we were visiting the upper realms, it wouldn't be too much of a problem. But we'll be emerging into the deepest pit of Tartarus; it would be suicide for a demigod. For you, it may be a life sentence at the mercy of the Titans. And you, son of Poseidon, would be loathed to find an ally. Not even Hades himself ventures into the lower realms."

"But you've been there, and you returned," Joal said, a spark of hope in his voice.

"I was able to return because my mother defied Hades. She allowed me to continue on below the deepest pit of Tartarus, where I emerged back into the human world. She was punished severely for it. I will not ask for her help again. Not under any circumstance. Do you understand?"

"Who is your mother?" Joal asked.

Dante sighed. "My mother is Styx."

Joal shook his head. "So that's why my dad assigned you as a protector. Your mom is both a sea goddess and Underworlder?"

"Yeah," Dante shrugged. "And I happened to be in the area."

"And who's your father?" Joal asked.

"Prometheus."

"The god of fire? I thought he was married to Pyrrha."

"You're not the only one who's dad is a douchebag."

"Is there a god on Olympus who doesn't cheat on their spouse?" Joal scowled.

"I'm sure there are. But, that's a debate for another time."

"Right. So, is this where you exited the Underworld?" Joal asked.

"No." Dante's eyes gained a far-off look. Worry crept into Joal's mind just before Dante shook his head and said, "We will not be exiting the same way I did. Not if we can help it.

"What I need you to concentrate on now is survival. There are four main rules you must always obey when traversing the Underworld. First, don't eat anything. Second, don't trust your eyes. Third, if you feel threatened, run first, ask questions later. And fourth, stay away from any body of water, bad things happen to people who enter the waters of the Underworld. And that goes for humans, demigods, and sea-gods as well."

"I understand most of what you said, but what do you mean don't trust my eyes?"

"In the deepest parts of the Underworld, reality twists and bends. Things may not be as they seem. In this case, it's not your life you should be worried about. It's your sanity."

"That's disturbing."

"Tell me about it."

"So, when you were down there the first time, did it... make you go crazy?" Joal asked.

"I don't want to talk about it."

Joal took a long look at his friend. "That would be a yes, then."

"Just keep focused on rescuing Jemma. If you do that, you'll do better than I did. And I'll be there to help. We have the two of us."

"What if we get separated?"

"Let's hope that doesn't happen," Dante said. "But if it does, don't try to find me, we're looking for Jemma and Cassie. They're the priority. Once you find them, get them out."

"Through this entrance?"

"Yes."

"Can't I just transport to you?" Joal asked.

Dante turned and looked at him like he'd just grown a second head. "I don't know why I didn't think of that. We could just transport to Jemma and Cassie and then transport all of us back here. You're a genius, Joal."

"Okay, that was a stupid suggestion."

"You think? No one transports through Tartarus. Otherwise, the Titans could easily escape."

"Do we need to speak to Hades before we begin our search?"

"Only if you want him to search for Jemma himself with the intent of destroying her."

"No," Joal growled.

"Then let's avoid Hades and if by chance we do see him, tell him anything but the truth. Jemma is the biggest threat his Underworld has ever seen."

Joal swore.

"Yeah," Dante said.

Joal looked at the entrance. "So, the plan is, we go in there, get Jemma and Cassie, and then get out."

"Right."

"Okay, Let's go."

Dante shook his head. "I can't believe I'm insane enough to do this," he said, not looking at Joal. Taking a deep breath, he added, "See you on the other side." Dante stepped through the doorway and was immediately swallowed by the blackness.

"We're both totally insane," Joal said just before he took a big breath and followed Dante into hell.

Λ

Something sharp bit into Jemma's cheek as music filtered into her consciousness. *Where was that music coming from?* Peeling her eyes open, the first thing she saw was the bumpy expanse of dirt and dry weeds. How had weeds managed to grow in this forsaken place? She stretched her aching, cold, limbs, trying to work some feeling back in her fingers and toes.

What she wouldn't give for a nice warm bed and plush blanket. Or… a warm tub and Joal's arms cradling her. The memory filled her mind and made her heart long for the past. How long had she been down here? A day? A week? There was no sun to measure the passing of time. Sleep came and went fitfully and in short clips. How much longer would she be here? Was this a life sentence? That seemed a bit harsh for dating outside your… what would they call it? It wasn't a race, was it?

Staggering to her feet, she brushed the dirt off the filthy dress, her finger catching on a tear. She was definitely not dressed right for this occasion. The material was practically disintegrating. She sure hoped she didn't end up naked down here. It was frigid. If she had any lingering doubts about being a supernatural being, they had dissipated. Now she knew she was. Any regular person would die from hypothermia. She almost wished she were human; the relief of death would mean not having to endure the elements in Tartarus.

"Jemma." A ghostly voice floated through the mist brushing against her skin. Who was it? Her heart picked up the pace when she considered that it may be Cassie again—or whatever entity had been impersonating her. Though, if it were someone impersonating her, they'd played her character to a tee—that is until a switch was turned and she went all psycho on her.

"Jemma." There it was again. Malevolent fingers of fear clutched her heart. She would bet her life the voice calling to her was evil. It felt evil.

Turning away from the voice, she ran, her feet kicking up dirt and rocks as she sprinted, the bite of the stones forgotten in her fear-driven run. If only she'd had her wings. She could have flown out of here. She may have only had them for a short time, but she'd grown really attached to them.

"Jemma."

The sound seemed just as close, despite her run. Her foot struck something hard and down she went, even harder. Her palms felt as if they were slicing against a cheese grater. Ignoring the pain, she pushed up off the ground and scrambled back on her feet.

"Jemma."

Seriously? She should have either outrun the deranged voice or it should have caught her. What was it doing? How long would she have to run?

Skidding to a stop, she stood and listened. Maybe she could hear it running after her? Maybe—

"Jemma."

She pressed her brows together and pursed her lips, her anger igniting.

"What?" she shouted. "What do you want?"

Silence. There was no answering voice. No—

A force slammed into her. She flew back about twenty feet, skidding across the uneven ground. A scream built in her throat as the pain exploded from her open flesh. But before the scream could escape, the force followed, slamming into her, an invisible weight crushed her as she was pressed against the hard ground.

I can't breathe! Oh, please, I can't breathe!

The exhalation of an invisible creature warmed her face with its breath. Panic assaulted her mind as an inhuman growl formed words. "Pathetic creature. Where is your power? Why have they brought you here?"

Did he expect her to answer him? How could she when she couldn't even take a breath? The weight pressing against her lessened and she was finally able to squeeze in some air. "Who are you?"

"I am the abyss," his gravelly voice spoke as the ground shook. "I am torment. I am suffering. My name is Tartarus."

Jemma's heart raced at the animosity in his words.

"What are you going to do with me?"

Tartarus chuckled deeply.

"Jemma." Once again, she heard her name, but this time it was different. There was a softness, a warmth to the voice.

"I will relish each shriek of terror," Tartarus said, oblivious to the other voice, "devour each howl of pain."

"Your enemy is close. Remove the ambergris from his ears so he can hear you. And then sing to him," the feather voice brushed her ears. *"Sing softly, so only he can hear."*

"Cry out, siren," his voice rose, rumbling like stones tumbling against each other. "Wail long and loud so the world can hear you. Free me from their torment!"

"Do not listen to him. You can sing but sing softly. But first remove the ambergris."

Ambergris, wasn't that the wax that Odysseus had his men stuff in their ears to protect them from the siren's voice? She was a siren, but this was Tartarus, the Titan feared by all— gods and goddesses alike. Would her voice have power over him?

"Sing, like a whisper, daughter, let your voice flow."

Jemma's heart leapt. This was not just any voice. It was the voice of her mother—her real mother—she could feel the connection, the love. The pressure lessened as coldness, so sharp it burned, enveloped her bare fingers and toes, and then crawled up her limbs. *"Release yourself from his grasp."*

The pain was excruciating, but she managed to reach up and feel the outline of his head, her fingers searched for and found his ears and the waxy nubs. She tried to pull them out, but he jerked away as if he knew what she was doing. Still, as he pulled away, she held one ball of wax between the fingers of her right hand.

Without hesitating, she opened her chattering mouth and sang, though it sounded more like a groan. The titan froze, his stale breath coming slow and steady. The icy cold seeped away from her hands. The hum of her voice rose like a gentle breeze from her throat and the pressure lessened even more. Was it really her causing the monster's reaction? The sound of her voice was barely a whisper from her lips. What if she were to sing as loud as she could? It was obvious he'd wanted her to. Just like evil Cassie had. But why?

Squirming from beneath the invisible form pressing against her, Jemma was able to crawl out from under him and scramble to her feet. She stumbled away and then ran, hoping the thing would remain incapacitated for a long while—at least long enough for her to hide. But hide where? This whole place is— Jemma's thoughts seized as she skidded to a stop. Here, where the frozen lake hung the lowest, she could now see what was contained in the lake. She shuddered at the sight. Static figures were frozen in time, their arms, legs, faces, and torsos trapped in the ice, which was filled with limb upon limb, the faces showed various states of horror. It was only then she remembered that detail from *Dante's Inferno*. According to the book, this lake contained people who had committed the most heinous of all crimes—betrayal.

Her attention caught on the face of a woman, she was inhumanly beautiful, with high cheekbones and a delicate nose. Her face was fully encased in ice. Next to her was a man, his face open to the air. She looked closer. His eyes were closed, but still, he looked... dead, his skin white, his eye sockets sunken in. Then, his eyes fluttered open. Jemma's heart slammed against her chest wall as she sucked in a breath and jerked back. His eyes narrowed as they pierced her with a glare. Then understanding lit his face as despair melded his features. "Jemma," he rasped in a ghostly whisper.

Jemma's eyes widened. "You know me?"

"Yes." The word escaped his lips like the hiss of a snake.

Jemma looked through the ice, searching for recognition. She saw some gold threads and an arm close to the surface. It was heavily muscled, despite the emaciated face. Who would know her down here? A thought drove fear into her.

"Zeus?" she ventured a guess.

"Yes," he confirmed, "I'm your father."

A million questions flooded her mind, but only one word surfaced. "Why?"

"Why what, Jemma? Why did I destroy your mother? Why did I banish you to the human realm? Why did I steal your powers?"

His voice raised goosebumps over her already chilled skin. She nodded, unable to speak.

"Because I craved power. And you, and your sisters, as well as your mother, threatened that power."

Jemma could feel the being before her was completely powerless. "It looks like you lost it anyway. All of it."

"Yes, and without it, I'm thinking more clearly. I truly regret what I did to your mother. I regret what I did to you. If I could do things again, I would change a great deal."

"You're talking about the woman who gave birth to me, right? You turned her to stone. But I can hear her down here."

Zeus coughed a laugh. "Yes. She is nearby and she's exceptionally powerful. Once, I considered marrying her."

"But I thought you were married to Hera."

He scoffed. "Hera is weak and pathetic. I stopped loving that sorry excuse for a goddess ages ago."

Jemma looked him up and down. If there were anything weak and pathetic now, it would be him.

"I know what you're thinking," Zeus snarled. "But *they* did this to me—the Aethers, with the help of my brother— unworthy king of the gods."

"I thought you were king."

"I *should* be," he snarled. "I'm the most cunning, the most ambitious. My brother doesn't even appreciate the power he has. He allows those weaker than him to have a say in how they are ruled. He allows them freedom to make their own choices. Power should be respected. Power should be feared. Like your power, daughter. You have the power to control others with just a whisper. With a shout, you can lay waste to civilizations. You can destroy even one as powerful as Petros."

"I don't want to destroy anyone," Jemma said. "I don't want to control anyone."

Zeus sneered at her. "And that is why you are unworthy of your power. That is why it *should* be mine. I created you. I have a right to it."

"I thought you regretted taking my power."

"I regret not raising you myself," he sneered, "Without my influence you've been corrupted. You're no longer worthy of the power you hold. I've peered at you from time to time over the years. You've become a colossal disappointment. Befriending the weak, showing kindness to humans with broken bodies and minds. It's all such a waste."

"I don't see helping others as a weakness. It's a strength."

Zeus laughed hoarsely. "You're a fool. Strength is controlling and subjugating others, bending them to your will."

Jemma was stunned into silence by the malice of the man who was her father. What he'd done to her. What he'd done to others. It was unfathomable. Something built in her, a well of indignation grew in her chest. She had to try to make things right for her mother and her sisters. Let Petros handle the rest of the world. Zeus took Jemma's family from her. Jemma always had a strained relationship with her mom, the mom who raised her. And though she'd always love her, she wasn't the mother Jemma was supposed to have. And hearing the tender voice that had been guiding her down here, Jemma could feel love woven in that voice. Now, more than anything, Jemma wanted her true family back.

"Where is my mother?" Her voice was hard, determined.

Zeus scoffed. "Even if you could find her, there's no releasing her."

"Where is she?" Jemma repeated.

"There is a frozen lake between us. She's far enough from you; you can never reach her."

"Why do you hate her so much?"

"I don't hate her. She was... stunning, powerful, and I loved her."

"You turned someone you loved to stone?"

He smirked, with a wicket glint in his sunken eyes. "I love power more."

Jemma scoffed. "Look where that got you. You're the one who's pathetic."

Zeus snarled, "And you're trapped with no chance of escape. Eventually, the Titans will get what they want. They will be released, and you will be trapped here, forever."

Acid built in her stomach, and she felt all kinds of disgust when she said, "I'll have *you* with me."

Zeus smirked. "No, you see. I've made a deal with the Titans. I know things, things that can help them regain their power. And they have agreed to let me go when they escape."

"You may be able to escape, but *your* power is gone."

"That's temporary. As soon as I find out who has it, I'll strip them of it and destroy them in the process."

"How are you going to overpower them when you're so weak."

"I have my ways." His expression held no hint of doubt.

"And you really think the Titans will hold up their end of the bargain?" Jemma sneered.

"They swore on the River Styx."

"And that means...?"

"If they lie, they die."

"But they're already in Tartarus. Isn't that like already being dead?"

"Not for a god—or Titan. Death to a god is ceasing to exist."

"But I thought you couldn't kill a god."

"We're not easily killed, but there are ways. Crossing Styx would do it."

Jemma heard a crack behind her just before she was pulled against a hard chest. Her back flared in pain as arms like vices surrounded her and a hand slapped over her mouth. Zeus smiled as the ice around him also cracked and broke apart as shards rained down. In moments, Zeus stood before her, smiling. "Didn't expect that, did you?" He chuckled. "You see, I am the bait, you are the fish, and Heracles, he's the hook."

Jemma squirmed and fought, but the arms were locked around her.

"Funny thing about the waters that feed this lake," Zeus said, strolling around a frozen shard, she lost sight of him for a moment, and when he re-emerged, he was only a couple of feet away. "These waters come from the rivers of the Lethe which causes forgetfulness and the Mnemosyne which brings remembrance. I'm sure you're wondering why they don't cancel each other out. Well, in my brilliance, I created the perfect prison for my enemies, and I did it by combining the power of the rivers with the powers from Pandora's box. I put sickness, death, agony, despair, and all other horrors into the waters of Mnemosyne, so that they will always be remembered, and then I put hope into the Lethe so that prisoners would forget any hope they have of escape."

"That was one of my more brilliant acts. It is the perfect prison, for all but me. Since I created Pandora's box, I am immune. My enemies must not have known that little tidbit when they put me here. However, escaping this place will still be a challenge. That's why I need you, my dear daughter. Because of you, I will be able to leave Tartarus and regain my power. And having an army of Titans will help me gather all from Olympus, those who betrayed me, so I can trap them here in our place.

"Now, my daughter, it's time for you to lose the powers you are so unworthy of." Zeus pulled out a bottle from his robe and removed the stopper. White mist poured from the jar.

Jemma trembled in fear.

Chapter Twenty-eight – Joal

I am the way into the city of woe,
I am the way into eternal pain,
I am the way to go among the lost.
——Dante Alighieri, *Inferno*

TRAVELING to the Underworld had to be the most unpleasant, horrible journey Joal had ever gone through. Measuring time was impossible in the void. It might have been days or hours; he had no idea. But the worst part, he couldn't breathe, like literally he couldn't take a single breath for the entire time. Eventually, Joal found himself lying on the ground, gasping in stagnant air. "Hades, that's a journey," he continued to gasp, "I never want to take again."

"What took you so long?" Dante asked, seemingly unfazed by the trip.

"Oh, I don't know. I thought I'd stop and sightsee on my way here." He sat up, lifted his arm, and tried to check the time and date on his smartwatch. "Hades, it's completely dead. How long were we in there?"

"Hard to say, but your watch is not dead—well, it's dead here. It should have power again once we leave the Underworld." He grabbed Joal's hand and pulled him off the ground. "Come on. Look at where we are." Dante looked above them.

Joal followed his gaze, and he froze, stunned at the sight. The ceiling was dark, with a faint green glow—somewhat translucent with shards hanging down.

"This doesn't look right," Joal said, shaking his head. "I thought this entrance led to the highest level of Tartarus."

"It does, for most. I took us down a different path. One that only I know about."

Joal turned to him. "How is it that only you know about it?"

"I've spent a lot of time here."

"Were you imprisoned?"

He shook his head. "I was looking for someone."

"Did you find him?"

"It was a her, and no, I didn't."

"Who—"

"I don't want to talk about it."

Dante's tone told Joal he was finished with the conversation.

Dante walked forward and Joal followed. He had to sidestep a spike that was long enough it stabbed down into the earth. An irregular-shaped shard hung nearby. His blood chilled when he saw five fingers encased in the ice. "That's an arm!" He stepped back.

"Yeah. This is the Cocytus, the wailing lake."

"Nobody's wailing," Joal said.

"They're frozen, but just because you can't hear them, doesn't mean they aren't screaming for release. Every frozen person in here is conscious of their state. Their torture is immense. We're beneath the lowest level of Tartarus. The frozen lake above us imprisons betrayers."

"Betrayers?" Joal remembered what Sara had called Zeus. *The Betrayer*. "Do you think Zeus is in this lake?"

"I think that is exactly where he belongs," Dante said, looking up. "But the Aethers chose his punishment. I hadn't heard what they'd done to him, just that he'd been dealt with."

"Jemma couldn't possibly be here," Joal said. "She was no betrayer."

"She's probably not in the lake, but she and Cassie could be down here." Dante shrugged. "*We're* here."

"But I thought nobody else knew of this place."

"The Titans have been here for many millennia. Who knows what they've been doing."

An ear-piercing scream rented the air as power washed over them. Joal and Dante whipped around and raced toward the sound, their feet skidding across the dirt floor as they ducked under shards of ice-encrusted limbs. Cassie's frantic face appeared before them, and Joal's breath caught. Her face was bruised, swollen, and bloodied.

"Cassie?" Joal said, "What happened?"

"Joal? Joal! We have to get out of here!" Joal looked down at what she cradled in her arms—a small chest. It looked ancient, made of wood with intricate carvings and it radiated an unusual power. His heart slammed against his rib cage when he recognized the box.

"Is that what I think it is?" Dante asked the question that was on the tip of Joal's tongue.

"Probably," Cassie said, "and we don't have time to talk about it." She turned to take off running again.

Joal was just about to ask her what they were running from when he heard an inhuman roar. It made his blood freeze in his veins. He and Dante turned to each other, their eyes wide just before they scrambled after her.

They were running at breakneck speed. Cassie could run fast, for a human. In and out, and around the tree trunk sized shards they sprinted. Cassie looped back and then turned again. It's almost like they were running through an invisible maze. "Where in the *hell* are we going?" Joal said, keeping pace with Cassie.

"We're in... Tartarus...," Cassie said, "so—"

"All of this is hell?" Dante said, shaking his head and then narrowing his eyes at her. "Very funny."

"I thought... so," Cassie said.

"You've been here before." Dante said it as if it were a fact.

"Nope," Cassie answered.

"Then how do you—"

"—know which way to go?" she said, slowing to a stop. "I just know."

Dante pulled her to a stop and then jerked her around to face him. "No one knows how to navigate beneath Tartarus, so how do *you* know?"

"I'm... an oracle," she said, continuing to breathe hard. "Jemma... figured it out."

Joal's heart leapt when he heard her name. "You've seen Jemma?"

"Yeah," Cassie frowned, "we were trying... to find a way out, just before... we were attacked. I couldn't see what was attacking us, but I think something posed... as me. Jemma kept saying... my name and telling me to stop. But I swear I didn't hurt her. I'd never hurt my best friend."

"Why do you have Pandora's box?" Dante said, his voice strained.

"I found it."

"You didn't open it, did you?" Dante said.

"Yes, but don't worry. It was empty when I got it." She panted.

"Do you realize what you could have done?" Dante said.

"I had to. It was the only way I could carry all of them."

"Them?" Joal said.

"I don't know who they are." She breathed. "I just know I had to rescue them."

"There are people in there?" Joal said.

"Yeah, sort of." She shrugged. "They're in bottles."

Joal shook his head. "Like genie bottles."

Cassie chuckled. "That's funny."

"Not genies," Dante said, "Syphers."

The creatures that stole god powers? Joal swore.

"Did you get them all?"

Cassie shrugged. "I think so. At least I got all there was on the shelves. I didn't have time to look around much."

Joal shook his head. "There's nothing more we can do about that. But, Cassie, where's Jemma?"

Cassie sighed. "I don't know, but I have a feeling she could really use our help about now."

Λ

Jemma couldn't breathe as white mist poured from the bottle and took the shape of a beautiful woman with sad eyes. She looked at Jemma. Moments later, the woman flew toward her and disappeared into her chest. Jemma shook her head, as the mist enveloped her. Weakness seeped into her fingers and toes and spread through her limbs, through her body, and then to her head. The pain in her back faded as her legs gave out, but with the strong arms around her, she remained upright.

Zeus shouted, triumphant. "Let go of her. She can do nothing now."

Jemma collapsed in a heap on the ground. She looked up and glared at her father. "You're a monster."

Zeus laughed. "I've been called worse. Oh, and your precious Joal, I'm going to cut him into a thousand pieces and feed the pieces to a thousand different birds of prey that will scatter all around this world. Let's see if you can put him back together after that." He sneered, the cruelty in his eyes turning her stomach.

Jemma's blood boiled. She'd kill him, she'd kill her father! If he laid one hand on Joal, she'd destroy him herself. She may no longer have any power, but she'd never give up fighting. Leaping to her feet she attempted to throw herself on Zeus and strangle him with her bare hands. Heracles grabbed her before she could reach him and squeezed her hard against his chest.

"Believe me." Heracles chuckled in her ear. "You don't want to do that."

"Yes, I do," she shouted, fighting against his grip. "If you harm one hair on Joal's head, I'll kill you."

"And how would you do that? Your powers are gone, and in a moment, you won't care one bit for that sea-god. In a moment, you'll be loyal, only to me."

"I'll never be loyal to you!"

"Yes, my dear," Zeus smirked. "You will. Once you drink the unadulterated waters of the Lethe." He pulled out another bottle and thrust it toward her face as Heracles lifted his hand and drove his meaty fingers into her mouth and forced it open. The bitter liquid poured down her throat and Jemma coughed and sputtered.

She fought against... against...

Shaking her head, she felt dizzy. Stunned. Strong arms surrounded her in a vice grip. She could barely breathe. "Let go of me," she said. "What do you want?"

"Nothing but for you to stand right where you are," a

handsome man smirked at her as the arms holding her, let go. She stumbled forward, almost falling. "Now *you* are the bait," the man said.

She looked around as her heart took off in a sprint. "Bait? Bait for what?"

"For Joal," he said.

"Who is Joal?" she asked, confused.

The man chuckled. "He's no one. At least he will be in a moment. Just make yourself at home, my dear."

She looked around at the dark cavernous expanse of dirt and jagged ice. How could she make herself at home in a place like this? What was she doing here anyway? Where was her home? At that thought, she was stunned to realize she had no idea where she lived, where she was from, people... she... she couldn't remember a single person. Why couldn't she remember? "What did you do to me? Who are you?"

"Why Jemma, I'm your father, Zeus," he answered.

"My father?" she could hear the doubt in her voice. If he was her father, shouldn't she remember him? And he called her Jemma, was that her name?

"I am king of the Greek gods, and you are devoted to me," he said, stepping forward and putting his hand on her shoulder. At his touch, his words sounded like truth. She *was* his daughter, and... she was devoted to him? He said she was. But was she? If she were, how could she have forgotten? Still, he was her father, she knew he spoke the truth..., about that at least. "What do you want me to do, father?"

"Take this. You'll need it in a moment." He placed something cool and smooth in her hands. She grasped the item. Looking down, she saw it was a bottle, milky white and made of stone with a small stopper in it.

"Jemma!" a voice called out.

A young woman emerged from the darkness and then stumbled to a stop. Two young men appeared behind her, and nearly ran the girl over before they too stopped. All of them looked from her to the other two men, gaping at them.

"What is a human doing with Pandora's box?" her father snarled as he looked at the girl and then each of the other two men. He closed his eyes and took a deep breath. "Ah, I see. You want my power for yourself."

"That power no longer belongs to you," the darker figure said.

Jemma had to be seeing things because it looked like flames were burning across his skin, yet he wasn't burnt.

"Dante," Zeus said. "I'm happy to see you."

"The feeling is not mutual."

"Ouch. That hur... no. Doesn't hurt a bit. And you're right, the power in that box may not belong to me." He then nodded to the fairer of the two men. "But the power Joal has stolen does. Those are my powers, sea-god."

Joal? This was the man her father said she would be the bait for. What did that mean?

Zeus turned to her. "Jemma, open the bottle."

"That's not going to work," the girl said.

Her father sneered at the girl. "What do you know, human?" He practically spat out the word *human*. He turned to her and looked at the bottle. "Jemma."

She hesitated a moment before saying, "Yes, father."

Horror and disbelief blossomed on Joal's face as he turned to look at her. "Jemma, what are you doing?"

She ignored the pull of Joal's words. Zeus was her father, he loved her, he had to. And he would want to protect her. Right?

Pulling the stopper from the bottle, a white mist billowed from the opening as her father chanted. A spectral figure materialized and flew toward the stranger, and then the girl was there, holding another bottle out and mumbling under her breath. The figure once again dissolved into mist and poured into the girl's container. The girl put a stopper in it and said, "No one ever believes me!"

"No!" Zeus shouted. "You think you've won? You think I haven't planned for this? Dante, Joal..., you may have escaped once before, but your fate is sealed. While you've been wandering around, lost and ignorant, looking for your precious Jemma..."

Jemma's eyes darted to her father. Confusion filled her. Why was her name said with disdain? And he'd called her *their* precious Jemma. Wasn't she precious to her own father? Had he lied to her?

"...my followers have been busy," Zeus continued, pointing up to the ice above them.

Jemma followed his gaze to see limbs, bodies, faces... a tangle of people she didn't recognize.

The girl gasped as she whispered, "Tao." Her eyes were locked on a frozen face in the ice.

"Kahula," Joal said.

"You see?" her father sneered at Joal. "The people you love, those you truly care about have been taken from you. Even Jemma," he said as he put his arm around her. Then he turned to Dante. "And then you," Zeus paused, "do you recognize this woman?" He stepped away from Jemma and brushed his hand over the ice, wiping away the haze from the surface. A stunningly beautiful face came into view.

Dante's eyes widened as flames roared, an inferno rising from his skin. Joal swore. "Dante, calm down. Don't listen to him."

Dante's gaze was locked on the face of the woman when he breathed, "Beatrice." His voice was filled with a mixture of agony and rage. "What is she doing down here? This is a place for betrayers."

"And that's exactly what she is. She was married to another

when she declared her love to you and you declared yours in return, was she not?"

"But we never even touched one another. Her body never betrayed him."

"But her heart did."

"She was forced into the marriage."

"Doesn't matter," Zeus waved as if Dante's words were inconsequential.

The flames rising across Dante's flesh radiated an immense amount of heat. Still, Zeus continued to taunt. "Do you know how much she suffers, your one great love? There is no existence as torturous as one trapped in Tartarus's frozen prison. And this is where she'll remain for all eternity!"

Confusion flooded Jemma's mind. Her father was acting... heartless, cruel. What kind of man was she supposedly devoted to?

"Dante?" Joal said. "You need to calm down."

Jemma backed away as Dante's flames rose.

"Cassie," Joal said.

The heat swelled, unbearably hot. A hand grabbed Jemma's and she turned to see the girl with the box. "We really need to get out of here," the girl said, echoing her feelings as she tugged her away. "Joal," Cassie shouted. Jemma wanted to argue, but she didn't. Instead, she turned and ran. Moments later, a fiery shockwave knocked them off their feet. They fell, tumbling across the rocky ground as the hard ground jarred their bodies and tore across their skin. Jemma pushed off the ground and sat up, nursing her injuries.

"And here comes the flood," Cassie said as Joal reached them. The girl scrambled to her feet, the box still in her hands. Cassie yanked Jemma from off the ground, and nearly jerked her arm out of its socket as she pulled her along, racing away. A staircase came into view in front of them. "Go, go, go!" the girl said.

Jemma didn't argue but took the stairs two at a time. The sound of rushing water and wailing cries followed them as they scrambled up the stone blocks. The staircase looped up and around and then opened up. Jemma skidded to a stop at the sight of a man, clean shaven and handsome.

"Why, hello young goddess! I bet you're looking to escape this place."

Cassie was at her side at that moment. "Don't listen to him. We need to keep going up."

"No!" the man shouted. "Follow me. I know the way."

Cassie pushed Jemma toward more steps on their right. Joal came up behind them and said, "I'll go first."

"I have gold, silver, jewels... if you would just follow me," the man said behind them as Joal raced up the steps. Jemma followed and Cassie rushed, coming up behind them. The man was obviously lying. Why would he be offering them riches?

As the next opening came into view, Jemma's heart stopped when a large man with a mace swung the spiky ball at Joal's head. Joal ducked and the mace blasted chunks out of the stone wall. Without missing a beat, Joal spun and kicked the man. He flew back and skidded across the ground. Jemma shrieked when she saw a whole mob of men and women scrambling over the fallen man on their way to get to them. Their hands held a whole array of weapons—swords, spears, axes, even modern guns.

"Keep going, I'll hold them off," Joal shouted, holding a trident in his hands. Where had that come from?

Cassie and Jemma didn't slow as they took the next steps.

"You think you're gods?" A woman with white frizzy hair said just as they reached the next opening. "There's no such thing as gods, or prophets, or oracles... it's all a bunch of nonsense."

Joal's voice came at them from behind them, shouting, "Keep going."

The next flight of steps took them to a group of men and women simply shouting at them. They didn't try to attack; they just swore at them, faces contorted in anger. The next level was a bit more traumatizing. A man rushed forward and grabbed Cassie's box, Joal acted quickly, punching the man in the throat, and then pulled the box from his hands as the man continued to grab at it. This time Joal kicked him, and the man collapsed in pain. Joal turned to Cassie, and she snatched the box back from him and they continued up.

The next few levels weren't so bad, but still horrible... emaciated people begging them for food, people attempting to grope them and asking for sex. Joal bloodied a few faces before they got past that level. Finally, they reached a level that wasn't horrible, the people there paid them little attention, just wandered around as if in a trance. Then they finally spilled out onto the top with no more staircases in sight, just the opening of a cave lit by torches. Jemma and Cassie collapsed in a heap, sucking in breaths. Joal reached the top just behind them, but he didn't even look winded.

"That was..." Jemma breathed, "really weird."

"You're..." Cassie gasped, "telling me."

"Jemma," Joal breathed her name and Jemma tensed. "... are you okay?" He looked hesitant to approach her. This man was her father's enemy, and probably hers as well. Afterall, she released the ghost that had tried to attack him.

"How do you know me?" Jemma asked.

He looked...devastated. "That's a long story."

"Everything happened just as they planned," Cassie said. "And now he and all the Titans are one step closer to being free."

Jemma shook her head. "I don't understand. Who are you two? And... why did you save me?"

"I know you're not going to believe this," Cassie breathed, "but Joal's your boyfriend and I'm your best friend."

Jemma tried to remember. She really tried. But she couldn't. There was nothing, nothing beyond what happened in the cavern below. "How do I know you're telling the truth?"

"You don't," Cassie said. "You won't... not until... Oh, gods, I don't know. I don't know how to get your memories back. But I should know, you told me yourself I was an oracle—"

"I did?"

"Yeah, but I don't know what..." Cassie trailed off. "What's that?"

Jemma blinked, wondering what Cassie was talking about at first, and then, the whole place rumbled, the ground trembling beneath their feet. Was this an earthquake?

"Crap!" Cassie said. "And my heart had just stopped pounding out of my chest."

"Is that—" Jemma began and then a giant hand appeared through the opening of the cave and then she was being crushed and lifted off the ground.

"Jemma!" Joal shouted as Cassie screamed.

Jemma felt open air in her face as the view spun around and she saw not just one, but a sea of ugly faces all scrunched up together— bristled hair covered their heads, more bristly strands covered their bearded chins, their eyes had various color irises, but each were blood-shot, bulging, and watery. Many were smiling with crusty yellow teeth. And their breath... she nearly passed out from the putrid force of it. "What...?" she said, but then trailed off when she noticed the arms—branching out like the pedals of a flower with countless heads in the center of the blossom. This was the ugliest flower ever. One of the arms also had Cassie clutched in its grasp as several of the heads were sniffing her. There were at least fifty heads and a hundred arms all together. Rumbling steps had

Jemma turning around to see two other giants with countless heads and arms lumbering toward them.

"Put them down!" Joal's voice boomed, rumbling like thunder.

Jemma looked down. She was about thirty feet above the ground. Falling from here would definitely leave a permanent mark. Joal looked so small, standing far below them, but then a curious thing happened. He grew as well, not near as large as the giant holding her, but he had to be at least fifteen feet tall with electricity crackling over his skin. The giants stumbled back as they eyed him curiously. Over a hundred noses sniffed the air as many said, "He smells like Zeus."

The highest of the heads said, "Silence brothers. Let me speak." All the other heads quieted down and then he said, "You do not look like Zeus, but you smell like him. Are you the Betrayer? Petros said if he tried to escape, we must not let him go."

"Do I look like the Betrayer?"

Many shook their heads. "No, but—"

"I have replaced Zeus. His power is mine, but I am loyal to Petros."

"What is your name, god with the power of Zeus?"

"My name is Joal."

"And who are your parents?"

Joal sighed. "My father is Poseidon, and my mother is Vedava."

"Sea-gods?"

"Yes."

One of the heads spoke looking up to the tallest head. "This is not without precedent. Pallas, the Dagonian..."

"Yes, yes, I know, I still do not think we should let them pass." He turned to Joal and said, "Why were you in Tartarus? What crime have you committed?"

"None," Joal said, "we were sent here by King Petros and

his granddaughter, Sara to rescue Jemma, daughter of Zeus and Peisinoê, and we were also to retrieve Cassandra Troy, the human oracle."

Peisinoê is the name of my mother?

"How do we know you are not lying to us?" the giant said.

A head several feet below him, with shaggy red hair said, "It doesn't smell like a lie." Many other heads mumbled their agreement.

"I'm not lying," Joal said, "And if you do not let them go, you will face my wrath." Joal raised his hands. Lightning gathered across the sky, their branches converged in one thick bolt, striking the ground in a deafening crack that shook the earth and caused the giants to stumble.

"Do you doubt my power?" Joal bellowed, his voice shaking the ground as much as the lightning had, but then another bolt struck the ground even closer to the giants than the first. Fear lit their wide eyes. The heads spoke, their voices rising in confusion. It was hard to make out what any one of them was saying until the highest head shouted, "Quiet!" They went silent, and then he grumbled. "I hear you, brothers."

He turned a curious eye to Joal. "No, we do not doubt you have the power of Zeus. And it is reasonable to assume the only way you could have Zeus's power is if the fates have gifted them to you for a purpose."

"They have. You need to let me, and my friends go!" Jemma felt the ground rumble at his voice.

"My brothers and I must speak in private to deliberate on this."

"Do what you need to do, but we *will* be leaving."

The giants turned and lumbered a few paces away from Joal, which for them was actually quite a distance. Jemma tried to listen to them, but their voices hummed like a thousand bumblebees. She couldn't understand a thing. Minutes later, the giants ambled back.

Jemma hit the ground so hard, she stumbled and landed on her butt.

"Ouch," Cassie said.

"You may leave, but I warn you. Do not return unless..." His voice trailed off. A rumbling sound seemed to draw the giant's attention. In moments, the rumble turned to a roar of sound, making it impossible to hear. At first Jemma thought it was the heads talking all at once again, but their mouths were not moving, and they looked confused. The voices were coming from somewhere else. Jemma turned to the cave housing the staircase they'd just escaped through, and shouted over the commotion, "Is that what I think it is?"

"The prisoners are escaping!" the giant said, staggering toward the cave entrance.

Joal grabbed Jemma's hand. At his touch, a shock reverberated through her, though it was not unpleasant. She looked over to him and, oh, wow. He was really handsome! Having his hand in hers caused her to feel warm and tingly all over. But this was so not the time to be thinking about that. Joal pulled her along as he said, "We've got to go, like now!"

"What do we do about Tao and Kahula?" Cassie asked. "They've got to be somewhere in the crowd of prisoners."

"Let's hope they're with Dante," he said and took off running, pulling Jemma with him.

Cassie followed and said in a shaky voice, "I really hope they didn't burn to a crisp."

Jemma hadn't really gotten a good look at their surroundings, but now she could see they were outside, and they were running around and through a bunch of animals.

Cows.

Like a whole herd of them.

The sound of a monumental scuffle came from behind

them. Thundering footsteps, roars, and shouts filled the air. It sounded like the prisoners had reached the giants. The sooner they could get away from the battle, the better.

On the other side of the bovines stood mountains. Jemma's eyes followed the mountains to the sky. It was amazing, a kaleidoscope of colorful constellations, each star a pure and brilliant color and then beyond that, a dark sky filled with purple, blue, and magenta nebulas. The sight was beyond words. Jemma may not remember everything, but she knew in that moment, she was definitely not on earth. Her heart pounded when she asked, "Where are we?"

"We just came up from Tartarus and now we're in the Underworld," Joal said.

Jemma realized she was still holding his hand. He may be hot, but she still wasn't sure if she could trust him. She pulled her hand from his grasp and said, "But I thought the Underworld was underground. This is out in the open."

"It's a parallel dimension," he explained.

Jemma looked back to see a flood of people spilling out of the cave leading to the stairs. The giants were flailing around, snatching them up as quickly as they came through. "Wow, so who are all those people?"

"They were prisoners of Tartarus. Some of them are Titans, but most are like the ones you saw coming up the staircase, evil, depraved humans."

"Were you a prisoner there?" Jemma asked.

"No, I came to rescue you. Hades, I wish you had your memories back." He glanced back. "Cassie, any idea how to fix this?"

"No," she gasped, shaking her head. "But all this running is killing me. And I haven't had a meal in I don't know how long. My suggestion, let's look for something to eat."

"Absolutely not," Joal said. "If you eat anything here, you can't leave."

"What?" Cassie said. "What if I'd already eaten something?"

"You'd be stuck."

"Okay, but drink, we have to drink something."

"We need to leave," Joal said.

"No," Cassie said forcefully. Jemma's eyes widened at the finality of the word coming from Cassie's mouth. "Jemma needs to drink." Cassie said in clipped tones, enunciated each word.

"I do?" Jemma asked.

Cassie looked at her, her eyes intent. "Yes, you do." She turned back to Joal. "I may not know everything, but when I know something..., I just do. Jemma needs to drink."

"Okay," Joal said, "Okay." He nodded and held out his hand. "Lead the way."

Chapter Twenty-nine –
Jemma

CHAPTER 29

> But the stars that marked our starting fall away.
> We must go deeper into greater pain,
> for it is not permitted that we stay."
> ——_Inferno,_ Dante Alighieri

THE PALACE of Hades was immense and black as midnight, with high, thick walls lit by the glow of torches with a dozen towers topped with cauldrons of fire burning orange. The blazing fire and plumes of smoke from the cauldrons made the shadows surrounding Jemma dance in the light of their flickering flames. Jemma, Joal, and Cassie ducked behind a boulder, keeping out of sight as they observed Hades' home.

Jemma looked over at Joal. He looked back at her, and she could see a mixture of hope and despair in the depths of his eyes. Emotion filled her, emotions she didn't understand, and she looked away. Whatever Zeus had done to her, had wiped him completely from her mind. She didn't have a flicker of a memory.

"We can't be seen," Joal said. "We'll have a hard enough time leaving the Underworld as it is. If Hades knows we're here, we'll have no chance."

"What do you mean?" Cassie said.

"Outsiders that come here, stay here—well, except for Hermes, the messenger of the gods is the one exception. And we still need to get past Charon, the ferryman," Joal said. "And then crossing the river Styx will be... to tell you the truth. I don't know how we're going to do it. If Dante were still with us, his mom could take us, but he's not."

"Well," Cassie said, "aren't you a bundle of good news."

"I'm just being truthful," Joal said. "If you could just use your oracle powers and let me know how we're going to escape, I'd be a lot happier."

Jemma saw movement coming from the direction of the castle. Was that a person coming toward them?

"I can't just snap my fingers and tell you everything you want to know," Cassie said. "That's not how it works."

"Shh. Guys," Jemma whispered.

"It would sure be nice if you could," Joal said, apparently, he didn't hear her.

Jemma grabbed Joal's arm and jerked him around. "Shh!" she whispered, "there's someone coming."

Joal swore as he looked around. He stiffened when his eyes found the dark figure strolling toward them.

"What do we do?" Jemma whispered. "We don't have any other place to hide."

"I think they've seen us anyway," Cassie said.

"Hades," Joal growled.

"It's Hades?" Cassie asked.

"No, I was just... it's just an expression."

They went silent as the figure came closer. Joal couldn't even hear anyone breathe. When the figure was just a few steps away, it stopped. Or rather, she stopped. The shape of the figure was clearly female.

"Joal, Cassie, Jemma..." she nodded to each of them as if her vision pierced the shadows, allowing her to see them clearly. "I've been expecting you."

Electricity crackled across Joal's hands as he emerged from behind the rock. A beautiful woman's face was lit up by Joal's sparks as her brunette hair glowed with a golden halo from the fiery torches behind her.

"You'll want to put that out," she gestured to his hands. "You wouldn't want my grandfather to see you."

"Who are you?" Joal dimmed the light. "And who is your grandfather?"

"I'm Gretchen, and my grandfather is Hades, of course," she answered.

"And you're the daughter of whom?" Joal asked.

"Thanatos."

"Death?" Joal said.

"To a lot of people, he is." She shrugged. "To me he's just, dad."

"You don't talk like an Underworlder," Joal said.

"That's probably because I was raised in the human world." She nodded. "Like you."

"You're a demigod?" Joal asked.

"Not exactly. My birth mother was a mermaid. My other grandfather is Triton, your brother. Sara sent me here to help you."

"Yeah, well," Joal said, "you'll have to tell Sara things didn't go according to plan."

"That's highly unlikely. Sara doesn't get things wrong... well, not anymore."

"Yeah, you should tell her Zeus is free and so are the

Titans. My friends are probably in Zeus's cruel hands right now, and Jemma's powers are gone as well as her memories."

Powers? What kind of powers did I have?

"Her memories, *I* can help you with," Gretchen said. "As for her powers," she turned to Cassie, "Cassie can restore those, can't you?" She looked down at Pandora's box and then back at Cassie. Joal realized how much of a miracle it was that she'd held on to the box after all they'd been through tonight.

Cassie was wide-eyed. "Yes, I think I can."

"Okay," Gretchen said, "first things first. Jemma needs to drink from the pool of Mnemosyne." Gretchen pointed to a grove of trees on their right. "That will restore her memories to her. Then Cassie can do her thing with a bottle in Pandora's box. Then you'll need to continue on, heading in the direction of the brightest blue star, it will take you to Charon." Gretchen reached into her pocket and handed Joal three gold coins. "Give him these and he'll take you across to the human world."

She turned to Jemma, "Once you return, you'll need to get your wings back, siren."

I'm a siren?

Gretchen glanced at Joal, "You can take her to them."

"I don't know where they are."

"Your mom kept them close," Gretchen said. "Shouldn't be too hard to find." She turned to Jemma. "Then you'll need your sisters. One will be more difficult to locate than the other. But you'll need them both."

"To do what?" Jemma asked.

Gretchen raised a brow. "To save your mom, oh and save your world. Another war involving the gods, the Titans, and others... well, let's just say, it would be bad. Like, really bad."

"But... but I couldn't possibly...," Jemma said. "You're asking me to save the world?"

Gretchen smirked and stepped toward her, putting her

hand on her shoulder. "Believe me, I know exactly how you feel." She tipped her head. "You can do this." She looked from Jemma to Joal to Cassie. "With help, you can."

When Gretchen turned and strode away, Jemma wanted to call her back. How could they defeat Zeus and the Titans? "This is crazy. We're just a bunch of teenagers."

Joal looked at Jemma and her heart took a stuttering beat. He was so beyond good looking and if she believed Cassie, he was her boyfriend. Did he love her? From the way he was looking at her, she thought he just might. Saving the world with the help of someone like Joal may not be so bad.

"Let's go," Joal said, taking Jemma's hand. Her eyes widened at the gesture, but she didn't shake off his grip this time. Did she love him in return? The warmth of his hand in hers and the fluttering of her heart had her believing in the possibility.

As they approached the glowing Pool of Mnemosyne Jemma's breath caught. The waters swirled, glowing green and lapping at the shore. It was a small pool, twenty feet wide at the most, but it seemed deep. And now it was time, time to get her memories back, time to learn the truth—that is if Gretchen wasn't lying and playing a cruel joke on her. Maybe the water would turn her into a snake or a toad or something.

"It's okay," Cassie said. "It's not going to hurt you."

"How do we know it isn't?" Joal said, echoing Jemma's thoughts. "We don't know this Gretchen woman."

"I know she's telling the truth," Cassie said. "I can feel it. This pool will restore Jemma's memories."

Jemma hesitated. *What choice do I have? Who am I if I don't have my memories?* Reaching forward, she took a breath, scooped some water in her hands, lifted it to her lips, and sipped. It was cool and tasted pure, rejuvenating her body and her mind.

"How could you know anything?" Joal said.

Jemma lifted her head, a floodgate opened, memories filled her mind, filled her heart, and everything lay before her in perfect clarity. She was Jemma Ryan; she was head over heels in love with Joal Forsetti; she and Cassie have been BFFs since, well, forever; and she was a freaking siren who recently had her wings cut off by her boyfriend's mom. That really sucked!

Cassie stomped her foot. "I can't tell you how sick I am —"

"Can you both please shut up?" Jemma said. "Cassie, you know why people don't believe you, I'm sorry, I know it's frustrating, but that's just the way it is. And Joal, you really should believe Cassie's impressions. She does have the gift of prophecy, but the curse of no one believing her—for that she can thank the jerk, Apollo."

"You're back," Cassie squealed and ran forward to give her a massive hug. Jemma squeezed her friend back just as tight.

When Jemma pulled away, she turned to Joal as he took a step forward. His eyes drinking her in. "Do I get a hug too?" he asked. She shook her head and he winced.

"You get more." A smile broke out on his face as she ran to him. She threw her arms around his neck and kissed him. He kissed her back, lifting her off her feet. She wrapped her legs around his waist, and he spun her around. When she finally pulled away, she was beaming, but then her smile wavered. Something wasn't right.

"Wait a minute," she said, pulling away and then she pushed him back.

Sadness colored his features as he lowered her down to stand on her feet.

"What happened to you?" she said. "You look older. How long has it been?"

"A couple of days," Joal said, shrugging.

"No... you..." Jemma stammered, taking a step away from him.

"It was Sara," Joal said, "you know the woman Gretchen mentioned, she's the goddess of fate *and* time. She spun my biological clock forward about three years so I could have my full powers."

"You're twenty-one now?"

"Just my body, not my mind."

"So, you're technically not robbing the cradle? Right?"

He smirked and shook his head. "You're still more mature than me."

"And..., oh, gods, and..." Jemma's eyes widened. "Your powers... Zeus said you have his powers."

Joal shrugged. "Yeah. My mom kind of freaked out and disowned me."

"What? Seriously?"

Joal shrugged. "It is what it is."

"I'm so sorry."

"Now we're both orphans." He cracked a smile that didn't quite reach his eyes. "But we have each other."

"Yeah, we do." Jemma took a faltering step toward him. He met her halfway and wrapped his arms around her.

"Okay," Cassie said, "now that you've had your reunion and your lips have gotten reacquainted with each other, I think it's time to give you your powers back."

Jemma shook her head. "I don't know if that's a good idea."

"Why not?" Cassie said.

"Did you forget what happened at the dance? It was a complete disaster. And I have to say, despite the fact that flying is really cool, now that I'm human again, my back is not an open wound anymore. It's such a relief to not be in pain. If I get my powers back, I've a feeling my wound will come back, and the pain is excruciating. So, my vote is no, at least not until I get my wings."

Cassie sighed. "I don't like messing with this. If we lose

these bottles, there may be no way to restore you at all. Besides, your powers aren't simply gone. Someone has them and is using them."

Jemma's eyes widened. "But...," she paused, confused, "Who has them?"

"I don't know," Cassie said. "Probably Zeus."

"But wait. You could have given me my powers long before now. Why didn't you?"

"The truth?" Cassie said.

"Yes."

"I didn't trust you yet," Cassie said. "You were like doing Zeus's bidding and all."

"I guess I understand."

"Either way," Cassie said, "you need them restored before Zeus can wreak havoc with them."

"I know." Jemma sighed. "Okay, let's get this over with."

Cassie closed her eyes.

"Are you sure—" Joal said.

"Shh!" Cassie whispered harshly as she opened her eyes. "I need to concentrate; gods I really hope I can do this." She closed her eyes once again. Her breathing steadied and she visibly relaxed, then a low, other-worldly voice spilled from her lips, "*Kóri tou aithéra, pagidevméni mésa stin Tzéma, vres katafýgio edó.*" She unstopped the bottle.

Jemma recognized the feeling at once. She'd felt this way in the cemetery months ago. The air around her filled with mist, but this time, she didn't see a face or a ghostly figure, the mist was simply sucked into the bottle. Jemma did, however, once again end up on the ground, gasping for breath. Joal's arms were around her in a heartbeat.

"Are you okay, baby?" he asked.

Jemma couldn't yet speak, but instead, nodded. Pain made her gasp. Her back... Hades, her back was once again on fire.

Joal jerked away from her, his eyes on his arm. There was blood smeared across his forearm.

When he spoke, his voice was hoarse. "I don't think I'll ever forgive my mom for what she did to you."

Jemma didn't know what to say about his monster of a mother. Instead, she said, "Let's just get my wings back."

Chapter Thirty – Jemma

Out of sight, out of mind
—— *The Odyssey*, Homer

JEMMA THREADED her fingers through Joal's as they sat, leaning into one another on a wooden bench in Charon's boat. The Underworlder never made eye contact with them, even when he had accepted their coins and directed them into the boat. Charon looked ancient, like you would expect someone who is thousands of years old—with wrinkly, pale skin that hung limply from his skull, and wisps of grey hair draped over his shoulders. The Underworlder was silent, in fact Charon hadn't said a word at all. Jemma wasn't even sure he could speak. Cassie was also uncharacteristically quiet on the ride along the River Styx. Jemma suspected she'd been worrying about Tao. Considering what Zeus had said, there was a lot to be worried about. Jemma herself had been so tightly wound that she found herself emotionally spent.

The lapping of the water against the hull hushed Jemma's

frayed nerves. Despite the fact they were in the Underworld, the air was fresh, with the scent of wooded pines and mossy shores. The stars dimmed as light seeped into the sky, brightening the expanse as if the sun were about to rise.

"Is there sunlight in the Underworld?" Jemma said.

Joal shrugged. "Sort of. The sun doesn't actually rise above the horizon here. The brightest it gets is the equivalent of twilight, or so I've heard. The phases of day and night coincide with the cycles in the human world, when it's day here, it's night in Greece, and vice versa.

Jemma's chest tightened when she noticed something strange. At the edge of the horizon, straight in front of them, the light seemed to be enveloped by a darkness that gyrated and pulsed, almost like it was alive. "Do you see that?"

"I see it," he said. "And it looks like that's where we're headed."

"So, that's the exit?" Jemma said. "We're not going to end up in Greece, are we?"

"I don't know." Joal shrugged. "If we do, I can transport us home."

Those words filled her with awe. Her boyfriend was a god! Yeah, she'd already known that, but she was continuously dumbfounded by what that meant. "That's good to know," she said.

He must have heard the amazement in her voice because he turned, a hint of a smile spread across his lips as he leaned over and kissed her gently. She raised her hand, her fingers brushing over his bristly, unshaven cheek as she kissed him back. His face may be rough, but his lips were warm, soft, and... gods, she loved kissing him. Too soon, he pulled away. She sighed and then tucked her head into the curve of his shoulder.

Jemma continued to smile, watching the flowing mist as it cleared, and a stone precipice appeared hundreds of feet tall.

As they got closer, she could make out an opening, a cave in the rock. They approached slowly and then entered the cave. Jemma couldn't help but feel like their small craft was being swallowed by the mouth of a dragon. Joal's arm tightened around her. Blackness surrounded them, but it didn't completely envelop them. It was dark where they sat, but Jemma could still clearly see the boat and all who sat in it. The air felt strange, though... thick. It took more effort to pull it into her lungs. The river fizzed below them; bubbles rising to the surface. It seemed like they were floating in carbonated water.

"I don't feel so good," Cassie said, swaying. Joal released Jemma and lunged to catch Cassie before she fell over the side.

Charon waved his hand and fresh air breezed in. Cassie sucked in gasps. "Oh...., that's so much better."

"Are you okay?" Jemma asked.

"Um, yeah. I am now." She shook her head and pushed away from Joal. She turned to him and said, "Thanks."

"No problem," he said.

She looked to the ferryman and said, "And thank you too, Charon."

He didn't respond, didn't even acknowledge she'd spoken. She turned to Jemma and shrugged.

Light glinted off the rocky walls ahead as the air warmed. It looked like they'd reached an opening to the outside world. As the boat emerged, it slowed, and they found themselves floating toward a crumbling down wall, just a few feet away. It stood about eight feet high, topped with clear sky above. Jemma glanced behind them. She noticed an archway they must have floated through, though it was too short for them to have actually been able to fit. *How did we pass through it?* Above the archway was an inscription. It looked to be in ancient Greek. The boat turned to the left and they floated to where the ground sloped up out of the water.

Joal got out first, then Cassie. Joal held out his hand for Jemma to disembark. She stepped carefully over the rocky slope, the sharp stones pressing into the pads of her feet. When she turned back, Charon and his boat were gone.

"Well, I think it's safe to say we're not in Garden Grove," she said, looking around.

"Yeah," Joal answered. "Definitely. The writing over the arch is in Greek."

"What does it say?" Cassie asked.

"It's a dedication to Hades and Persephone," Joal said.

"Hmm," Jemma said. "Makes sense. Okay, first, we go to Joal's to get my wings back." As she thought about her missing appendages, her back flared in pain. She took a breath and then continued, "Then..."

"We figure out how to stop Zeus and the Titans from taking over the world," Cassie said.

"The first thing we need to do," Joal said, "is figure out how to get home."

"I thought you already knew how to do that," Cassie said.

"In theory," Joal said. "I've never actually done it before. Well, at least not with passengers."

Jemma sighed. "What do we do?"

"I need you both to take my hands."

Jemma took his hand in hers. Cassie grabbed on with both of her hands. When Jemma looked at her, Cassie shrugged. "I don't want to accidentally get left behind."

Jemma's grip increased.

"Okay," Joal said, "now I want you to think about my house, just inside the foyer. Does everyone have that picture in their mind?"

Jemma closed her eyes and pictured the open foyer with marble floors. "Yes," she said.

"Um... uh...yep," Cassie answered.

Jemma felt power wash over her, like static prickling her skin, then there was a breeze... a cool, humid breeze.

"What in Hades?" Joal growled.

Jemma opened her eyes. Something was seriously wrong with the sight.

"Oh, gods," Cassie gasped. "I'm so, so sorry. I just... I couldn't stop thinking about this place."

They were standing in the center of a... cemetery? But the sight was so unbelievable. All the tombstones were knocked over. The rot iron entrance sign was bent in half and part of it was missing so that it read "ates Cemetery." A swirling black vortex rotated, gyrating not more than thirty feet away.

They were in Heavenly Gates Cemetery! Jemma had almost forgotten what had happened there. Gods, the portal was not only real, but it was still there, much larger and foreboding than she remembered! There were muddy tracks leading away from it in a path of destruction that left broken down trees, fences, and even several overturned, mangled vehicles.

Jemma's eyes followed the scene of destruction and she gasped at the sight in the distance. The valley below glowed orange with plumes of smoke rising. Jemma pointed toward the smoke. "Is that Garden Grove?"

Cassie nodded her head.

"Yes," Joal gasped, "It is."

A murmur of shouting voices caught her attention and Jemma turned to see the source. Her eyes landed on two figures running toward them on the left. "Joal!" one shouted and the other yelled, "Cassie!"

Cassie took off running as she shouted, "Tao!"

Jemma and Joal followed. It was Tao and Kahula. The relief at seeing them alive and seemingly well, was overwhelming.

"What happened?" Joal asked Kahula. "Where's Dante?"

"Do you want the long version or the short version," Kahula asked, as he skidded to a stop.

"We don't have time for the long version," Joal said.

"We don't know where Dante is, we followed Zeus and the Titans, and they led us here." Kahula pointed to the smoke, "Now there's that."

Joal swore. "We need to get Jemma's wings back, but given what's happening down there, I don't know if it's a good idea to transport to my house."

"Yeah," Kahula said, "for all we know, we'd be transporting in the middle of a war zone."

"We could transport to *my* house," Jemma said. "It's kind of on the outskirts of town, and I doubt any of the Titans have claimed it for their own."

"Joal's house is the safest," Cassie said.

"No," Kahula said, "his mom could be there. For all we know—"

"She's not there," Cassie said. "She's not even on this continent."

Kahula raised his brows. "How could you know?"

"She just knows," Jemma said.

"And I know we need to go to Joal's house," Cassie said, her tone stopping any protest.

"I hope you're right." Kahula said.

"She is," Jemma said, certain.

Joal took her hand and then looked at the others. "Everyone needs to hold hands. I'll transport us there. And this time..." he looked at Cassie, "no detours."

Moments later they were standing in Joal's living room. Joal turned to Jemma and said, "I think I know where your wings are."

Jemma followed him, desperate to get them back. She felt so incomplete without them. They passed through the great room and headed to a door. Joal opened it and turned on the light. The room was like a museum, hardwood floors were lined with glass cases containing treasures and artifacts. One case had what looked like a ram's horns. Another housed a white fur coat. And still another, the skeleton of what appeared to be a person, only it was about a foot and a half tall.

Jemma searched the room, taking notice of her reflection in the mirrored back of a case she passed by. Her face, though smudged with dirt, glowed with goddess like perfection, her hair was unbrushed, but still looked soft, with rich, copper hues. Her clothes, on the other hand, were dirty, tattered, and falling apart. Good thing she wasn't missing anything important from the fabric, at least not anything that would make it embarrassing for her. Jemma gasped when her eyes fell on *them*.

At the far end of the room was a large case housing the missing pieces of her soul. Her wings hung majestically, and even appeared to glow in the incandescent light. She sprinted, with Joal on her heels and skidded to a stop when she reached the case. Joal turned the latch of the glass door, and it swung open. Jemma stepped forward, tears burning in her eyes. "I didn't think I'd get so emotional." She reached in and brushed her fingers over the plumage. The wings shuddered, as if they were still alive and sensed her presence.

"Do you mind?" Joal asked as he nodded toward them.

Jemma shook her head.

Joal carefully lifted the wings and pulled them out of the case. "Okay, turn around."

Jemma did so and she felt a jolt of energy the moment they touched her back. Within seconds the pain in her back was gone and she felt an immediate connection to her wings. The relief was palpable. She tucked them against her body but didn't put them away. She relished the feel of them too much. Turning around, she threw her arms around Joal, pressed her cheek against his chest, and let her tears fall. "I feel complete again."

He pressed a kiss against her head. "I'm so glad you got your wings back."

She shook her head as she raised her eyes to his. "It's not just my wings. It's you too. I missed you so much!"

Joal was smiling as he lowered his lips to hers. Gods how she missed this—being in Joal's arms, kissing him, feeling all the sensations of them, together, it was simply perfect. She ran her hands over his chest and around his shoulders. He felt different—larger, more solid, his body more mature. And now the feelings he elicited from her; they had matured as well. Too soon, he pulled away.

"Mmm," she said. "Why did you stop? Don't you want to kiss me?"

"Oh, I want to, but... the others are still waiting for us. Besides, Garden Grove is in danger from Zeus and the Titans right now."

"Why do you have to be so practical at a time like this?"

Joal shrugged. "Well, I am three years older than you."

"That's totally not fair."

"Sorry, babe." His face morphed into surprise. "I'm twenty-one, and you're seventeen."

"Seventeen? Wait! What's the date?"

Joal looked at his smart watch, and sure enough, it was working fine. "It's October second."

"You're in luck, Joal Forsetti. I'm an adult too. My birthday was—" The glass cases around them shuttered and clinked, cutting off her words. The floor trembled under their feet and then the room swayed as she and Joal staggered, trying to stay upright. "Is this an earthquake?" she asked. One of the taller cases tipped and crashed onto the floor. Pottery inside smashed into tiny pieces. Then another case fell over as the entire room rolled and her stomach dropped.

Joal took Jemma's hand. "Come on," he said, "we've got to get out of here."

"Joal! Jemma!" Tao shouted from the other room.

Jemma and Joal scrambled around the broken pieces of furniture and artifacts and then ran out of the door into the open room.

"What's going on?" Tao asked.

Movement from outside the wide window had Jemma's heart smashing against her rib cage. A face as large as Garden Grove itself peered down at the town.

"We've got to get outside," Tao shouted.

"Who is that?" Jemma asked, pulling Joal to a stop as she pointed toward the window.

"I know who that is," Joal said, his voice filled with wonder.

"What are you talking about?" Kahula said, his eyes searching, but not focusing on what he should be seeing.

"I don't see anything," Tao said. "We need to get outside." He took off running, dragging Cassie behind him. Joal and Jemma looked at each other and then followed out the back door. A thundering roar bellowed around them as soon as they opened the door. Jemma ran across the deck to see they were perched over a waterfall. It seemed as if it flowed from beneath the house and fell into a pool a hundred feet below them.

"I don't think this is the best place to be," Tao said, "I don't know how you were able to get a permit to build a house over a waterfall, but it does not look like the safest foundation. And if this deck collapses, we're dead." As he spoke, the shaking stopped, and everything went still.

"He's gone," Joal said.

Jemma nodded, relieved.

"Who was it?" Kahula said, awe in every word.

Joal answered but Jemma didn't listen to the answer. She

was too distracted by the color of the sky—the blue was tinted, more of a turquoise than sky blue. And the sun was more of an amber color.

"Look at that," Tao said, pointing up.

Jemma was already looking at what he was talking about. The smoke from the fires below rose, only to pool against the top of an invisible barrier, a thousand feet above them.

"Do you feel that?" Joal asked. "There's no wind. Not even a hint of a breeze.

"We're trapped," Cassie said.

"What?" Jemma asked. "What do you mean?"

She pulled out a bottle from Pandora's box and held it up. It was made of clear glass but had a yellowish tint. "We're under a dome made of the same stuff this bottle is made of."

Jemma and Cassie remained silent as the rest of the group exploded in a flood of expletives.

"There's no way," Tao said.

"What about the innocent humans?" Kahula said.

"This is insanity," Tao said. "Whose plan was this?"

"It had to come from Petros," Joal said.

"Who the Hades is Petros?" Kahula asked.

"Okay, everyone just... calm down," Joal said. "Take each other's hands."

"That's not going to work," Cassie shook her head as Tao snatched her hand.

"Jemma!" he shouted at her back as she strolled toward the railing overlooking the town.

"It won't work, Joal," Cassie said, more adamantly. "We can't escape here." She said, reinforcing what Jemma already knew. But then Cassie added more. "And Garden Grove is now invisible to the world."

"What do you mean?" Kahula asked. "No one can see us?"

"Or remember us," Cassie said, her voice void of any hope. "This is a prison, a dome created for captives to be forgotten."

Dazed, Jemma leaned against the railing. Through her supernatural vision, she could see everything. Her heart broke at the chaos below. The Titans had declared war on the demigods and humans. Fires burned. People, friends, families…, all ran in fear. Women huddled, clutching their children against their chests, praying their lives would be spared. She saw it all; she comprehended it all. They'd been left here to die.

Jemma knew what she had to do. She could feel it, a song tugged at her mind, begging, pleading to be released. So, she did what she had to do. She took a deep breath, parted her lips, and sang.

Also by Holly Kelly

THE RISING SERIES

Rising (Book 1)

Descending (Book 2)

Avenging (Book 3)

Raging (Book 4)

Acknowledgments

I'd like to thank CTP Publishing for giving me my break over a decade ago and sticking with me through all my crazy ups and downs.

I also want to express my eternal thanks to my husband, for his unwavering love, patience, and support which has carried me through hard times, and for fighting to stay by my side through challenging health problems that threatened to take him, not only from this world, but from by my side.

Then, for my children, I'd like to thank them for the love and support they've given me and their dad, and for giving us a reason to keep fighting through impossible odds.
Finally, to those who have supported my writing–my beta readers, author friends, extended family, editors, and unwavering readers who have given me the desire to keep writing and creating.

All of you have earned my everlasting gratitude because you have made this journey not only possible but enjoyable and rewarding. Thanks again, from the bottom of my soul!

About the Author

Holly Kelly is a mom who writes books in her spare time: translation-- She hides in the bathroom with her laptop and locks the door while the kids destroy the house and smear peanut butter on the walls. ;)

She was born in Utah but lived in Salina, Kansas until she was 13 and in Garland, Texas until she was 18. Now back in Utah–"happy valley" she's married to a wonderful husband, James, and they are currently raising 6 rambunctious children.

Her interests are reading, writing (of course), martial arts, visual arts, and spending time with family.